D1389378

THE OTHER HALF

The Other Half

CHARLOTTE VASSELL

faber

First published in the UK in 2023
by Faber & Faber Ltd
Bloomsbury House,
74–77 Great Russell Street,
London WC1B 3DA

Typeset by Typo•glyphix, Burton-on-Trent, DE14 3HE
Printed and bound by CPI Group (UK) Ltd, Croydon, CR0 4YY

The right of Charlotte Vassell to be identified as author
of this work has been asserted in accordance with Section 77
of the Copyright, Designs and Patents Act 1988

*This book is a work of fiction. Any references to historical events,
real people, or real places are used fictitiously. Other names, characters, places, and
events are products of the author's imagination, and any resemblance to actual
events or places or persons, living or dead, is entirely coincidental.*

*Every effort has been made to trace copyright holders and to obtain permission
for the use of copyright material. The publisher would be pleased to rectify any
omissions that are brought to its attention at the earliest opportunity.*

A CIP record for this book
is available from the British Library

ISBN 978-0-571-37493-9

MIX
Paper | Supporting
responsible forestry
FSC® C171272
FSC
www.fsc.org

Printed and bound in the UK on FSC paper in line with our continuing
commitment to ethical business practices, sustainability and the environment.
For further information see faber.co.uk/environmental-policy

2 4 6 8 10 9 7 5 3 1

For my late, and much missed, nan.

What men or gods are these? What maidens loth?
What mad pursuit? What struggle to escape?
What pipes and timbrels? What wild ecstasy?

'Ode on a Grecian Urn', John Keats

★ ★ ★

He was misanthropic and gifted with the sly,
sharp instinct for self-preservation that passes for
wisdom among the rich.

Put Out More Flags, Evelyn Waugh

THE OTHER HALF

SATURDAY

1

A girl is dying. A girl who wears bespoke perfume. She wants you to inhale her deliciousness; to know that she is untouched by the dirt, the smog, the filth of your London. Pathetic men rub their underdeveloped legs against her arse as they commute to their piteous 'careers' on the hamster-cage tube. She wants other women to covet her manicure as she types an 'empowering' Instagram post about her 'inner glow'. People follow her. A be-legginged messiah to the inflexible, undesirable, slovenly masses. She drinks spirulina, kombucha and matcha, but she doesn't eat wheat or dairy. She's faking an allergy to mask her disordered eating, which she won't seek help for because it feels so very normal nowadays. It's a shame, she used to like eating bread. She waxes everything. Everything. She is filthy. Filthy. Used to do anything, absolutely anything, if it meant he'd stay with her.

A girl is dying. She is savvy. Astute. Commercially minded. Clever. She's clever. She knows that all she really has to sell is the idea of her beauty, her youth, her long rolling vowels, and she does. In the old stories Pygmalion made Galatea, but this new Galatea made herself and streamed it live. She put it on a T-shirt, on a tote bag. Got paid for sharing a link to organic date and cashew nut energy balls (£6.50 for four, not including postage). She believes in self-improvement. She practises her poses and reads her prose. She believes in love and practises that too. She has put so many hours into practising, hours and hours, tears and tears, and yet . . . She can be droll. She'd buy you a drink if you made her laugh. More than once had she bought a *Big Issue*. She'd gone to charity fundraising galas, because it would get her into the society pages of *Tatler*, but still she went and clapped loudly and exclaimed 'how brave' at the survivors of whatever hideous disease the whole thing was in honour of and handed over a cheque. She is vain, and angry, and sad, so very sad. Of course she is sad. Miserable. Wretched. Plain old unhappy. How could she not be? The poor thing.

A girl is dead. A girl who was flawed. No, not the pores on the nose, those were perfect. Resolutely perfect. Her head had spun but the world hadn't noticed; it callously carried on spinning as she suffocated on her own bile, writhing there amongst rotting leaves, her hair infused with the stench of mulch and stomach acid. She deserved better than to die there. To die because of him.

2

Midsummer Night, North London

The McDonald's in Kentish Town had seen some sights, but this was something different. At 6 p.m. an elegant man strode through the automatic doors. Wing-collar shirt, cummerbund and silk bow tie. Expensive shoes: Italian. They made a clipped noise when he walked, much like his vowels when he spoke. He strolled up to the counter and asked to speak to the manager. The server peered around him nervously, looking for a non-existent camera. The manager was dutifully found and propositioned like a comely whore. The gentleman, and there really couldn't be another word for a man dressed in such a manner, was going to use the upstairs area – usually reserved for children's parties on Saturday mornings – for a private gathering that evening. His guests were arriving at 7.30 p.m. and the staff were to bring food upstairs (the order had already been courteously written out in fastidious copperplate) at 8 p.m. for them. They were not to be disturbed after that. The gentleman made it very clear that they were to be handsomely recompensed for their efforts, and their silence. No one who worked there was to mention it again and CCTV was to be turned off. The gentleman paid in cash – crisp £50 notes – and gave all the staff, including the poor, poor cleaner, who would have to deal with true horrors tomorrow morning, a nice little tip for all the trouble he was about to cause. A young woman with rippling, flame-coloured hair brought in vase upon vase of flowers. The smell was divine. Not enough to cover the smell of chip fat, burger grease and blocked coronary arteries, but heavenly nonetheless. A butler took case after case of champagne upstairs. And it was champagne, direct from a vineyard in Champagne, not from Tesco. Only plebeians drink supermarket plonk, let alone prosecco. The formal invitation stipulated that the dress code was black tie, photography was strictly prohibited, and it was BYOC (Bring Your Own Coke).

★ ★ ★

For once Nell wasn't overdressed; she was, however, uncomfortable. Her feet already hurt from a pair of architecturally complex shoes that she had bought from a pompous boutique in Spitalfields Market. She'd spent a whole month's food budget on them, but she considered that a win-win. Nell's dress was an artful creation of pale lilac gauze and twisted embroidery that she had made herself, the effect of which was somewhere between a drowned innocent from a Millais painting and wrath personified. She was a diaphanous, tortured cobweb. In the soft June breeze, Nell delicately floated like a resplendent vision of Hell. She was waiting outside Kentish Town tube station for Alex – nothing earthly could have persuaded her to go to Rupert's birthday party on her own, and indeed it had taken much poking and prodding, cajoling and coaxing from silver-tongued Alex to induce her to go with him. They were going to go for something strong beforehand, a nip of liquid bravery. The flower seller on the corner of Leighton Road was packing up for the day. Five minutes earlier Nell had enjoyed spectating as a panic-stricken man sprinted from the tube and bought a large bouquet in a frenzy.

'Anniversary or birthday?' Nell asked the florist, as she sauntered over and mused over a few bedraggled hydrangeas.

'Sorry?' she replied.

'The bald man just then, he looked like he'd forgotten an important date.'

'Oh yeah, he said his missus just had a baby at the Royal Free. Wanted some pink flowers.'

'Ah, how sweet, a gender-conforming baby girl. Did he realise that he'd caught the wrong branch of the Northern Line?'

'I didn't have the chance to tell him.'

Nell looked at the leftovers of the florist's day. The severed head of a luckless ranunculus the colour of a good claret floated in a bucket of water.

'How much for that one?'

'You take it, love.'

'Thank you,' Nell said, shaking the water from the flower and tucking it into a roll of her hair.

'Big night?' the flower seller asked, tacitly acknowledging Nell's remarkable appearance.

'I'm going to Satan's birthday party.'

'A normal Saturday evening then.'

'Pretty much. Thank you for the flower,' said Nell as she turned back to face the tube. She was just in time to see Alex rise from the gaping mouth of the station. He was tall, which she thought was the only important quality a man should possess, but clearly feeling uncomfortable in his penguin get-up. Nell thought it suited him. A shapely young woman gave him a second glance before she unceremoniously tumbled through the barriers

'Thou art a sight for mine poor wretch'd eyes,' he said, kissing Nell on her rosy cheek. They turned up the road and towards the pub.

'You should dress like this more often, you'd get laid all the time,' she said, holding on to the crook of his arm to steady herself. Her pinkie toes hurt.

'I have a lot of sex. Specialist stuff too. Deviant things that you don't casually mention at dinner parties.'

'Corpses? You need to stop reading *Vice*. It's bad for your soul, Alex.' They stopped at the crossing as a police car hurtled past, siren blaring.

'Is this pub all right?'

'As long as they serve spirits.'

'The spirits of thy vanquished enemies? The damned party starts at 7.30 p.m. I say we should aim for after 8 p.m.,' Alex said, holding the old saloon door open for her. The pub was a Victorian temple to the English drinking problem, with high ceilings and floral plasterwork. Mismatched chairs and ironic posters. Creaky floorboards and media luvvie clientele.

'I'm amazed that we're going at all.' Nell peered round a column before spotting an empty table near the back and pouncing on it like a lioness after a lame gazelle at a watering hole. 'I'm not sure how you convinced me.'

'You share my morbid curiosity,' Alex said, taking his jacket off. That wasn't why he was going. It was a test, a field exercise to calculate his chances with Nell now that she was single.

'What do you think Phlegm will be wearing? I shouldn't call her that. I'll say it to her face accidentally-on-purpose.'

'Clem? Pelts made from the supple skin of tuberculosis-riddled, cockney orphans? Silk woven from the purest evil thoughts of neo-Nazis? Nothing, absolutely nothing, like a witch on her Sabbath? You have to feel sorry for Clemmie though. Imagine dating bloody Rupert for ten years.'

'I couldn't imagine it.'

'The crap he must pull . . . I'm sure he cheats on her.'

'I'm sure he does too.'

'What do you want to drink?'

'Anything that burns,' Nell said, watching him try to elbow his way to the bar through a throng of unique individuals all wearing Uniqlo and unanimous disdain for everyone else's uniformity.

'Tequila it is,' Alex yelled, turning back to look at her as he dodged a woman in a stripy turtleneck and a pair of utilitarian shoes. He stopped still for a short moment as he evaded the woman's flailing arms. To Nell those seconds were an age, as through the window the low-slung sun hovered above his head like a lazy halo. He turned and looked at her in all her glory. 'You look rather lovely tonight,' he shouted over the crowd.

Nell didn't acknowledge the compliment and instead stared at the patterned ceiling, trying to divine some order out of its chaotic design. She felt a buzzing. She opened her bag – a quirky Kate Spade that she'd pillaged from eBay for a song – and took out her phone:

Rupert: 18:34
I hope you're nearby. I am so looking forward to seeing you. Let's go for brunch tomorrow. Just me and you. I miss us and our little jaunts x

Alex returned with two tequilas and two vodka and lime sodas. 'A shot each, and then something to take the edge off before we go over the top.'

'How's work?'

'Dull. Lots of spreadsheets.'

'At least you got seconded somewhere warm. Imagine doing taxes for billionaires somewhere miserable, like London.' Nell smiled to herself as she flicked her despicable shoes out to the side and admired them. 'Why *are* we going tonight?'

'I'm going for the story. Something hideous will happen. I could write a bestselling novel off the back of it and never have to work again.'

'They're both monsters.'

'And monsters should be slain by heroes. I'll be your knight errant.' Alex looked at Nell and began pressing the supposed rationale of his experiment again. 'This is our old college gang's last hurrah. Of course, you don't have to go if you don't want to, but I would appreciate your company.'

'The last hurrah. Goodbye Rupert, and goodbye to all of Rupert's nonsense.' Nell toasted the thought, and they downed their tequila in remembrance of the friendship that had once been. There wasn't any salt or lime to distract from the taste, from the bitterness.

'Last hurrah.' Alex leaned back in his chair and fiddled with his phone as Nell stared intensely at a knock-off Belle Époque absinthe poster. 'What did happen in Greece?' he tentatively enquired. He could guess, but he wanted to hear the sordid tale from her own mouth, and such a pretty mouth it was. Perfectly full.

'What?' she asked, feigning absentmindedness as she stared at a flirty green fairy with prominent nipples and an impossibly small waist.

'What happened between you, Rupert and Clemmie, when the three of you came to visit me in Greece last month?'

'Nothing.'

'I go to the office in Athens for a couple of days, I come back to the villa, and then that evening Clem swings for you over dinner.'

'Bad spanakopita?'

'Don't insult my people like that.'

'Clem was just high. She'd taken a load of MDMA or whatever.'

'And?'

'And they had a fight the morning before about something, something really stupid, and she took it out on me.'

'Like what?'

'I think it was about that temple we'd visited.'

'They had a fight about a ruin?'

'It was bizarre, I didn't get what the fight was about. I don't think the ruins were the problem,' Nell said, hoping that this was the end of the discussion, but then failing to stop herself from talking. 'Clem refused to go after breakfast, so me and Rupert went on our own and it was just weird. She spent the evening in a foul mood.'

'Weird? What did he do?' Alex asked, eyebrow arched.

'Rupert did that self-satisfied, smug thing he does. He drove us there in that little toot-toot convertible he'd rented. The sky was blue and the light just . . . everything felt golden, and the temple was appropriately numinous. And Rupert, well, he was Rupert. When we got back, Clem was high and he tried to kiss me, which set her off even more. I . . . He . . . And I . . . And I don't want to talk about it. Please. I don't need to talk about it. It was nothing. Absolutely nothing. Just the flicker of a kiss.'

'All right.' Alex was desperately relieved that was all it was.

Nell swilled her vodka around the glass and then drank it in one gulp.

Alex fiddled with his phone. 'Rupert is a . . . You shouldn't let him take advantage of you. It's not fair. He treats you like a second girlfriend, but all you get is the crap, the meltdowns and the 3 a.m. drunken rants. You deserve more than that.' Silently he added, 'You deserve me.'

'I'm sure that's the advice I'd be giving myself too. I haven't spoken to him since the plane landed back at Heathrow. He's taken it better than I thought he would. I need to kill our friendship properly. Stab it in the heart with a wooden stake and bury it under a crossroads.'

'Do you want another?' Alex asked. He was liking his odds of romping home considerably more than he had on the tube journey over. This might be it. He'd played a long game and was about to win.

'Another vodka please, mister consultant.'

'You make me sound so dull,' Alex said, smiling as he got up to go to the bar.

'I don't think you're dull at all,' Nell yelled after him.

Alex laughed exaggeratedly for Nell's benefit as he strode across the pub. Looking back at her from the bar, he saw the most magnificent and the most melancholic face in all of London. Nell felt his gaze upon her and looked up as Alex gave her a smirk. He bought two drinks from the bearded barman with the painfully obscure eighties cartoon character on his T-shirt.

★ ★ ★

Alex and Nell stood on the pavement across from McDonald's as they watched Rupert prowl up and down the street outside like an impotent tiger in an especially sad, underfunded zoo that you might sign a petition online against and then forget about moments later.

'Clemency really, it started thirty minutes ago and I'm getting annoyed. It's terribly rude. It would've been nice if you'd have bothered to come early to help with the set-up. Poor Minty has been run ragged and looks terribly pitiable for it. If you're not here by 9 p.m., then you can move your shit out of my house.' Rupert was trying to control himself, but he was making enough commotion that two girls in a Fiat 500 beeped their horn and cackled wide-mouthed and toothily at him through the open window as they trundled past. It isn't every day that a man who looks like the suave villain from an Oscar Wilde comedy crunches the bones of discarded chicken wings into a North London pavement. Rupert was handsome in that dashing-white-knight sort of way that often proves fatal to any damsel moronic enough to fall for it. To let their hair down for him to latch on to. To have slumbering lips, soft and tempting.

'He just can't help himself,' Alex said, smirking at Rupert in all his glorious ridiculousness.

'The thing about Rupert, the thing that people find attractive, is his obliviousness to the age in which we live. He revels in a nostalgic world of his own making, like he's some bastardised character from *Brideshead Revisited*. He just doesn't care for our time, not a jot.'

'No, not at all.'

'He's a dangerously charming oddball. A patrician weirdo. Does he unironically have a teddy called Aloysius? How do you become like that?'

'A noxious concoction of boarding school from six, reading Byron at too early an age, and rapacious genes. Do you know how his family first came into money?'

'Slavery?' Nell asked, her nose wrinkling.

'No, but that's how they bought that absurd house in the Chilterns.'

'Remember his twenty-fifth birthday?'

'I can't remember much of it at all. No, the illustrious first baronet was a nabob. "Found" a diamond the size of a household tabby in the Punjab,' Alex said, as Rupert's ancestral crimes lingered among the toxic fumes from an articulated lorry that had just crawled past.

'Have you pressed the button for the green man?' Nell asked, looking at the traffic light.

'No. I'd rather stay out here with you.' Alex went to hold her hand but panicked, and instead crossed his arms and tucked his hands under his armpits like a four-year-old whose mummy had told him not to touch.

Nell leaned over him to press the button and Alex smelled her hair – vanilla. 'He still hasn't noticed us, has he? This is it, the last hurrah. Look him dead in the eye, spit, turn and flee.'

'Beauchamp! Rupert. Rupert, you bellend,' Alex yelled across the road with considerable bravado, choking with shock an old lady who had joined them at the crossing with her shopping trolley. 'Apologies for my language, madam, but in this case it is accurate. He's a paying member of the Conservative Party, and I once saw him kick a dog. The dog only had two front legs, it had little wheels at the back. And it was blind.'

The green man flashed and the three of them crossed the road.

'*Salvete!* Don't you smarten up well? Where's your suit from? Moss Bros.?' Rupert asked Alex with his arms outstretched, awaiting an embarrassed embrace that turned into mutual back slapping.

'It's from Favourbrook. I'm not a pleb,' Alex said, turning to face Nell, his eyes wide as Rupert surveyed his shoes and estimated how much they'd cost him.

'Prick,' muttered the old lady at Rupert as she shuffled past. He didn't notice, of course, he never noticed, although Nell did. As she tried to swallow a howl, Rupert turned his attention to her.

'Well, don't you look charming,' Rupert said in a softer, more hushed tone, trying to cosset her.

'Thank you,' Nell said coolly.

And then no one said anything for twenty seconds. The triumvirate looked at each other expectantly. A double cheeseburger wrapper whistled silently through the middle of them like an unhealthy tumbleweed.

Alex broke the silence. 'Would a strawberry milkshake make a good mixer for vodka?' He pulled a hip flask out of his pocket and gave it a little shake. Alex started as if to move inside when he realised that Rupert's feet were planted firm, and Rupert expected Nell to stay too. Nell was stuck, unsure, as if she'd forgotten how her legs worked. Nell: deer. Rupert: headlights of an especially obnoxious 4x4 driving down a narrow country lane.

'That sounds disgusting, but I'd like to try yours,' Nell said, staring at a fifty-pence piece on the floor. She nudged it with her foot. Some trickster had glued it to the pavement in gleeful anticipation of frustrating the good citizens of Camden Borough who might be sufficiently desperate to try and pocket it.

'Vanilla would probably be better. A McRussian, like half the US establishment,' Alex said, going through the automatic doors. The sickening smell of junk engulfed him, that peculiar smell that every McDonald's has. A butler in full tails greeted him and directed him to the next floor, but before Alex turned upstairs, he stopped and watched Rupert touching Nell on the cheek and playing with the flower she'd put in her hair. Too intimate a gesture for him to continue watching, too much frisson, too much tension for his flimsy heart to withstand. The experiment had failed. Nothing had changed except for him, and evidently that wasn't enough.

★　★　★

17

Rupert brushed Nell's cheek in a gesture that he hoped was paternalistic enough to justify standing too close. 'I texted you earlier, I don't know whether you've seen it yet? Have you? I think it would be nice for us to go for brunch tomorrow. I booked us a table at this lovely place in Chiswick. It's on the river.'

'I can't.' Rigid, she stood. Eyes cast down. *Spit at him*, Nell told herself. *Look him in the eye and turn him to stone, buy cement, be your own Medusa.*

'Why not?' he asked, assuming she was playing hard to get as always.

'Yoga. I'm going to a yoga class with my cousin,' she lied. Tell him the truth, she told herself, don't spare his poxy feelings. Tell him you don't want to see him ever again after tonight.

Rupert rolled his eyes at the mention of yoga. 'Clem's started an Insta for yoga. Apparently, she's popular.'

'Of course she is. Where is Clemmie?'

'Running late, of course. Always has to make an entrance, does Clemency. Although this is really her grand exit.'

'We should go inside. It is your birthday party after all.' Nell started for the automatic doors. 'Trust you to do black tie in a McDonald's.'

'It's amusing, isn't it.'

'It's cruel,' Nell said, acknowledging the butler with a slight nod. The poor staff behind the tills looked utterly bewildered. She hoped Rupert was tipping them and generously at that.

'What, McDonald's? Their eggs are free range, look at the posters,' Rupert said, following Nell's wiggle as it climbed up the stairs and past a picture of a 'happy' chicken.

'Yes, McDonald's,' Nell said, stopping on the mezzanine. She looked at Rupert and smiled her best happy-fake teeth-baring grin, like a delirious young mother in a toothpaste commercial.

'White Russian vanilla milkshake?' She always knew that she was a coward deep down. She liked to think she was brave, but here was the moment, the moment to prove her mettle, and she had failed.

'That would be delightful.' Rupert beamed. He could always count on his Nell.

★　★　★

Alex was avoiding her. She kept trying to make eye contact with him across the crowded room, full to the brim with the great and good under thirty-five, but he was listening intently to a girl who Nell knew for a fact was a crashing bore. Tibby, Nell thought her name was, or was it Nibbs? Nippy? No, Minty, that was it. Some childhood friend of Rupert's who bred prize-winning gladioli, or something else quaint and cottagey and far too tedious for a woman still in her twenties to care about. Wasn't she at Saint Cecilia's College when they were at Oxford? A botanist perhaps? She looked rather like a gladiolus actually. Gangly and rather too brightly coloured. Her dress was a peculiar colour for a redhead to choose. Was her father a viscount? Rupert drags her out when he wants a mention in the society pages. Nell sat alone on a pleather banquette to save her feet. She could see the disabled toilet from where she was perched and could hear squeals that incrementally increased in pitch coming from within. The door finally popped open, and Jolyon and Tabitha came out looking perky, as evidenced by the powder clinging to their nostrils. Nell was nursing a vanilla milkshake sans vodka. Alex still wasn't acknowledging her. There was vodka on the table, but it wasn't his, so she didn't want it. What music was this? Who hires a string trio to play Drake? She could smell the fries. They smelled calorific. Naughty. Sinful. Rupert slyly kept looking at her. Clemmie's friend, Becca, whom Rupert referred to as Porridge Face, gave Nell a spiteful once-over. Where was Phlegm? Jolyon had spotted Nell and started slithering through the room towards her.

'Hullo, you. You look pretty, and pretty girls shouldn't be alone at parties,' he said, plonking himself down with a thud on the banquette and leaning in a little too close to Nell.

'Hi, Joly. How's tricks?' Nell asked, angling herself away from his porcine face. He had once been a passable rugby player for their college team at Oxford.

'Not bad. Just started my own company.'

'Really, what are you doing?'

'I am consulting.'

'On what?'

'Marketing strategies for luxury watch brands trying to crack the British market.'

'I see. As long as it keeps you busy, eh? Something to kill the time between now and your inevitable early death.' He didn't hear the end part. Something shiny had distracted him.

'Are you drunk enough to have sex with me yet? I don't believe I've ever had the pleasure and I've discovered that the disabled loo is surprisingly spacious. Rupert would kill me, but it would be worth it.'

'No, Joly. I'm not that drunk.' There was not enough tequila, vodka or Jesus fucking Christ (the holiest of spirits) in the whole world to get Nell drunk enough for that to happen.

'Not to worry. I'll be back in an hour or so to check again,' he slurred, hauling himself up.

Nell felt like she might need to powder her nose (peel her flesh from her bones) after that encounter, her skin crawling and all that, so she fled to the ladies. Someone was having the longest, loudest piss. She rifled through her bag and found her lipstick. Nell had read an article in a women's magazine when she was fifteen that said she should pick a shade and stick with it. Make it yours. And she did. She wore the same lipstick to weddings, funerals, first dates, job interviews, the supermarket and smear tests. It worked for her – she had a reputation as the girl who wore red lipstick to the most inappropriate events. Tabitha came out of one of the stalls. She was wearing a navy blue silk dress that was probably in fact a nightie.

'Helena bloody Waddingham. Fuck, you look sexy.'

'Tabs, how are you? It's been a while. We should get a coffee or something soon?'

'Yah, it has, hasn't it. We should do that. You still in publishing?'

'Unfortunately. What are you up to?'

'Oh, I just started my own business,' Tabitha said, proudly sucking in her cheeks and pouting.

Here we go again, Nell thought. 'Wow, what are you doing?'

'I'm a professional stylist for child stars.'

'That must be exciting.'

'You wouldn't believe it. I've just taken on the children from the *Les Mis* cast. So thrilling,' she said leaning in, pupils wide.

'How's Casper?'

'He's Casper. I'm so glad you two broke up. You're way too good for my idiot brother. Your tits look great in that.' Tabitha reached across and copped a feel. 'Are these yours or did you buy them?'

'They're mine,' Nell said, as the door to the women's loos swung open.

'Lesbians!' Jolyon yelled from the corridor. 'Threesome?'

Rupert immediately appeared – as if supernaturally sensing

the pseudo-sapphic energy Tabitha was oozing – in the hope that he could watch whatever was going to unfold, but when he realised it was Nell, whose face was that of a tempest, he changed course. 'Joly, Tabs, in the sin bin you go,' he commanded, directing them towards the rainbow-coloured ball pit. Nell stood in the doorway of the loo watching Jolyon give Tabitha a piggyback to the children's play area as Rupert herded them into what must have been one of the highest concentrations of cold germs per square metre in North London. Rupert trotted back. 'They've just got engaged, you know.'

'They're perfect for each other.' Nell attempted to retreat to the safety of the pleather banquette.

Rupert put his arm up across the door frame. 'I'm taking you for dinner next week. Somewhere nice.'

'No, you're not, Rupert.' She still loved him after everything. She knew she did. She knew she would for beyond forever. The bastard. 'I hate that you're so beautiful, Beauchamp.'

'Come to dinner with me, Waddingham.'

'No. I've given up eating.'

'Nell, darling, be serious. I want to take you out to dinner. I said to you that I would, and here I am asking you properly. Go out with me.'

'No, I don't think we have anything to say to each other any more.'

'We have plenty to say. I turned thirty today and I'm breaking up with Clemmie tomorrow morning. I want to get serious. I want to get serious with you.'

'No, Rupert. I said no. This is the end. I came here tonight to say goodbye. So, goodbye.' Nell went back to her seat. She wanted to leave. She wanted to leave with Alex. She wanted to fuck him, fuck Rupert out of her system. She picked up her milkshake, took a slurp and then threw it against a wall. The chaos of the bacchanal had gained such momentum that barely anyone took notice as the sludge slid down the shiny paintwork.

★　★　★

Alex had managed to empty the entirety of his hip flask into one milkshake, and it had been a surprisingly palatable way to get smashed quickly. He needed to shake Minty, Rupert's childhood friend, soon though. Just when you think that the country exists in the twenty-first century, you get cornered by Jane Austen's virgin aunt at a party because you have 'kind eyes'. Poor thing, she was probably worried about a repeat of Rupert's twenty-fifth (scene of the infamous Great Pond Incident) and had picked him as a safe person to hide behind. She'd been chattering away at him like a nervous squirrel about her new company making floral sculptures for events for a good forty-five minutes. Should he get a double cheeseburger? Should he get a double cheeseburger and a glass of port? Knowing Rupert, it would be very good port. Fuck it, he'd get them both and an apple pie the temperature of the earth's core. 'Excuse me, I'm so sorry, Minty, but I just need to check my emails. Tokyo,' Alex said to Minty.

'Tokyo? Even on a Saturday?' she asked.

'Yes, they're very polite, but as clients they can be quite demanding.'

'Oh, yes, of course.'

Alex smiled broadly and walked over to the table with the food on it as Minty melted into the background. He browsed Twitter for a few moments, yelled out 'Oh, Shigeru-san' – over-committing to a gambit was a gentle sin of his – and then picked up a congealed cheeseburger.

23

'Body is a temple, mate,' said Rupert, smacking Alex on the back so hard that his kidneys rattled.

'Yes, but to which god?'

'That's the curse of the classicist. Which one do you pick?'

'They pick you,' Alex replied. That was Rupert distilled. He had the temerity to be above the heavens: he thought he had the right to choose his fate.

'Do you like redheads? I have a penchant for them personally.'

'I don't have anything against redheads per se.'

'You've met Bella before, right? Works in PR,' Rupert said, slyly gesturing towards a young woman engaged in what appeared to be, but in reality couldn't have been, a sparkling conversation with Teddie, Mungo and Julian, three lugs from their rowing days. They had all gone to seed now that they had steady professions behind desks and weren't getting up at 5 a.m. every day to do 5km before lectures.

'The one who cried about Keats at your twenty-fifth birthday party?' Alex asked.

'Yes. That one. She's got a massive thing for you.'

'Is Keats worth crying over? If it were over John Clare, I could understand it.'

'Great rack, direct descendant of Charles II.'

'Nell Gwynne?'

'Barbara Villiers, I think.'

'You're not selling her to me.'

'Women aren't a commodity, Alex. I would have thought you knew better.'

'Pass the port,' Alex said, changing the topic. 'Where's Clem?'

'Fuck knows,' Rupert said, handing Alex a bottle of Graham's 1986.

Alex poured himself a glass. It sloshed around and spilled

onto his cuff. It pooled like a blotch of blood. 'What have you done this time?'

'Clemmie's been leaving bridal magazines in odd places around the house for the last year. She finally stopped the other week, thankfully. What man wants to look at wedding dresses when they're taking a shit?'

'Are you going to marry her?'

'No, of course not. Not the right sort.' Rupert tried not to move, but Alex saw the tension in his shoulder as he resisted looking around for Nell. Alex had lost sight of her too, but he was trying to be cool about it.

'Best to break it off before it gets any worse.' Alex didn't think this advice was in his own best interests, but the booze had loosened his resolve. He remembered the nasty little vignette Rupert and Nell had posed for on the pavement earlier.

'I've decided that I'm kicking her out tomorrow. For good this time. I've been meaning to do it for a couple of months – well, years. Who doesn't turn up to their boyfriend's birthday?'

'Clemmie, evidently,' Alex said, sniffing his lapels. 'My jacket smells like fat. Where's the afterparty?'

'I have a little idea – might go skinny dipping in the Heath, but we'll have to see how trolleyed I am.'

'It's unlike you not to have some further grand, elaborate scheme.'

'Is this not enough?' Rupert asked, arms spread wide, gesturing at his guests.

The room was full of the sort of people that *Tatler* thinks you should know. Droll. Eyebrow-archingly amusing, achingly so. Distressingly beautiful. And rich, but the sort of rich that makes you interesting because you never talk about it. Second homes and literary aspirations. Boarding school Ancient Greek and au pair French. Long legs and taut torsos honed by expensive yoga studios and treks up Machu Picchu. From the banquettes to the ball pit, the room was replete with people like Rupert.

Alex laughed. 'More than enough.'

'I used to be jealous of you.'

'Why?'

'You're so simple,' Rupert replied.

'Thank you, I think.'

'You don't need much. You're some bucolic relic.'

'Is this about my grandfather again?'

'How could it not be? He was a Cypriot shepherd. How magical! Mine was just an MP.'

'Why do the English idolise sheep?' Alex asked, not expecting an answer.

Bella the busty redhead appeared. 'Rupe darling, you were going to tell me earlier about your novel.'

'Tell you what? That he hasn't written it despite banging on about it for the last decade?' Alex interjected. 'Excuse me.'

Rupert puckered his mouth, steam practically emanating from his being, as Bella stood there embarrassed by the slight. A disturbing cacophony of panting noises could be heard coming from the ball pit.

★　★　★

Alex stood in front of Nell. He'd joined her at a dimly lit industrial-looking cocktail place round the corner from the party as she sat at the bar. She was reading a book and ignoring the martini she'd ordered and the man across from her who kept trying to make eye contact. 'It's reassuring to know that England is still England and that you are still terrible at parties.'

'Why are you mad with me?' Nell asked him, not looking up from her book.

'I'm not mad with you. I'm grieving. I have given you up for good,' Alex said, sitting next to her, the misjudged mixing of wine and spirits having made him hyperbolic. 'I have given up the girl who I have been desperately, pitiably in love with for the better part of a decade. I have given up the one girl who takes copies of Marcus fucking Aurelius to parties. In the original Latin, too . . .'

'I am not a girl; I am a woman.' Nell took an unsoiled napkin from the bar and used it as a bookmark. She put the slight volume into her bag. 'Are you coming home with me or what?'

SUNDAY

3

Hampstead Heath

Caius Beauchamp was jogging on the spot at the bottom of Parliament Hill, trying to psych himself up for another doomed attempt at the summit. He had been dumped three weeks ago by Héloise: a sarcastically eyebrowed Parisienne poet who saw beauty in the oddest things and cruelty in everything. One day, he had thought, she would be the mother of his children. In penance for whatever flaw, whatever fault, whatever failing that had led her to desert him for some other man (a mystery that he had yet to solve), Caius had made self-improvement his *raison d'être*. Some addled, lovesick part of his brain had told him that if he got his act together then he might have a small chance of getting her back. Thus, he'd designed a regimen for both body and mind. He'd taken up running and YouTube yoga. He'd designated Tuesday as leg day. Caius was also now on first-name terms with the staff at the library around the corner from his flat as he slogged his way through all the books that he knew he should have read but had previously been unbothered by. The next stage of his overhaul was to acquire a new level of Euro-chic consumerist sophistication. So far he had bought a black polo neck jumper (this time not from Topman but a menswear pop-up shop in Shoreditch), a new pair of glasses from a Dutch online optician far more *élégant* than his usual Specsavers, a 5kg tub of chocolate-flavoured protein powder from a Swedish fitness company that he couldn't pronounce, and new bedsheets from a Danish brand stocked only in Selfridges (in the sale – some habits die hard). He'd even started going to the farmer's market on the weekend to touch up obscure varieties of organic squashes. The only squash in his upbringing had been orange. What else was a stodgy, lower-middle-class English policeman with a chip on his shoulder and an Estuary accent to do other than buy his way to bourgeois refinement and back into Héloise's heart? He thought it could work, and he was sure that was what he wanted. Adamant. Although, when he'd gone to purchase his ticket for the Eurostar that he was catching later that afternoon, he'd forgotten the PIN for his credit card (despite it being 1234). He wondered briefly if his subconscious was trying to tell him something deeply important, but he suppressed it. His train was at 3 p.m., but first he had to conquer Parliament Hill.

Caius started slowly up the hill, dodging dogshit as he ascended. It was steeper than he remembered it. Feeling prematurely triumphant, he increased the pace, but soon the embers of that dreaded burning sensation began to blaze in his calves. He tried to think of other things – he tried to think of what he'd do that afternoon. His train got into Gare du Nord just after 6 p.m., but then what? Caius hadn't yet worked out a plan. He did not know what to say, what to do. He would make an impromptu grand gesture and hope for the best. At the Louvre? No, too cringey. Jardin des Tuileries? Somewhere they could take their children and say: 'This, this is where it all happened.' He wasn't sure where, but he was sure that he wasn't going to make it to the top of Parliament Hill today. It had become something of a pilgrimage for Caius. The thought of conquering the city's twenty-third highest point had become the only thing that had got him out of bed this last week. He wheezed a third of the way up before deciding to walk the rest of the steep path to the top. Maybe he should go to the GP to check if he had asthma? It was probably just the pollution.

London is a filthy city. A dirty, putrid metropolis. What was he even going to do in Paris? What a ridiculous idea. Héloise didn't want him. She'd said as much, but in French and therefore much more expressively.

A pigeon loitered on a bench halfway up the hill, strutting across the breadth of it. Caius breathlessly flapped his arms and flung himself down. The bird was stubborn. 'I suppose we shall just have to be friends then, pigeon,' Caius said to the bird. It flew off. He pulled out his phone and checked the distance that he'd run – far enough to drop casually into conversation. Caius thought he deserved to walk back to his flat. He'd earned a slower pace, although he probably should do some theatrical stretches in case anyone he knew saw him. He'd seen a pretty woman in bright pink leggings at the bottom of the hill. A few lunges later and Caius strolled towards the trees north of the bench. He did a loop through a patch of woodland and then started to lightly jog down the hill towards the gates. Caius walked past the trees that ran along the park's boundary, not knowing the names of any of them. That might have been a birch, or an elm, or a horse chestnut. Some flowers here, a dull brown bird there.

And a stiletto oddly poking out the bottom of some scrub that probably warranted closer inspection, as did the corpse that was wearing it.

* * *

'Detective, you were the one to find the body. I thought you were in France?' asked Barry, the masked pathologist looming over the open body bag.

'I was out for a morning run before I caught my train. Better me than a dog walker. Makes a change from Carol and her diabetic Labrador,' Caius replied to the shrouded face.

'Cats are better.'

'Whoa, big chat for a murder scene, buddy.'

'*Un gros* chat?'

'I see what you did there,' Caius said, feigning amusement. His impromptu Paris trip was as dead as the girl whose shoe he had seen. 'What's your initial assessment?'

'The victim is a Caucasian young woman, mid-to-late twenties. Dead around fifteen hours or so. I'll be more precise after the post-mortem. She had her wrists bound before she died. A fox, by the looks of it, has had a bit of a go on her.'

'Her throat was slashed posthumously?' Caius stared at the gash on her neck. At a glance you could have mistaken the gaping flesh for a delicate choker of rubies. It was only when you looked closer that the true horror was revealed: the deep purple bruises on her wrists, her hacked-at neck, the stench of vomit coming from her ball gown. The poor woman.

'Yes, you can tell by the lack of blood. Her heart wasn't beating. Not sure of the blade yet. However, the position of the stain on the front of her dress suggests she threw up on herself before the throat slitting. Cause of death was asphyxiation. She choked on her own vomit. It's been dry out so there aren't any impressions on the ground, but we're looking for stomach content nearby. We found the other high-heeled shoe, size six, in the thicket too.'

Caius looked at the dead woman's face. She had been beautiful and hadn't yet been dead long enough for her features to become horribly distorted. The press was going to go bonkers for this case.

'DI Beauchamp,' a voice called from in the thicket, 'we've found her bag.'

'Any ID inside? A bank card?' Caius yelled.

34

'No, just a lipstick, a compact mirror and a business card for a hairdresser's,' came the reply.

'All right, get it into evidence,' Caius called.

'Detective, I wanted to point out the flower crown,' Barry continued, pointing at the floral arrangement on her head. 'It's got a pagan sacrifice vibe to it, a bit *Wicker Man*.'

'It's something else, isn't it? Thanks, mate. Oh, could you please get someone from your team to bag everything in the bins?'

'Do you have any particular bins in mind?'

'Bag all of them in the park. We've no way of knowing which way the killer went. They might have discarded the knife as they fled,' Caius said, as Barry went back to zipping up the body bag.

Caius walked out of the wood and into the open meadow that, but for the police tape, should soon have been filled with respectable picnickers and sloppy teens passing around glandular fever.

'Here comes my favourite himbo,' said Matt, Caius's DS. He was looking Caius up and down with some amusement. 'What are you wearing? I was worried that I would look a bit informal without a tie, but never mind.'

'I was out running. The lycra makes you more aerodynamic.'

'When is leg day?'

'Tuesday, you gobshite.'

'Aren't you supposed to be on holiday?'

'I spoke to the grand pooh-bahh, and as I had the displeasure of finding the young lady so dishevelled, I will postpone my break. It's probably not a bad thing.'

'You're not a fan of the Chief Superintendent, are you.'

'Keith the Chief wears novelty clothing all year round.'

'Damning,' Matt said, smirking. 'There has to be more to it than that?'

Caius ignored his question. 'Barry's team have just found her bag, so hopefully we can use it to identify our Jane Doe.'

'Hampstead Heath Constabulary have closed the park and there are officers stationed at all the exits taking statements. The dogs are going to do a sweep once forensics are done with the immediate crime scene. It's so much easier when people get killed in their own homes.'

'Murderers can be so inconsiderate towards the police. I'm really looking forward to all the foaming tweets about closing the park for forty-eight hours.'

'I hate the public.'

'That's the only rational response to this job. Everything under control, Matt?'

'Yeah.'

'I'm going to go home and change. These leggings . . . I feel exposed.'

'Yeah, you should go before HR gets involved and gives you another warning.'

'See you at the station,' Caius said, stretching his calves. He jogged off down the path until he was out of Matt's sight and then he slouched home at a crawl.

4

Nell's flat, overlooking Victoria Park

Sunlight dappled Nell's bedroom with the soft touch that hang-overs demand. Nell was a slut in the original sense – she hated housework. Her room was cluttered with the detritus of her messy existence. Half-read books, half-empty teacups and half-dead house plants. Fabric oddments, jars of buttons. Untouched copies of the *LRB* that she could neither be bothered to read nor cancel. Nell's head thumped and she felt sticky. It was too early to be up on a Sunday. Alex rolled over and into her arms. He smelled almost edible.

'You've been practising since college. I would never have thought you'd be that good at oral,' Nell said to Alex's sleep-filled face.

'In defence of twenty-one-year-old me, I had been given a lot of morphine that day.'

'Oh yeah, you broke your finger.'

'It's still wonky,' Alex said, holding up his other little finger for comparison.

Nell touched it. 'Your poor hand. That was a funny evening, wasn't it? I feel like I should make you a rosette or something. A little trophy for your mantelpiece. Get it engraved: "Best Improvement".'

'I'm offended. I have many previously undisclosed talents,' he said with his eyes still half shut.

'Like getting kicked out of taxis.'

'Like getting kicked out of taxis by prudish drivers. Your Uber rating must have plummeted. I can't blame the man though. I'm also very good at pétanque.'

'What a useful skill for a tax consultant.' Nell rolled out of bed – she was glad that she'd changed the sheets the day before. 'I have a horrible hangover, although I barely drank a thing.'

'Tequila,' Alex replied. He wanted to know what this was. Was it a one-time thing? He didn't want that. 'We should go out for breakfast. Bacon makes hangovers disappear.'

'I'm a vegan now,' Nell said, leaving the bedroom and wandering into the open-plan kitchen-diner-cum-living room-cum-store for Nell's ex Casper's painting crap.

'I saw you eat a double cheeseburger last night,' Alex said, getting up and scrabbling around for his boxers.

'Minor slip-up.'

'All right, a vegan fry-up to get you back on the wagon. This is Hackney, so that shouldn't be too hard to find. I hear that vegans breed like rabbits round here,' Alex said, as Nell came back with two glasses of water. 'It must be the number of carrots they eat.'

'Here you go.'

'Cheers. Could you please explain what a tofu scramble is? I keep seeing them on my feed, and they confuse me.'

'It's sadness on toast. Also, the toast has no butter.'

'So double the sadness?'

'The chickens and the cows are delighted though.' Nell went over to her dressing table and started searching for a reusable replacement for cotton wool to remove her make-up. She'd seen them online and felt guilty enough to buy them. Cotton, what an immoral little plant.

'You're not really a vegan, are you?'

'I dabble.' Nell started trying to scrub last night from her cheeks.

'Are you dabbling with me right now?' Alex asked, sitting on the edge of the bed.

'That depends.'

'On what?'

'On you.'

'I don't want this to be a dabble. I want this to be a thing. A thing thing.'

'A thing? Books are things, so are toasters and mosquitoes.'

'Mosquitoes are a life form, not an inanimate object.'

'Always the pedant. Are you going to spank me for not conjugating a verb properly?'

'*Amo, amas, amat.*' Alex looked sternly at Nell. 'You want me to say it, don't you.'

'Of course I do.'

'All right, Helena Waddingham, I think we would do well together.'

'We would do well together, would we? Have you been watching bodice rippers again?'

'Just the Emma Thompson version of *Sense and Sensibility*. I downloaded it and watched it on the flight over from Athens.'

'Such a talented woman,' Nell laughed as she played with her hair, which desperately needed a cut. Her waves were like seaweed. Ready to ensnare and drown overboard sailors who swam through her depths. 'I don't normally go for nice boys, and as a courtesy for having made me come thrice in the last six hours, you can take me out today. We've always had a little something, right? The potential, but not the timing, to be more than friends. We shall just have to see where it goes.'

'You're wicked.'

'And yet you still asked me out, so I'm doing something right. Besides, I sort of like you. A little bit, just a little bit.'

'I can work with "sort of like",' Alex laughed as he watched her at her toilette. 'I'll go back to my hotel and change after breakfast. I can't wander around East London in a wing-tipped collar on a Sunday.'

'This is Hackney – you'll fit in better than you'd think. What if I join in? We can have a dress-up day where we pretend we're Victorians. I can cough into a kerchief and have consumption.'

'I'm not a fan of that sort of English nostalgia.'

'Not being creepy or anything – it's not some weird sex game – it's just that there's a wardrobe of Casper's least favourite things, and you're about the same size. Would it be weird if you wore my ex's clothes?'

'Yeah. When is he coming to collect them? You broke up three months ago.' Alex was feeling territorial. To say that Alex hadn't been a fan of Casper's would not have been a lie. Casper, Casper, Casper. How would Alex describe Casper Thorsson? Cold, beautiful. Casper was Tabitha's blond half-brother. He was tall. He was mercurial. He was an artist and the closest thing to perfect this side of Rupert. Nell had a type.

'Casper owns the flat – his dad bought it for him, and I'm barely paying him anything to live here. He probably feels guilty, poor sod. I'll move out when he gets back from his artist's residency in Bristol. I don't really care.'

Alex climbed off the bed and started trying to find the rest of his clothing. His bow tie was strung across Nell's mirror on her dressing table. He picked it up and shoved it in his pocket. He couldn't find his cufflinks and there was no way he was going to amidst all Nell's trinkets. 'Get dressed, and we'll have some breakfast.'

'I know the perfect place.'

★ ★ ★

Alex slouched back in his chair, their table smothered with the debris of a good breakfast. They were sitting side by side at a table outside a Turkish restaurant on a busy road in Islington. It was an excellent spot for people-watching. And dog-watching. Judging by the high grooming standards, Islingtonites spent insane money on their Labradoodles. Alex saw a minuscule puppy that looked like a teddy bear. He thought he'd like to have one of those someday soon, and a house with a garden, and a wife and a baby or three. The whole adulthood starter kit. 'It's too early in the day to order baklava, isn't it?' Alex asked, not needing a response.

'What's Turkish for baklava?' Nell sipped her apple tea and watched a couple across the road have a fight. They were trying to be discreet but had perfectly failed. The woman seethed with quiet, inaudible rage as the man unsuccessfully tried to placate her with tiny hand gestures.

'I think it's the same word. I might order some to go. Although I doubt it would be as good as the baklava in a Greek restaurant.'

Nell's phone buzzed, again. Rupert had rung. He'd also sent her a text, a Facebook message from that stupid, anonymous dummy account of his and a WhatsApp. 'How do you ghost a friendship?'

'The easy thing is to delete and block him. He won't accept the affront though. He's never been treated like that before.'

'I will start small and unfollow Phlegm on Instagram.' Nell flicked through her feed and giggled at Clemmie's pathetic attempt at guruhood. Sure, she could do the poses correctly, but she was dead behind the eyes. A woman so devoid of sincerity and joy; a black hole crammed with lip fillers and empty platitudes.

'I need to go back to my hotel.'

'Are you not staying with your parents?'

'They've finally moved to Cyprus now that my dad has retired. They've let their house out, so I'm stuck in a very sad budget hotel in Farringdon. I am going to go back, change out of this get-up and check my emails.'

'They make you check your emails on the weekend?'

'It's expected once you reach my pay grade. How about I meet you at the V&A at 2 p.m.? If you want to, that is?'

'I adore the V&A.'

'Lovely.' Alex signalled to the waiter. Nell did the I-can-pay-we-can-go-halvesies shuffle but acquiesced when she noticed the Platinum Amex slip out of his wallet. Alex leaned across the table and kissed Nell on the cheek before he left. It felt rather chaste, considering.

Nell finished her apple tea, and the waiter came and passive-aggressively started clearing up around her. She asked the waiter for some baklava to take away.

5

The Police Station

Caius sat at his desk feeling proud of its neatness. He'd had a 'little tidy' last week so that it would reflect his new, Spartan sense of discipline. Héloise didn't believe in owning things. She was a Catholic minimalist who dabbled in Zen Buddhism. Caius had a mug of green tea brewing. Organic, of course. Loose leaf, brewed with one of those doodads that you put straight into the mug. He had bought it in IKEA last week. It was shaped like a tiny house with love hearts for windows. He'd changed out of his running clothes and into a pair of grey trousers that grazed his ankles, a white linen button-down shirt with the sleeves rolled up, and a pair of brown suede loafers. No socks. Caius went to lengths not to look like a plod, although he might have gone a bit far, a bit too ad-land today. Caius was looking over the missing persons reports from the last week and failing to find anyone closely resembling the girl in the body bag. The smell of greasy chips wafted through the incident room as Matt appeared with a McDonald's bag. 'Lunchtime, Matt?'

'Yeah, what have you got today? Something sprouted?'

'You're going to die young,' Caius said, getting out of his chair and moving towards the break room with his mug of bitter, over-brewed green tea. The tannins made him wince.

'I was supposed to be at a barbecue this afternoon, so this is my pitiful replacement,' Matt said, taking a seat at the table.

Caius opened the fridge and looked at his lunch. It was lamentable. Healthy but tragic, in an 'on my deathbed I will regret not eating more burgers' kind of way. 'Quinoa, salad and grilled chicken.'

'Mate,' Matt said, leaning in, 'I know you're my superior and whatever, but I think we've become pretty good friends over the last couple of years, and stop me if I'm overstepping, but if you want to talk to someone about what happened with Héloise then I'm a walking ear.'

'I'm good, mate. I'm good.'

'Cool,' Matt said, taking a bite out of his burger. 'How's your quinoa?'

'Perfectly seasoned.'

'What's that? Fresh dill?'

'Yep.' Caius poured the olive oil and lemon juice dressing he'd made from a minuscule pot that he had bought specifically for the purpose of transporting vinaigrettes around with him.

'You're so sophisticated.'

Caius stabbed some spinach with his fork. 'Thank you, Matthew.'

'Any time.'

'I actually like quinoa.'

'Me too. I hate the whole class-based food-shaming thing.'

'Right? I bought this in Lidl.'

'I have a recipe for sweet potato and quinoa burgers that's amazing.'

'You're so much better than my last DS.'

6

A cafe on Exhibition Road

Nell had walked from Islington to the V&A. No better way to kill a couple of hours waiting to go on a date with your long-standing friend who you angry-shagged last night than with a brisk panic-stroll through Central London. She had put her headphones in and listened to a science podcast or six. An overdose of pure facts to clear her mind. Learning about astrophysics made her feel comfortingly small, her problems minute, her life insignificant. Nell had arrived early and taken a selfie for her Instagram in front of the building, angling it so that the main entrance's carvings curved around the top of the picture with only her eyes visible. She was wearing a pair of oversized sunglasses that she'd seen in an abandoned copy of *Stylist* on the tube. They were blocky and quite ugly, but they made her feel like a sophisticate. Nell didn't fancy milling around on the benches out front with all the tourists in the heat, so she'd walked a loop around the Royal Albert Hall. The Victorians were such an earnest, assured and complacent people. They believed in progress so fervently, Nell mused, as she took in the frieze that skirted around the outside of the hall like the ribbon on a birthday cake. They thought they'd rule the world forever. That industry, invention and their 'obvious' superiority would naturally cause relentless progress.

She'd then gone to one of the overpriced cafes at the bottom of Exhibition Road and was now queueing for two iced coffees to go. It was too hot outside, and the shop had large windows that they'd opened out fully onto the street. People were lounging about at tables under the shade of a tasteful lilacky-grey canopy watching the world and their Boden-clad toddlers go by. She hadn't brought a reusable cup with her and felt terrible that she didn't feel terrible. That mistake had cost her an extra twenty pence. The barista was taking their time, so Nell did an awkward demonstrative dance with the woman at the till indicating that she was going to go to the loo. The loo was vile and lacking in hand cream, but when she came out the coffees she'd ordered were waiting. Her phone buzzed and she pulled it out of her culotte pocket – she endeavoured to only own clothes with usable pockets – and was going to answer it on the assumption that it was Alex, but when she saw it was Rupert she sent the call to voicemail. To her horror she heard an all-too-familiar voice booming in the street.

'Nell, it's Rupert. Wanted to check that you're all right. Quite an exit! I'm disappointed that you left so early. Let me know when you're free. I'm desperate to catch up. Coffee perhaps? Just the two of us. I would, of course, prefer it if you let me take you out for dinner.' He coughed. 'I'm dumping Clemmie today, when she finally crawls out of whatever hole she slept in last night.' Rupert walked past the cafe's open windows and towards the V&A.

Nell froze. Was this a coincidence, or had Rupert followed her to the museum? Her phone rang again – this time it was Alex.

'Hey, sorry I'm a bit late. Had to send a few emails. I'm just coming out of South Ken tube now.'

'I'm at the swish coffee shop at the bottom of Exhibition Road, next to the ice cream place,' she choked.

'Are you all right? You sound funny.'

'Yeah, I'm fine.'

'I'll be there in a moment.'

'This may sound bonkers, but try to be discreet,' Nell said before hanging up. She moved towards the door and leaned her head out. She saw Rupert cross Cromwell Road and turn out of sight towards the museum entrance. She stepped into the street and straight into Alex, who had jogged the hundred metres from the station.

'Coffee? Is that for me?' he asked, now dressed like a normal person in a pair of shorts and a loose-fitting shirt. He took the second coffee from her.

'I like that print,' Nell said, admiring the hundreds of tiny, snarling tigers that emblazoned his chest. Their teeth were bared and their claws unfurled.

'Thank you. What's up?' he asked, observing her demeanour. 'We could not do this. If you've changed your mind that's fine. I'm an adult, I can take rejection.'

'No. No, I want to do this,' Nell said, walking out onto the pavement. 'We just can't go to the V&A. Not any more. I'm sorry, it's my fault. It's always my fault.'

'What's your fault?'

'It's Rupert. He's here. I was early and I posted a picture of me in front of the museum, and he must have seen it and now he's here.'

'You're sure it was him?'

'Positive. He walked right past. I heard him leaving me a voicemail. I shouldn't have gone last night. I knew I shouldn't have. Everyone thinks he's so charming.'

'But?'

'But . . . He's got worse, hasn't he? He used to be fun, but a bit of a dick. Would get me to lend him my lecture notes because he was too hungover to turn up. I'd have to pick up a can of Coke for him on the way to his room in college and then sit on the end of the bed while he'd tell me a version of whatever fantastical thing he'd done the night before. But he's got worse over the years.'

'At least you weren't there to see it first-hand. He had a horrific reputation even amongst the scum of the earth in the rowing team.'

'He was so charming and sort of hopeless, I'd just do stuff for him. Now he makes me feel icky.'

Alex put his hand on her arm reassuringly. 'You don't have to be friends with people you don't want to. Maybe you should put that in writing and then block him? Either way, I think we should go somewhere else.'

'Sorry, this is a terrible date.'

'Hardly, I've got a free coffee out of it so far.'

Nell grinned a coy little smile and pulled out a plastic box from her bag. 'And some baklava.'

'Oh, goddess!' Alex said, his eyes bright. 'How about we go to the Saatchi Gallery instead? We can laugh at how we don't understand what's going on.'

'I'd like that. I don't get contemporary art.'

'No one does,' Alex said, taking her hand and quickly glancing over his shoulder for any roguish blonds.

They walked past South Kensington tube, heading towards the King's Road.

'Have you ever seen *Pygmalion*?' Nell asked with a skip in her step.

'Years ago, perhaps,' Alex replied. He hadn't seen it, but he didn't want to admit it.

'George Bernard Shaw got very annoyed with the first few productions because they made out that Eliza went back to Professor Higgins, married him and they lived happily ever after in Wimpole Street. He didn't like that so he wrote a little explanation saying that, and I'm paraphrasing now, if Eliza went back to Higgins then she would spend her life fetching his slippers, but if she went and married Freddy instead then he would spend his life fetching hers, and so she did. Colonel Pickering bought the Eynsford-Hills a florist's in South Kensington station and they got by on Freddy's schoolboy Latin and her new accent. Bernard Shaw acquiesced in the end and allowed the sentimental performances to continue, but I like to think about Eliza Doolittle and her little florist's every time I pass through this station.'

'I love your little lectures.'

★ ★ ★

Alex and Nell walked into a room in the Saatchi Gallery. It was pure white, like standing on the inside of a sugar cube. No paintings hung on the walls. No sculptures stood in the middle of the cavernous space. No videos were projected onto screens and no audio recordings played overhead.

'What do you think it means?' Alex whispered deferentially.

'I don't have a clue,' Nell replied, wandering around the empty room.

'Is it a comment on the bleakness of material possessions?'

'Or perhaps that we are born from nothingness, a blank slate, and when we die we return to that nothingness, the slate wiped clean?'

An authoritative young woman with an artfully edgy haircut and an odd pair of spectacles came into the room. She had a walkie-talkie at her hip and wore a pair of limited-edition Doc Martens covered in Renaissance cherubs. She was quite clearly in charge. 'I'm sorry, this room is closed in preparation for an exhibition opening next week.'

'That solves that question,' Nell said, bouncing out of the room as Alex trailed behind her. 'It meant bugger all.'

They walked out of the gallery and into the late afternoon's gentle warmth. An ice cream van was parked at the bottom of the Lilliputian square and a small queue of people had formed.

'Can I buy you an ice cream?' Alex asked, joining the queue.

'You can.' Nell slid her hand into his as they waited.

'Two 99s with raspberry sauce, please,' Alex said, getting a tenner out of his pocket as they reached the front of the queue.

Ice creams in hand, and very little change in Alex's pocket, they wandered over to a bench. The queue had subsided, and the ice cream van started playing 'Greensleeves' before pulling off.

'I can think of no sound as much like summer as that,' Nell said, pulling out the flake from her ice cream and taking a bite. 'Thank you, by the way.'

'You're welcome.' Alex put his arm round Nell's shoulders. 'So?'

'So?'

'So? Did you enjoy today?' Alex spotted a crumb of flake that had fallen from Nell's lips and had landed on her exposed chest. It was melting.

'I did. What are you doing tomorrow evening?'

'You tell me.'

7

The Police Station

Caius had been thinking about what their strategy should be before he got called in by the Chief Superintendent. Caius dreaded the inevitable pep talk sprinkled with golfing metaphors that the grand pooh-bahh would relish making. He rummaged through a drawer and found some Post-its. Generic versions – times were tough: cuts to the budget equals inferior stationery and fewer police officers on the streets.

'Who murders young women?' Caius asked.

'Serial killers, but it's usually the boyfriend,' Matt replied.

'Right.' Caius wrote *partner* and *serial killer* on separate sticky notes and put each one on the empty whiteboard behind him. 'There are no ongoing investigations with the same MO, so probably not a serial killer. We're waiting on forensics to confirm, but the initial assessment is asphyxiation after choking on her own vomit and then someone went back later to mutilate the corpse. Are the killer and the mutilator the same person?'

'You'd have to really hate someone to mutilate them after they've already been killed by someone else.'

'True. I think we can safely assume that they are one and the same. The dress she was wearing looked expensive. It was fancy, like she was going to the opera. However, her jewellery's pretty cheap – all sterling silver: a chain with a key on it and a pair of mother of pearl studs. We need to see her bag.'

'Forensics said that they'd get it to us first thing tomorrow morning. It could be a drug gang?' Matt wondered, chewing on a pen. He bit it too hard and it started leaking. 'Went out in

Camden, did too much coke, pissed off the wrong person, found herself dead on Hampstead Heath.'

'It doesn't feel right,' Caius said, passing Matt a box of tissues from his desk. 'If you can afford a dress like that, you can afford a drug habit. I'm going to go through the statements uniform took from people in the park now. I doubt anyone saw anything. The body was probably dumped at night. Put a request in to TfL for the CCTV footage for Gospel Oak, Hampstead Heath and Kentish Town for all of yesterday. I've looked through the missing persons for the whole country. Thought she could be a party girl who sniffed more than she could snort on a weekend away. She was dressed for a night out.'

'She's the sort of girl people miss when they're gone.' Matt dabbed at a spot of ink that had stained his shirt.

'Exactly. You should call it a day once you've spoken to TfL. It's getting late.'

'Bright and early tomorrow then.'

'Tomorrow. Oh, and Nigella, send me that recipe, please.' Caius stared at the board: *serial killer* or *partner*. It's always the arsehole boyfriend. He took the serial killer Post-it down, screwed it up and aimed it at the bin. He missed and had to go and pick it up. He didn't want to get in trouble with the cleaner again.

MONDAY

8

The Police Station

Caius hadn't slept well, despite his soft new bedsheets and a valerian diffuser he'd bought for his bedside table. He found himself at his desk at 7 a.m., propelled by an offensively large almond croissant that he'd gobbled on his bus journey in and a travel mug of instant coffee that didn't taste of anything but was effective in its caffeine load. He'd left flakes of buttery croissant all over the bus seat. He felt guilty about that now – the mess, that is. One should never feel guilty about a croissant. Caius thought that if there's one lesson to be learned from the French, it is that pastries are a daily pleasure, not a sin. However, the thought of all those old ladies sitting in his crumbs on their way to the Marks & Spencer food hall, or wherever they go, wasn't a pleasant one.

Caius spent an hour trawling through ancient cold case files trying to find another case with the same MO, but nothing suggested that it was a serial killer. No matching missing persons reports had arrived overnight, but he had had an email from forensics – the post-mortem was that afternoon, and the handbag was on its way over. They will have had Freedom of Information requests from the press by now. You can't close Hampstead Heath without anyone noticing. A wonderful reason for the Chief Superintendent to come and patronise his desk. Appeals for information from the public had only elicited responses from the usual fantasists. The crime scene photos were already at his desk when he arrived. He took the photo of the dead woman's face, placed it on the board and wrote 'Jane

Doe' next to it. The flower crown felt particularly despicable. It was quite beautiful, the glorious colours of a summer twilight: radiant blushed oranges and beaming pinks. Bright and aglow, like glimpsing dusk.

Matt appeared just after 8.30 a.m. with a spring in his step, which could only mean he either got laid or had had an idea that he was proud of.

'*Guten Morgen, mein Liebling,*' Caius greeted him.

'*Bonjour, mon ami.* Any updates?' Matt asked as he plonked himself on his swivel chair.

'Non-updates really. The sweep of the park failed to throw up anything remotely capable of causing the mutilation,' Caius said, before getting Matt up to speed.

'I had a thought last night.'

'NSFW?' Caius had seen this acronym on Twitter recently and had had to find out what it meant.

'I saw a friend of mine.'

'A friend?' Caius asked, his eyebrows raised, and his lips pursed.

'Maybe more than a friend, I don't know yet, but she's Swedish and she said that they celebrate Midsummer, which was Saturday, and they all wear flower crowns. She said there's a big party every year in Hyde Park. Perhaps the victim got the wrong park?'

'Our victim is blonde, although I would say it came out of a bottle,' Caius said, nodding as he considered it. 'Can you ring the Scandi embassies in case they've had a call from a concerned parent in Stockholm or Oslo? I doubt an post-mortem would throw up whether she's a Viking. Would you like a cuppa? I've not eaten yet today. I'm going to make myself a green tea to go with my porridge.' He had refused to acknowledge the croissant after all. So much for his new-found sense of Gallic epicureanism.

'Builder's, six sugars.'

'You can have a fruit infusion,' Caius said, opening his drawer and grabbing his tin of loose leaf, his strainer thingy, and an individual serving packet of organic oats (with added cinnamon, chia seeds and ground goji berry), before going to the break room. As the tea brewed and his second breakfast waltzed around the microwave, he stared out of the window. Héloise was probably sprawled across her bed wearing nothing, musing about some concept beyond Caius's comprehension so violently poignant and grotesquely profound that it would make choirs of seraphim weep from the devastation. The microwave pinged and he returned to his desk, and the reality of a North London murder.

Matt was on the phone, bobbing his head to holding music. 'It's Grieg. These Norwegians are classy. Got through to the Danes, nothing amiss.' The music stopped abruptly. 'Ah, hello, this is Detective Sergeant Matthew Cheung of the Metropolitan Police . . .'

Caius looked up and saw the Chief Superintendent pacing down the corridor. Their eyes met as he pushed open the glass door to the incident room. Caius sat up straight in his chair. 'Good morning, sir.'

'Morning, Caius, Matt. Where are we with the Hampstead Heath case?' The Chief Superintendent's cufflinks were extra special today: a police helmet on one wrist and a truncheon on the other.

Caius moved towards the board, gesturing to the photo of the flower crown and explained Matt's Midsummer idea.

'Interesting theory. Not concrete enough to keep the press at bay. Hopefully, you'll soon have something more solid than what Comms have put out already.'

'I'm positive we will, sir. The park is still closed, and officers are continuing to sweep the immediate vicinity. They should be done by this afternoon. Hopefully more physical evidence will reveal itself over the coming days.'

'The tabloids are going to be all over this case.'

'Yes, sir. There are some late nights ahead of us.'

★ ★ ★

Matt had drawn a blank on missing Scandinavians, but they'd received the handbag from evidence. Forensics had separated the contents into individual plastic wallets which Caius and Matt were poring over.

'One lipstick, YSL. Expensive – she must have got that from a department store not a pharmacy,' Matt said, picking up one of the plastic wallets before moving on to another. 'One compact mirror. Sterling silver hallmark on the back. Silver isn't worth much, but it could still be pawned. She didn't have her purse or her phone on her.'

'Robbery doesn't fit the MO. The handbag is designer. Why not steal all of it if you wanted to make some money? You could sell the bag on one of those vintage sites. Her phone and her purse might have been taken to hide her identity. Anyone can track a lost phone online.'

'If they didn't want anyone to find the body then why leave a foot sticking out of the bracken? Why dump her in a busy public park for that matter?'

'Good point. A rush job? Oh, this is interesting,' Caius said, looking at a small paper card through its plastic bag. 'Which barber shop do you go to?'

'The one on the corner of the high street.'

58

'Why?'

'Because it's near work.'

'I go to the one at the bottom of my road, because I'm also lazy.'

★　★　★

Cythera on Kensington Church Street was one of the most millennial places that Caius had ever set foot in, and he was one. The walls were powder pink, the floor had chessboard black-and-white tiles, and the counters were pale grey marble. The fixtures were polished brass, and the lighting was soft. It smelled like orange blossom and aspiration. Caius and Matt stood outside the shop, trying to get their bearings. Matt had scrolled through their Instagram as they drove over, hoping that their victim might have tagged herself, but found nothing. A blonde woman with a swishy ponytail sped past them on the pavement and onto the waiting high street.

'The Sweaty Betty sale must have just begun,' Caius said as he watched her bob out of sight.

The salon was quiet – there was only one woman getting a blow-dry at the back of the shop and one bored-looking young woman at the till. There were three empty nail bars at the front and four more empty hairdressing chairs.

'I'll do all the talking and you look out for anything weird. You like weird,' Caius said, straightening his Ralph Lauren tie – also purchased in the Selfridges sale.

'Weird is why I come to work every day.' Matt straightened his tie too – he didn't need to, but it felt appropriate. 'That, and the glamour.'

Caius opened the door to the salon. 'DI Beauchamp, and this

is DS Cheung. Could we please speak to your manager?' Caius flashed his badge while trying to be discreet.

'Please take a seat, I'll be one moment,' the young woman replied, a little flustered. She turned and nearly knocked a perilously placed charity donation box off the reception desk. The box was bright purple and complemented her baby blue and pastel pink hair. She looked like a heavily tattooed mermaid on shore leave. She disappeared out the back.

'Why does it cost so much for women to get their hair cut?' Matt asked, looking at the salon's price list.

'Because they're willing to pay it,' Caius said, as the receptionist came back with a young woman dressed entirely in black. Pencil skirt, stilettos and wiggle. Vampy, bright red lipstick, pin-up-girl tattoo and cheekbones that could cut glass. Caius had gone through a goth phase in his early teens and women like her still held a preternatural sway over him.

'Hello, I'm Annie, Annie Mason. I'm the manager. You wanted to speak to someone?'

'You're exactly who I wanted to talk to.' Caius stood up and shook her hand. His handshake was firm. Annie was the stylist named on the appointment card.

'I am?' Annie asked, looking confused. 'Would you like to come through to my office?'

'Yes, thank you, Ms Mason,' Caius said as they followed her through to the back. The hairdresser doing the blow-dry failed to feign indifference as the three of them trotted past. It was a small room kitted out with all the necessities that a hip office would need, but on the cheap. A white table that served as a desk, elegant chairs that would hurt your back, and a miserable cheese plant. Caius recognised all the items from his recent trip to IKEA. Far less luxurious than the salon. Someone was trying to save money behind the scenes.

'Is this about the bins?' Annie asked.

'No, we're not here about recycling. My colleague and I need your assistance identifying one of your customers. Who had an appointment last Tuesday at 13.30, with you as the stylist?'

'Isn't this against data protection rules?'

'I'm not sure of all the legalities of the regulation, but I can get a warrant if you are inclined towards being uncooperative.' Caius cast her a smile, she took the bait, and he hooked her in.

'Oh. Oh God. I see. Let me check,' Annie said, going over to the laptop on the desk and opening up the booking system. 'What time on Tuesday was it?'

'One thirty.'

'Clemency O'Hara. Oh geez, is she – is Clemmie dead?' she asked.

'I can't comment on any ongoing investigations. Do you have contact details for her?'

'Yes, an email and a phone number.'

'If you wouldn't mind writing them down? Thank you. How long have you known her for?'

'A while, she's a good customer. Has her ends done every six weeks religiously. Been coming since we opened two years ago. She's a nice girl. Very pretty.'

'Did she talk about her life to you?'

'A bit. She works as an assistant in an art gallery.'

'Whereabouts?'

'Near Sloane Square I think, and she's always talking about her photography. She's really passionate about her art. Clemmie's also an influencer: she reviews books and does stuff on wellbeing which is pretty cool. She's got a boyfriend who's an aristocrat. Proper *Tatler* set.'

Matt took his phone out of his pocket. 'Ms Mason, do you know what Ms O'Hara's name was on Instagram?'

'Oh yeah, I follow her. Hang on,' Annie said, thumbing through her phone, before showing Clemmie's profile to Matt.

'Thank you, Annie. Do you know what her boyfriend's name is?' Caius asked, as Matt started searching. Matt nodded at Caius. They'd found their victim.

'I don't know, she just referred to him as her boyfriend. I think she thought they'd get engaged soon. If I'm being honest, Clemmie is, well, a bit of a trophy girlfriend. You know the ones, it's West London. They're everywhere: swaddled in cashmere and trust funds. Treated like show ponies. Trotted out to win Best in Show. Is she OK?'

9

Transcript of Clemmie's most recent video (posted eight days previously) as it was seen on Detective Sergeant Matthew Cheung's phone

[CLEMMIE is talking directly to the camera from a highbacked green velvet chair in a room with floral wallpaper. Her outfit perfectly matches the colours of her surroundings. There are links below to purchase all of her clothing. She is cradling a mug of tea in her hands and has tucked her feet beneath her. She's talking as if she knows you.]

CLEMMIE: Hello darlings, I hope you're all surviving Mercury in retrograde as well as can be hoped. So, I just wanted to give you a handy round-up of all my posts this week. I read an amazing book - the plot was so complex and the twist at the end left me reeling. It's a thriller called *Her Boyfriend Did It*. Link below to buy your own copy and then you too can join in all the CDC fun in the comments.

[A banner runs below the video imploring viewers to 'Become an official member of the Clemmie Book Club for £10 and receive a limited-edition, rose pink bookmark!']

I think you all are going to absolutely love it, and I'm so excited to hear all of your thoughts. I've also published a new 'What I Eat In A Week' video with accompanying recipes. Lots of delicious gluten-free wholegrains and spiritually fulfilling fruit. I've been experimenting with my yoga routine and have a new set of videos available to my subscribers, but here's a cheeky preview.

[A 10-second video clip of CLEMMIE completing yoga poses plays underneath before cutting back to the initial footage of CLEMMIE. Another banner runs at the bottom of the footage: 'Use the code CLEMMIE15 in the next two days to receive 15% off!']

For non-subscribers I've composed a cheeky review of my favourite yoga pants. Spoiler alert: it's not the brand you think it is! And . . . and . . . and . . . I can't say much yet but, let's just say that I have a very exciting secret that I may reveal this week. Love you, darlings!

#ad #affiliate

★ ★ ★

Matt mused on the video and then pulled out his notebook and scribbled:

- Private schools should be banned for the good of the nation

- Pushing ridiculously expensive leggings to women is more profitable than you'd think judging by the affiliate rate
- Either very clever or very stupid – can't tell yet

10

The Police Station

Caius and Matt charged through the doors of the station. It was lunchtime, after all, and they were famished. Caius was disappointed to find that someone had just microwaved a mackerel, so he would have to eat his wholewheat penne pasta with dairy-free pesto and side salad of spinach and Santorini plum tomatoes with a balsamic dressing al desko, because of the foul, foul stench.

'How's lunch going for you?' Matt asked with a grimace.

Caius huffed and glanced upwards to the heavens for mercy. 'Trying to increase my fibre intake – colon cancer is no joke, my friend – but wholewheat pasta is grim. It's a punishment, not lunch.'

'This isn't going great for me either,' Matt said, mulling over his store-bought sandwich complete with limp lettuce and taste-less tomatoes.

Caius caught a whiff of the offending mackerel from across the floor. 'That fish is haunting us. It wouldn't go down well if I wrote a sign for the kitchen, would it? What if I put a picture of a grumpy cat on the sign?'

'Not if you want anyone to talk to you at the Christmas party this year,' said Matt, returning to his sadwich.

'I have Clemmie's address in Kensington. Registered as cohabiting with a Rupert Achilles de Courcy Beauchamp, the homeowner,' Caius said, as he scrolled down the page and took a bite of his virtuous lunch.

'Any relation?'

'As if I have family in that part of town.'

'IT are downloading all of Clemmie's social media and her blog in case it gets taken down. I've skimmed through and it's fairly innocuous. In her last video she said that she had a secret that she may or may not reveal. She's an influencer; it could be about a brand partnership? Opening a vegan cafe or something?'

'Are those big enough reasons to be killed for? The hairdresser said she thought she would get engaged soon. That feels like a more plausible secret.'

'It's just as likely to be about charcoal cleansing.'

'Is this murder about sex or money? It's usually one or the other.'

'I found Clemmie's LinkedIn. She describes herself as a self-employed artist and influencer, but she's also been working at the Hesperides Gallery in Pimlico for over a year. I've just emailed you a link to their website.'

'Is it near the hairdresser's?' Caius asked.

'Not really, it's on Pimlico Road.'

'Damn it, I would have put money on it being near the hairdresser's.'

'Did the hairdresser's feel off to you?' Matt asked.

'Yes, it was too quiet. They're in a pretty pricey part of town where a lot of women don't work, only work out. You saw how busy the coffee shop over the road was. Rammed full of yummy mummies drinking turmeric lattes.'

'Maybe they're bad at cutting fringes?'

'I wonder why she went there. If it's neither convenient nor good.' Caius chewed on a pencil. 'We have to break some bad news to Mr Rupert Beauchamp.'

They were getting up to leave when a young detective

constable came over who Caius didn't fully recognise. She must be newish. 'DI Beauchamp?'

'Yes?'

'We've just had a missing persons report come through. Looks like your victim. Submitted by her boyfriend,' the DC said, as she handed Caius a copy of the report.

'Thank you. Noakes, isn't it?'

'Yeah, Amy,' she said, smiling as she left the incident room.

'Thank you, Amy,' Caius called after her. 'She's the DC who rugby tackled the Finsbury Flasher, right?'

'Yeah, he was lurking outside a primary school.'

'Yuck.'

'She was in Armed Response for a couple of years, I think.'

'Nice,' Caius said as he looked through the missing persons report. 'It was made fifteen minutes after we left the hairdresser's.'

'A coincidence?' Matt asked.

'Maybe.'

★　★　★

Caius and Matt pulled up outside Clemmie and Rupert's house. It felt incongruous: a reminder that London had once been a collection of villages. The surrounding buildings were Victorian mansion flats that had probably been built in its former substantial gardens. The flats were six storeys high, with discreet Ionic columns and mosaic-floored entrance halls. The house, which was called Thurstone, felt like a small corner of the Shires with a sushi bar at the bottom of the road. They walked through the front gate and were accosted by a garden that only Beatrix Potter could have conceived of. The smell from the blood-red roses was overpowering.

'Where the hell are we?' Matt asked, staring at the house. 'Will this guy have a monocle?'

'It's another world,' Caius said, badge at the ready. The knocker was in the shape of a green man. Caius grasped its beard and rapped hard.

A plummy voice boomed from within, 'There you bloody are!' The door opened. 'What the bloody hell have you been playing at, Clem . . .' The young man tailed off once it became evident that neither Caius nor Matt was the 5'7, blonde, plant-based artist-cum-lifestyle vlogger with whom he was cohabiting. 'Can I help you?'

Caius flashed his badge. 'Detective Inspector Beauchamp, and this is Detective Sergeant Cheung. Are you Mr Rupert Beauchamp?'

'I am indeed.' Caius saw him twitch slightly at their shared name. 'Is this about Clemmie?'

'May we come in, sir?' Matt asked.

'You may.' Rupert led them through the dark green entrance hall, with its floral wallpaper and parquet flooring, to a sitting room. The entrance hall was packed with suitcases. Matt nearly tripped over one. 'I've filed the report already. Do you have more questions about it?' The room was painted a cool duck-egg blue. There was a cast-iron fireplace in the centre devoid of wood, which had been replaced with a vase of the garden's haemophilic flowers. The room was lined from floor to ceiling with book-shelves. 'Clemmie's probably holed up in a hotel trying to get at me while charging it to my credit card. Two can play at that. She can get a pasting for wasting police time.'

'Please take a seat, sir,' Caius said. He'd never met a white person with his surname before. He knew they existed, but it was a horror nonetheless. It was a curious thing for him, to pass as white with a name like his – to sound like a member of the gentry when your blood had been exploited to build their Palladian monstrosities, fund their art collections, put their doltish children through the best education, and even now keep them living tidily off the interest of their stocks and shares.

Rupert sat down in a battered leather armchair. A notebook had been left open on the small cherry-wood table to his right elbow. Rupert caught Matt looking and promptly closed it shut with a snap as he tried to hide a blush. What an odd thing to do, Matt thought to himself. He must know where this visit is leading. Why be so preoccupied with a notebook with a few scribblings-in?

'I'm so sorry, sir, but we have a body that we think is Clemmie. Can I show you a photograph? It may be distressing,' Caius said.

'Yes. OK. Yah,' Rupert said, rolling his eyes.

'Is this your partner, Clemency O'Hara?'

'Yes. Yes, it is.' Caius had told enough people that their loved ones had perished, but he had never seen anyone be so uninterested, so bored by the news. No, wait, was that relief that flashed across his lips? It was. He was thankful that she was dead.

'Thank you, Mr Beauchamp. We will need you to come and formally identify the body,' Caius said, making his best compassionate face. He had been doing this job for twelve years, which was probably ten years too many.

'Of course, I can do that,' Rupert said. Stone. Granite. It was as if he had been chiselled. The cheekbones, the chin, the nose. He had a high brow. A face fit for a marble bust. Quite beautiful, but terribly cold. Unreactive. Emotionless. Blank.

'I appreciate that you're in shock right now, but did Clemmie have any enemies?' Caius continued.

'No, everyone loved her.'

70

'I'm sorry to ask, Mr Beauchamp, but where were you on Saturday?'

'Saturday was my birthday. I was with my friends the whole time.'

'We'll need to verify that with them.'

'Of course. I can give you their names now.' Rupert tore out a piece of paper from the back of the notebook he'd been shy about, started scribbling a list of names and then took out his phone to transcribe their numbers. Determined silence as he wrote. While Rupert held his finger up to keep the detectives quiet, Caius took the time to scan the room. There were no photos of Clemmie – there was a small picture on the mantelpiece of a rowing team and above it a decorated oar from Pious College, University of Oxford. Matt finally took the piece of paper from Rupert after a good few minutes of unnerving muteness.

'Mr Beauchamp, can I confirm that Ms O'Hara worked at the Hesperides Gallery on Pimlico Road?' Caius asked.

'Yes,' Rupert said, fiddling with his signet ring.

'Does Ms O'Hara have any relatives?'

'Did . . . Past tense. Her parents live in Singapore. I'll ring them in a moment. Her mother will be upset. Clem was an only child. I rang her on Saturday evening, frantically so. I left her a voicemail as I couldn't get through to her. She didn't come to my birthday party, you see. I can give you her number and whatnot so you can track her phone if you like? I thought perhaps she'd just run out of battery and was characteristically late. Then I thought she was punishing me.'

'Why would she punish you on your birthday?'

'I don't know. I never do a damned thing wrong. Who knows how the mind of a woman works?' Rupert caught the detectives quickly glance at each other, realised that he hadn't been helping himself and decided to give a straight answer. 'She wanted to get married and I didn't. In fact, I was planning on breaking up with her on Sunday. I thought she was trying to embarrass me at the party; trying to force my hand by acting up.'

Caius raised an eyebrow. 'When was the last time you saw her?'

'Saturday morning. We ate breakfast together and then she went to the gym. Clem was an artist, a photographer. She could get lost in the world if she found something that interested her. It wasn't unusual for Clem to go incommunicado for a day. Kept me on my toes – well, that's what she thought anyway. We weren't a logical couple.'

'Had she been acting strangely before Saturday?'

'She's always been a bit odd. We're quite independent of each other really. I don't know much about her at all any more.'

'In a recent video Clemmie said she had a secret. Do you know what that was? A new business venture, perhaps?'

'Not an inkling.'

'Do you know Clemmie's hairdresser?'

'I'm not acquainted socially with tradespeople.'

'Thank you, Mr Beauchamp. Do you have any friends nearby?' Caius asked. 'In these situations, it's best not to be left alone with one's thoughts for too long.'

'I can imagine that to be true.'

'Would you be able to come to the station tomorrow at 9 a.m. to formally identify the body? We'd also like to take a longer statement. Belt and braces, you understand.'

'Yes, I can do that.'

'We are sorry for your loss, Mr Beauchamp. Here's my card. Do feel free to call at any time and to pass my details on to Ms O'Hara's parents. The station address is printed at the bottom.

Do you mind if we have a quick look around the house before we go?'

'Of course not.'

'We'll show ourselves out after.'

'Detective.'

'Yes?'

'My name's pronounced "Beecham", not how it's spelled.'

★ ★ ★

Matt closed the door behind them, and they walked back to their car in silence. They pulled away and turned onto the King's Road. Matt looked out of the window. 'No monocle,' he said.

'Was he unemotional or just posh?' Caius said, musing over their first meeting with Rupert Beauchamp. 'That wasn't a normal reaction. I've seen enough people go numb, but the way he wrote those numbers down like that.'

'Socialite or sociopath?'

'He switched to the past tense very easily . . . I wonder where he buys his shirts?'

'I bet they're bespoke.'

'Oh yeah, definitely from Jermyn Street. Turnbull & Asser? I couldn't find Clemmie's phone. I'll order a proper search of the house ASAP. They have one of those magnetic knife strips in the kitchen, but they were all accounted for. Did you spot anything weird?'

'Nothing, but it felt like a museum. William Morris wallpaper, clunky furniture. Not the house of a young woman. Completely at odds with the image Clemmie projects online. It's very much his house.'

'They had some interesting books. A lot on classics and art,'

Caius said, feeling an Amazon binge coming on. 'I'll ask if we can have Amy Noakes on the case. She's on the ball. Get her to drill down into the victim's social media. Clemency O'Hara lived her life online. There must be something she overshared that'll help. Can you get the tech guys to track her phone?'

Matt was checking his email on his phone. 'Sure. The post-mortem report's come in.'

'What are the highlights?'

'Like we thought, asphyxia caused by choking on her own vomit. Likely due to a toxic element.'

'You don't get many poisonings any more. What was it? Something out of Agatha Christie? Cyanide? Arsenic? Was it thallium?'

'They've checked the likely suspects, but the results have come back inconclusive. They've sent samples off for further testing. The results will be back in a few days. Wrists were tied with a thick twine made of jute. There was bruising as she struggled.'

'And the throat-slitting?' Caius asked, as they drove past Hyde Park Corner.

'Definitely post-mortem. Death is around 5 p.m., give or take an hour or two either way.'

'Any alcohol or drugs in the system?'

'No to both. Oh, this is interesting. The victim had had sex earlier that day and a semen sample was found. No obvious signs of rape, she didn't have any typical defensive wounds and she didn't scratch anyone, but they're testing it against the database in case it's from a serial rapist.'

'Let's ask Rupert Beauchamp tomorrow for a DNA sample. We shall see if he suffers the indignity,' Caius said, mimicking Rupert's pronunciation of their surname.

'I think we've found Clemmie's secret. Approximately six weeks pregnant.'

'Oof that's rough, but there's a motive there once we know the particulars. She gets pregnant to force him into marriage?' Caius said, considering the facts. 'There's enough there to keep our glorious leader happy for two days.'

'What is your beef with him? It can't be purely sartorial.'

'I just don't trust him. He's old-school in the wrong way. Funny handshakes . . . I don't know.'

★   ★   ★

Caius was back at his desk in the incident room and had finally finished reading the full post-mortem report. Clemmie's poor mother had called, or rather sobbed down the phone to him. She didn't appear to know her daughter at all. Nothing useful came from that interaction. Caius had rung all the numbers of the people who could corroborate Rupert's alibi for Saturday evening and had one of them coming in shortly. The grand pooh-bahh had popped by for a little chitter-chatter and they'd been graciously granted Amy's full attention for the duration of the investigation. She currently had the joyous job of printing out and cataloguing Clemmie's blog posts.

'Caius?' she asked.

'Yes, Amy.'

'I've implemented a comprehensive filing system,' she said, gesturing to the celebration of stationery sprawled across the empty desk next to Matt. 'I've created four separate folders based on the themes that the victim filed them under: Recipes, Health, Travel and Fun. Each folder is organised chronologically, with each month as a separate section, and each individual blog post is labelled with the capital letter of the folder and a number.'

'Thanks, Amy. Go through them and create an index for each folder stating briefly what it is. Highlight any posts that seem pertinent to the case, especially anything about weddings, her boyfriend or babies, plus anything else that comes across as a bit odd. Creepy comments, overzealous fans. Use your judgement.'

'I'll get on it.'

'Cheers.' Caius appreciated stationery, and he really appreciated people who knew how to use it. His favourite shop was Paperchase; he could spend hours in there browsing through their pens, but a sense of shame prevented him from publicly admitting his love of highlighters. He was also partial to Muji and their little white cubes that puff essential oils. Tiny little scented clouds of delight. 'I know your skills lie elsewhere, Amy. I promise if there's a door to be kicked in then it's yours.'

Matt was at his computer looking annoyed. Caius wandered over holding the full post-mortem report and put it in front of him. 'How are you getting on with stalking Mr Beauchamp online?' Caius asked him.

'I'm not getting much. Went to Pious College, Oxford, and graduated in Ancient History and Archaeology. He's never had a real job. His LinkedIn says that he's a writer, but I can't find proof of anything that he's had published. He might have a pseudonym?'

'Why publicly describe yourself as a writer if you don't want people to know?'

'You know what these public school boys are like: discreet.'

'Or he fancies himself as a Booker winner while sitting on his inherited wealth.'

'You're quite the reverse snob, aren't you?'

'Behead them all and take back the commons. Eat the rich.'

'He might just be private – his school isn't on his profile, and I bet it's one of the famous ones. He doesn't appear to have any other social media, which is odd for someone his age.' Matt picked up the post-mortem report and thumbed it. 'She was tied up. Maybe it's a kidnapping gone wrong?'

'There hasn't been a ransom note. Whoever gave the poison to her went back to finish the job by slitting her throat, but she was already dead. They did it anyway because the blood-letting is symbolic and more important than the death itself. The throat-slitting denies Clemmie her humanity. Turns her into a beast, a piece of meat. It's more than just violence.'

'Do you still think it was the same person?'

Caius nodded. 'My gut says they're one and the same. Killers like to go back and visit the crime scene.'

'True.'

'If the foetus turns out not to be Rupert's then we have both a sexual and monetary motive for him. Wealth is meant to be inherited by your own children, and if she cheated on him but tried to pass it off as his child . . . We need to find out if Clemmie was having an affair.'

'I hate outdoor murders. There's never enough DNA floating about. The report suggests the blade was likely to be a standard kitchen knife. That's not that sinister, just practical.'

'Poison is organised, kitchen knives are spur of the moment,' Caius said, before turning his attention to a picture of the flower crown. 'There's something about the flowers. Are the flowers an apology?' Now there was a thought: maybe Caius should send Héloïse a bouquet. His desk phone rang. It was the front desk. 'God, that was quick. I'm going to go and confirm Rupert's alibi. We spoke to him, what, two hours ago and we've already got a Hooray Henry here.'

'Male or female?' Matt asked.

'Male.'

'I bet he's wearing red trousers.'

★ ★ ★

Matt saw Caius come out of the lift with a bewildered look.

'Red trousers and a monocle,' Caius said, shaking his head. 'His name is Jolyon and he has a triple-barrelled surname.'

'How old was he?'

'Thirty, but he looked like he fought at Waterloo. Says that he met up with Rupert at 7.30 p.m. and was with him until 11 a.m. the next day. They both slept on the sofas in Minty's living room in Highgate on Saturday night. Minty is apparently a childhood friend of Rupert's whose house was the closest to the party. Jolyon had a drunken row with his fiancée, who was also at the party, and she told him not to come home that night. It's not much of an alibi. Rupert still could have murdered her before the party and slipped away to mutilate the corpse. Minty is coming in tomorrow.'

'Bagsy Minty.'

'She's all yours. Rupert Beauchamp's birthday party sounds bizarre. Black tie in McDonald's Kentish Town, and then they went on a pub crawl up towards Minty's house.'

'They were heading north. Puts them right next to Hampstead Heath.'

'He was vague about the timings. They need to be probed on the specifics. Rupert Beauchamp. Something is wrong with Rupert Beauchamp. Could he get that many people to lie for him like that?'

'Maybe? One of them would mess up though and get confused,

or they all parrot the exact same facts like primary school kids in a nativity play.'

'We should go home soon,' Caius said, checking the time on his phone before leaning back in his chair and thinking of Paris. Thinking of Héloise. Thinking of Héloise sitting on the pavement outside a bistro arguing with a handsome man with a neat beard and twinkling eyes about Descartes, or Camus or whoever. She's sipping a glass of decent but surprisingly affordable white wine, her hair hanging loose, undressing her opponent with her eyes. She laughs to herself at the thought that she could've ever been so silly as to settle for a London policeman.

11

The National Gallery

Nell was sitting in the downstairs foyer of the gallery on a squeaky, brown leather pouffe. She'd come straight from her office in Bloomsbury and had made sure that she looked so hot that she was flammable, in a well-fitting skirt and a flouncy blouse. It was a vibe reminiscent of a Merchant Ivory production in which the heroine, having read too many novels, has an affair with an illiterate farm labourer on her father's estate. Her hair tumbled down her shoulders. Rossetti would have killed to have known her. Nell was waiting for Alex with Thomas Hardy. She had read *Tess of the D'Urbervilles* as an obnoxious teenager who'd raged against the demotic chaos of her sixth form in the Midlands. The first time she read it, she imploded in an immature, improper sorrow fanned by a nascent bluestocking's dire need to transcend the ordinariness of her parents' existence. To leave the pebble-dash, Findus Crispy Pancakes and caravan holidays of her childhood for London, and poetry, and silk scarves. Nell had tried to feel what she could not, to live through a sadness wrought of another's imagination. She had lacked real comprehension. Comprehension came with experience, and even if she couldn't yet face it, articulate it, she had since lived too much. Nell rooted around in her bag for her mirror and reapplied her lipstick. Nell's appearance was an exquisitely crafted performance.

Alex sat down next to Nell. 'These seats are uncomfortable.'

'They don't want us to loiter, but they don't want to look unwelcoming because they take so much lottery funding. It's a chav tax: the working class play the lottery while middle-class cultural institutions get given arts grants,' Nell said, putting her book away.

Alex was going to put his arm around Nell but thought better of it. She looked unusually brittle. 'Shall I go and buy us tickets?'

'No need,' Nell said, flashing the pair that she had already collected. 'I'm a member, I get invited to special viewings. Their shows are impossible to go to on the weekend, so I always come in the week. They ram so many people in that you can't see a damn thing. I got trodden on by a WI leader at an exhibit on Watteau.'

'A bit risqué for them.'

Nell tucked her arm through Alex's as they walked towards the exhibition's entrance. All she was missing was a folded parasol. They handed over their tickets to the attendant and entered the Artemisia Gentileschi show.

They wandered around the exhibit. Taking in the pictures. Reading the little white cards. Nell stopped in front of *The Artist as Saint Catherine of Alexandria*. 'I hate the word "survivor". It should only be used for shipwrecks.' Nell looked at Alex who had just caught up with her. 'The broken wheel. The defiance. The courage to take the fucker to court and suffer having her thumbs put in screws. Gentileschi tries to own her narrative, to reclaim it. Turn it into something stronger. By embracing it remove the shame, and the stigma, and the whispers. So what? Her story has become what we talk about. It's what makes her interesting to these day trippers. Why can't they appreciate her use of light?' Nell did not want pity from Alex.

Alex did not understand what she was trying to tell him. They had always been mutually incomprehensible through an over-reliance on metaphors and allegories. She carried on walking through the exhibit, stopping to look at *Susanna and the Elders*. The Elders looming out of the picture, spreading across the sky. 'Susanna uncomfortable'. The description to the side of the painting used the word 'uncomfortable'. Like an ill-fitting bra, not a pair of lechers trying to blackmail her into sexual acts. 'Let's look around some more. Then you can buy me a pencil from the gift shop, and maybe even take me to dinner,' Nell said as she stared at *Judith Slaying Holofernes*.

12

Caius's flat, Tufnell Park

Caius got back from work, changed into his skimpiest lycra and went into the garden of his ground-floor flat. His maternal, Irish grandfather had bought the building, a four-storey Victorian house, back in the 1960s when no one wanted to live in London any more, for seven feathers and a fistful of marbles. When Caius's mum had inherited it a few years ago, his enterprising builder father converted the house into flats and moved to the Loire Valley on the proceeds. Caius, of course, was living there rent-free so he could 'save' to buy his own place. He was embarrassingly aware that it is such quirks of family history that mark the difference between chronic debt and a large, dilapidated pile in rural France. This was how he'd met Héloise. Their parents were now second-home neighbours, although in this case the girl next door was not a quiet beauty but a combustible Parisienne poet with funny ideas about the safety of raw milk and an extensive collection of vinyl jazz records. Flowers. He really should send her flowers. But not ones that look like the sky before the sun crashes into the waves. Hydrangeas maybe, fresh and green, undecided about whether to be pink or blue.

Caius had let his new regime slip. Twenty squats. Twenty burpees. Twenty press-ups. Twenty crunches. Repeat five times.

Drip sweat on the patio. Cry on the inside. Google French florists. Buy a few books on Amazon – an art history reader, a biography on William Morris and a copy of *Pride and Prejudice*. Cry for real now. Shower so you don't know you're crying.

Read Wilfred Owen poems because Héloise thinks you're not in touch with your culture's poetic heritage. Really, really cry. *Dulce et decorum est* . . . Leave Héloise a voicemail in French. Use *tu*, not *vous*, because she's not lost to you yet. Ring back and leave another in English, for additional clarity. Cook some sort of spinach-based thing. Feel glum that it's going to be lunch tomorrow too. Lie on the floor, stare at the ceiling, think about the poor dead girl who had the sunset across her stony, cold brow. Panic when Héloise rings back and don't answer. Sleep, somehow.

TUESDAY

13

The Police Station

Caius was pacing up and down the incident room. He'd had a lot of coffee and not enough sleep. He was wearing his crispest shirt. Caius knew that to go up against a man like Rupert Beauchamp you had to look sharp, let him think for a moment that you might be an equal, but at the last minute prove yourself to be an idiot and then show him deference. Lots of 'yes, sir', 'frightfully sorry', 'would it be terribly inconvenient if' . . . Apologise like a cabinet member caught prowling for teenage prostitutes.

'Has anything interesting been found in the park bins yet?' Caius asked Matt.

'Nope.'

Caius got up, went over to the whiteboard and stared. 'I liked the Midsummer Theory,' he said, taking the Post-it down. 'Amy, Post-its are theories, pen is fact. If you have any ideas, voice them. Every Post-it from you becomes a pint.'

'I'm teetotal,' Amy said.

'Good for you. Well, whatever your poison is. Your poison . . . Amy, what does the victim like to eat?'

'Honestly, not much. I don't think she was very well.'

'Matt, give Amy the file of Clemmie's Instagram photos. Does she use Facebook? She's probably too cool for it. It's just nans sharing conspiracy theories on there now. Amy, I want you to go through the blog posts, YouTube videos and her Instagram, and tally what food and drink she consumes. Matt, have we had the footage back from TfL yet?'

'It's getting sent over this afternoon.'

'Chase them. We need to know what she did on Saturday. We don't have a damned timeline.'

Caius wrote on the whiteboard:

Saturday day:
- Has breakfast at home
- Goes to the gym – TBC
- Had sex with at least one man

Saturday evening:
- Approx. 5 p.m. – Poisoned
- Mutilated / Body dumped on Hampstead Heath

Caius's desk phone rang. Rupert had arrived and so had a selection of his closest friends. 'I'm going to take on Beauchamp, I'll be a while. Matt, you take the friends. Rope uniform in.'

* * *

DS Matthew Cheung's notes –
Beauchamp Alibi Interviews:

Edmund (Teddie) Witting – barrister, left at about 11.30 p.m. with Julian after getting kicked out of The Pineapple for throwing up purple sick on a bar stool. Would like us not to mention his name in any reports to the press as he doesn't want it to ruin his career. Thought Clemmie was a nice girl, had a lot going for her. She was unfathomably loyal to RB who he rowed with at uni. He wants to reassure us that he isn't a sexual predator.

Julian Hinckeley-Smythe – has own company that makes luxury dog collars and other pet accessories. Also rowed with RB – carried Teddie Witting into an Uber and stayed at Teddie's flat in Islington. Is annoyed with Teddie for throwing up in the back of the taxi and lowering his Uber rating. Thought Rupert could do much better than Clemmie, but there's no accounting for taste: vulgar.

Rebecca Jones – university friend of Clemmie's from Oxford Brookes. Works in a media agency. Sobbed through the whole thing. Left at midnight to go and buy a doner kebab – she produced a receipt of the purchase and showed a picture of herself cuddling the takeaway owner. There was chilli sauce in her hair. Last saw CO'H the week before when they went to an exhibit at the Tate Modern. Thought Clemmie and Rupert were the strongest couple she knew. Gutted, kept saying gutted. Didn't know what the secret could've been – seems unlikely then that Clemmie told anyone about the pregnancy.

Bella Villiers-D'Arcy – owns a PR firm that specialises in luxury candles. Went back to Minty's too, thought about shagging Jolyon but didn't want to piss off Tabitha – Minty talked her out of it and she went home instead soon after they got there, but not because of Tabitha, she went home because she felt nauseous and not very sexy. Uber receipt shows that she left Minty's at 12.34 a.m. Gave me a 10 per cent off voucher for an organic beeswax candle company. Not sure if this counts as trying to bribe a police officer – going to report anyway just in case. Not much of a fan of Clemmie's – thought she was after the title – and considers herself to be more Rupert's friend because they went to the proper Oxford together but had had some fun times with Clemmie in the past.

Mungo Harvington – owns a company making quilted gilets – can't remember much after 9.30 p.m. – blames a bad chicken nugget. Woke up in the disabled loo in McDonald's the next day – he'd accidentally locked himself in. Took a selfie with the cleaner who found him the next morning. Asked what happened with Bella and Joly in the end. Thinks Jolyon is a hound and Tabitha is better off without him. Tabitha apparently should never have left the Argentinian cattle rancher she met trekking last year. He's tempted to have a crack at her if they do break up. Thought Clemmie was pretty, but they weren't close.

Minty Gaunt – flower sculptor – google this job description? Not convinced it's a real profession. Might have been flirting, but also might have been nervous. With RB from 2 p.m. on Saturday helping to set up the party until 11 a.m. the next day – she drove him around town picking up bits of his outfit, went to the party, RB and Jolyon crashed at hers and then the three of them had brunch together the next day. Considered Clemmie one of her best friends. Said that Clemmie had been especially kind to her and taken her under her wing after a bad time of it. Had no idea what the secret might have been.

Tabitha de la Croix – stylist – confirms that she had a fight with her fiancé Jolyon Armstrong-Wille-de Fflouffe. He was flirting with Bella and she didn't like it, because she doesn't find Bella attractive in that way and didn't want to have a threesome with her. Left the party and went to stay at her other boyfriend's house. He can vouch for her. Thought Clemmie was a laugh – could be mean in a fun way – and was never boring.

Algernon/Arthur/Alfred/Edgar/Edwin/Inigo/Oscar/Orlando/

Umberto – interchangeable school friends of Rupert's who work in insurance/private equity/property/think tanks and arrived with their wives or fiancées. All of them thought the party was a little off/vulgar/unsightly. This was universally said with an incongruous smirk suggesting that they all enjoyed it really. They all left at around the same time, after the 'second ball pit incident'.

★ ★ ★

Caius and Matt looked at each other in the break room over their late lunch. Matt had a can of Vimto and a ham salad sandwich, and Caius had a green tea and the rest of the disappointing spinach thing.

Matt sipped on his Vimto. 'Rupert Beauchamp's alibi checks out; he was with Minty all afternoon, and I took several different alibis from his friends who between them can account for Rupert's movements from 7 p.m. to lunchtime the next day, so he can't be the mutilator. It's like they got a minibus.'

'I didn't learn anything new. Rupert happily let Barry swab him after I took his statement. He voluntarily left a set of house keys for us so we can sweep it this afternoon. I guess I was wrong about him. Didn't even need to get a warrant. Is he being overly helpful?' Caius asked, annoyed with himself. His gut had told him that Rupert Beauchamp was a guilty man. 'Matt, go to the McDonald's and all the pubs they named. Ask for CCTV, get the staff to confirm whether they were there. We need to bury that line of inquiry. I'm going to speed over to the gallery where she worked, and her gym. We're going to search the house with forensics at 4 p.m. I'll meet you there. We need to piece together the day she died. And where is that phone? IT have traced it to her gym and then nothing.'

14

DS Amy Noakes's computer

Amy's finger was cramping from scrolling so hard through Clemmie's Instagram. What had she learned so far? That she wanted to go to Venice too, and to Singapore, and the South of France. Clemmie seemed to travel a lot (read: took phenomenal photos in pretty places in exquisite clothes). Amy wondered what Clemmie's carbon footprint was, and whether Clemmie had cared about that too. What else had she learned? That Clemmie read some pretty heavy novels and owned some pretty impressive handbags. That rainbow vegan bowls look lovely but probably don't taste great. Who wants a meal that consists of strawberries, orange peppers, pineapple, Brussels sprouts and blueberries with a side of mixed white and wild rice all in one bowl?

Every Tuesday, Clemmie had posted under the hashtag #sippin. It was a double review of both a novel that she had read and a cup of tea. They appeared to be quite popular. The pictures were clever combinations of book covers and cups and saucers. Sometimes there were wildly blooming flowers, partially peeled oranges and lemons, bowls of raspberries; sometimes a slither of cake or a dainty macaroon in a pastel colour. All of them chosen to perfectly complement the book cover. A scarlet-bound book had been befriended by a red rose and a berry infusion. They reminded Amy of those still-life paintings that you see in museums. The reviews were service-able – nothing too deep, more like an account of the plot – and each post was accompanied by a link to Amazon for the book and a link to the tea company #ad #affiliate. Amy wondered whether there was a living to be made in hawking teabags to the good people of Instagram. It probably paid better than the Met.

15

Bloomsbury

Nell had taken her lunch break late. She didn't eat much normally, but she was starving and so indulged with a baguette. She couldn't help herself. Usually she'd microwave some frozen vegetables, have a cup of instant miso soup, perhaps a banana. She had piously counted her five a day by tallying it on her left palm in red ink. She aimed for seven, sod the government, what do they know about health? Nell worked in a niche publishing house that specialised in poetry. One of her jobs was to read through the submissions from all the miscreants who thought their dirty little ditties were better than Byron and Coleridge and Donne. Nell's office was in a pompous corner of central London surrounded by concept shops that sold expensive and impractical homeware and dreams of upper-middle-class material prosperity. You could buy a cushion with Frida Kahlo's face on from no fewer than six different shops, but you couldn't get a pint of milk – cow's milk, that is. There was an independent health food shop that sold every sort of nut milk that could be imagined by a corporate food scientist. There was a funny little store around the corner that was having a sale from 2 p.m. for an hour only. They kept weird hours and sometimes wouldn't open because the owner didn't feel like it. Nell wasn't sure of their business model, but she'd seen a vase shaped like the naked torso of a woman and was desperate to own it. To claim the form as her own again. She was walking back, victorious in her quest, when she saw a familiar figure crouched over on the steps of the Georgian town house that her office occupied.

'Rupert, what are you doing here?' Nell demanded, her hands placed firmly on her hips, like she was trying to make herself bigger. If it would scare off a bear, it might work on a Beauchamp.

'The receptionist said that you'd just popped out, so I waited. I hope that's all right. I don't want to inconvenience you,' Rupert said.

'I have to be back in the office for a call soon,' Nell lied. She didn't have to go on calls. She wasn't important, but she was too polite to swear at him.

Rupert stayed crouched on the steps. He looked smaller, like a broken puppet of a child. He stared at his shoes.

'What's going on, Rupert?' Nell asked, as she wondered whether this was a new tactic of his. She hadn't seen him try to use fragility to manipulate a girl before.

'Can we go and sit in the square?'

'I only have ten minutes.' Nell's curiosity was piqued. Something was wrong. It was a scorching afternoon. People were lounging on the yellowed grass eating ice lollies. An old lady waddled her miniature Schnauzer past them. Rupert spotted a vacant bench upon which he duly collapsed like a corseted, consumption-riddled Victorian heroine. Nell didn't think he could cry, but there he was. One solitary tear rolled down a cheek. It wasn't a terribly forthcoming tear, but she had thought that boarding from an obscenely young age had squashed every fibre of emotive sensibility out of the man.

'Clemmie's dead, Nell.'

'Oh God. What happened?'

'She was murdered. The police said that she was pregnant, and they swabbed my cheek.'

'Bloody hell.' Nell sat down on the bench next to Rupert. 'How could she have been murdered?'

95

'She wasn't late to my party, she was dead in a bush on Hampstead Heath.'

'Fuck. That's awful. Poor Clemmie!' Nell hadn't known anyone who had died that wasn't over seventy-five, let alone someone her own age.

'I feel so lost.'

'Oh Rupert, how dreadful. Is there anything I can do to help?' It just flew out of her mouth. Nell hadn't wanted to offer, but her respectable English sense of duty pushed her to do so. Convention over self-preservation.

'Can I stay at yours? I don't want to be alone,' Rupert asked. Of course he asked that. She now noticed the backpack he'd been carrying.

'Sure, but my sofa isn't very comfortable, and . . .'

'I could cope. How about we order pizza and watch *Troy*? We can get angry about all the inaccuracies, and I can read Homer to you in Greek.' Rupert reached over and squeezed her hand. 'You are the best thing that ever happened to me, Nell.'

'I doubt that very much.' Nell couldn't move her hand. It was frozen. She could feel her ancient habit pulling her under. A rip tide of her own emotional self-abasement. An addiction to a terrible man.

'No, it's true,' Rupert said, peering up at her from underneath his fine eyelashes. 'I failed you, Nell. I failed you and I am so sorry. Can you forgive me? I just, I love you and I slipped up. I got a little carried away, that's all.' He stopped, and watched a woman push a pram along the gravel path. 'I should have broken up with Clemmie months ago, years ago, but I couldn't. I can't explain why. Please don't ask me. I'm desperate for you. You know I wouldn't hurt you? Not really. I love you.'

'Poor Clemmie.' Nell stood up and brushed her skirt down. 'I would have done anything for you. Anything. I mean that.'

'We're meant to be together.'

'I think we both need to accept the truth.'

'The truth?'

'It's gone so horribly wrong over and over and over and over again.'

'No. No. No.'

'I know that you can hurt me. I know that you have, and I know that you always will if I don't walk away now.' Nell swallowed hard. 'I don't ever want to see you again. You have treated me with the utmost contempt for the better part of a decade. You've strung me along as some sort of back-up for when Clemmie's battery finally failed. And I am sorry that she's dead, I really am. It's awful. No one deserves that. Poor Clemmie. Poor, poor Clemmie. Saturday was the final number, Rupert. Our grand farewell. The band played me out and then I went home and fucked someone else. I love you, Rupert. I always will, but I can't be with you. Not now. Not after Greece. Not after everything else. Goodbye.'

Nell started walking across the square. She did her best to look composed, but as soon as she turned the corner and was obscured by an unruly rhododendron she ran back to her office. Greater than Orpheus, she did not look behind her, but Rupert was dead to her and should go back to Hades. She charged through the door of her building. Ali the receptionist, an affable Australian who'd fancied a change from Adelaide for a year or two, stopped her. 'Nell, you're popular today.'

'Am I?'

'A really cute guy just left these for you. He said he saw that you were in the park, and he didn't want to disturb you. He wrote you a note when he was here,' Ali said, handing Nell a pretty posy of white roses and a folded-up piece of paper from her desk pad.

'Thank you, Ali.'

'I thought people normally sent red roses?'

'Yes, I suppose they do. Do you know why roses are red?'

'Because that's the way they are?'

'I'll tell you in the pub one day.'

'Cool, is this another one of your ancient history facts?'

'Yes, sorry. It's what you get for working for a company that has a habit of hiring otherwise unemployable classicists,' Nell laughed, before the cheer abruptly left her cheeks. 'Oh, Ali, the blond gentleman who was here earlier waiting for me, his name is Rupert Beauchamp – it's spelled B-E-A-U-C-H-A-M-P but pronounced Beecham – and I wish nothing but suffering upon him, so if he calls put him through to my voicemail, and if he turns up here tell him I'm out of the office at a meeting across town and I won't be back in that day.'

'Ah, that's intense. Bad Tinder date?'

'Yes, something like that. Thanks, Ali.'

'No worries, chick.'

★ ★ ★

Nell put the flowers in a jug of water on her desk between a miniature Venus de Milo that she'd found in an Oxfam and a tidgy bottle of prosecco that she'd won in the work Christmas raffle. She read the note:

See me tonight? We need to talk about Rupert – Alex

Nell put the card down and picked up the statue. She stared at its expressionless face. Men may appear, proverbially, to arrive all at once. However, the real question is: why aren't men more like buses? By virtue of their scale and colour, buses are obvious. Unlike men who only make themselves obvious years later. The new buses even have multiple exit routes, unlike men. Bus shelters have little displays that tell you in real time when each bus arrives at your stop, and there are maps that tell you where each service terminates, unlike men. Who made men so careless that they afford you less consideration than TfL? Were London's buses ever white like roses? Did an unknown lover of Aphrodite's die in a cycling lane? Did she turn the buses red in honour of some new Adonis? Nell opened her drawer and pulled out a biography of Byron that she kept for moments when she had no work to do and tried to lose herself in tales of keeping bears in college and swimming the Hellespont.

16

Pimlico

Caius pulled the car up in front of the Hesperides Gallery. It was on one of those quaint little streets that tourists walk along and think is terribly charming, whereas proper Londoners just think it's terrible. The shop across the road sold antique chandeliers for the price of a terraced house in Liverpool, another sold moth-eaten taxidermy specimens of nearly extinct predators – a snarling wolf graced their window – and a third sold exorbitant room scents, although it tried to look like an alien pharmacy. There was a handwritten sign on the gallery's door that read 'Back in 20 minutes'. Caius had drunk too much coffee that morning and was desperate for a piss. There was a pub called The Grapes further down, which he waddled over to. Caius pushed open the cheerful stained-glass door and went in. The pub was empty apart from a bored-looking barmaid who, based on the repetitive sweeping motion she was making with her index finger, was on a dating app. She had a pierced nose, a large tattoo on her arm, and her black T-shirt had paint splattered on it – an art student, maybe? Not the look you expect from a West London gastropub, but then again the pub wasn't what you'd expect either. Every commercially minded boozer across the city, from Aldwych to Woolwich, had in recent years undergone some form of 'improvement'. They all now looked the same. Offensively neutral Farrow & Ball paint. Ironic artwork. 'Gin o'clock' scrawled in chalk on a rustic-looking slate. This pub, however, hadn't been touched at all. He looked over her shoulder and spotted a notice that said they would be closed for three weeks in August for renovation works. There goes another one.

'Hello, sorry. Would you mind if I just used your loo?' Caius asked.

'You'll have to buy something,' said the barmaid, not looking up from her phone.

'Packet of ready salted and half a pint of Coke.'

The barmaid looked up at Caius. 'Is Pepsi all right?'

'Sure, Pepsi's fine,' he said. Odd. Caius saw her relax at his response. 'Are the gents up the stairs?'

'Yeah,' she said, going back to swiping left.

A relieved Caius came back downstairs to a still empty pub. 'How much do I owe you?'

'Four pounds twenty, please.'

Caius fished for the change in his wallet and then found his badge in his pocket. 'DI Caius Beauchamp. Do you mind if I ask you a few questions?' he said, smiling at her, flashing his teeth.

'All right,' she said, tensing up. The smile hadn't worked.

'Don't worry, you're not in trouble. Do you know the girl who works in the Hesperides Gallery down the road?' Caius nonchalantly sipped on the Pepsi.

'The blonde, leggy one? After a bottle of rosé she tries to tuck her ankles behind her ears.'

'Yeah,' Caius said, getting out a picture kindly supplied by Rupert that morning. 'This girl.'

'Yeah. She comes in every Friday.'

'Did she ever get in any fights with your regulars?'

'No.'

'Anything stand out about her?'

'What, apart from shagging her boss?' she said, relishing the taste of the gossip in her mouth.

'Really?' Caius leaned in conspiratorially. Barmaids like a bit of rumourmongering.

'The silver fox with the beard. It's his gallery. They have mad chemistry. My mate who got me this job caught them at it a few weeks ago, out back where they keep the empty barrels. The silver fox knows the manager of the pub, or something, so it all got smoothed over.'

'Thanks. Here's my number, in case anything else comes to mind. Anything at all,' Caius said, giving her a card and a beaming smile as he took the unopened packet of crisps. He turned to leave when he spotted a purple charity fundraising box. He went in for a closer look: Help for Hippos. It made him laugh.

The barmaid was watching him closely. 'The landlord is an animal lover, I guess.'

'Thanks again.'

He walked back towards the gallery and saw that it was still closed. Next to the chandelier shop (or was it a boutique, or even an emporium?) was a small public garden with a bench in it. It was close to Victoria station – the house that should have been there must have been bombed in the war and never redeveloped. It was an odd feeling to find a patch of death that had grown so prosaically beautiful. There was a banal rose bush planted at one end, a generic geranium here and a drab pansy there. He was sitting on the bench eating his crisps when Matt rang.

'*Hola muchacho*, just got back to the station. All the pubs confirmed that Rupert and the others were there when they said they were – by the sound of it, they all got a bit messy – but the CCTV was on the blink at McDonald's so there was no footage,' Matt said.

'I have a new lead. Barmaid at the pub down the road from the gallery thinks Clemmie was having an affair with her boss.'

'That's a twist.'

'I think our gallerist has returned from his lunch break. I'll see you at 4 p.m. at Clemmie's house. *Auf wiedersehen.*' Caius hung up as a grey-haired man in a loose-fitting Nehru collar shirt, faded pink shorts and brown leather boating shoes unlocked the gallery door. It was reassuring to know that fifty-somethings with little pot bellies could still pull. The gallerist was holding a large rustic baguette under his arm as he went into the gallery. Caius put the empty crisp packet in a nearby bin and rubbed his hands on his trousers. It was no good shaking hands with salt-encrusted, oily fingers. He didn't want to make the wrong impression. He crossed the road and stopped outside the gallery. He took a picture of the splattered canvas hanging in the window and another of the description with the artist's name. Caius remembered doing something similar in primary school with marbles. He sent the pictures to his mum asking if she'd kept his portfolio of work from nursery, because they could make a killing if she had. He tried the door, but the proprietor had locked it behind him. He knocked on the plate glass and the silver fox appeared, pointing at the paper sign and wiggling his fingers. Caius wiggled his badge in response and was duly let in.

'DI Caius Beauchamp. Are you Mr Ned Osbald?'

'I am. Please come through, detective,' Ned said, bemusedly leading Caius to the back office. 'Would you like a cup of tea?'

'No, thank you.' The room was airy and bright. It had a small kitchenette with six or seven boxes of herbal tea piled up next to the kettle and a desk shoved into the corner. On it there was a picture of Ned and a stately looking woman in her fifties. 'Are you much of a tea drinker, Mr Osbald?'

'That stuff?' he asked, nodding towards the kettle. 'No, that's Clemmie's, she's my assistant. Made me one once. It smelled like garden cuttings and I refused to drink it. I don't drink hot drinks – sensitive teeth, absolute agony. Please excuse the mess. You've caught me on my lunch break.'

'I can see,' Caius said, acknowledging the baguette, a wedge of oozing Brie and an apple. 'How very French.'

'Is Francophilia a crime?'

'No,' Caius said, smiling to himself before straightening up. 'I've come to ask a few questions about Clemency O'Hara. When did you see her last?'

'We were both here until about six-ish on Friday. Why do you ask?'

'I'm sorry, Mr Osbald, Clemmie is dead. I assumed her partner had told you.'

'What? She's dead?' Ned stopped. This was news to him. 'No, he hadn't.' The lights turned off as he sunk into his swivel chair.

'Would you like a glass of water?'

'I'm fine,' Ned said, sitting up straight, both back and upper lip stiffening in the chair.

'Did she say what she was doing last weekend?'

'Not much. Something about her boyfriend's birthday party. He rang on Sunday morning to ask if I'd heard from her, but I didn't think she . . .' Ned trailed off.

'What did you think?'

'Oh, I don't know, girls like that.'

'Like what?'

'Difficult ones. Ones who grew up knowing they're beautiful. Confident. She's one of those private school yobs who's out for what they can get.' He struggled to find the words. 'Like a St Trinian.'

'And what was it she wanted?'

'Honestly, I think she was just so desperate to marry that . . . Evelyn Bore, that's what I call him. Never to his face, of course. Her boyfriend has a vision of himself as the leader of a new cultural movement like the Bloomsbury Set or the Pre-Raphaelite Brotherhood. She was determined to be a photographer just to keep up with him. God knows what she saw in him. I always thought she could do much better.'

'Was her photography any good?'

'No, not an ounce of talent, but she put a lot of effort into it. She kept trying to convince me to let her put a show on here. I caved in eventually. I was going to let her have the space for two weeks in August. No one is in London then. She was going to do some sort of ticketed preview event with her "followers". She was keeping it secret so she could do some big reveal on her channel. Followers. It's a funny use of the word. Imagine Jesus charging entry for the Sermon on the Mount.'

'Did you like her?' He meant 'did you love her', but he wasn't going to be that blunt about it. Not yet anyway.

'Did I just. She's a curious girl, a bit misguided, perhaps. She has a wonderful sense of humour. Brutally honest . . . I don't think I should say anything more until I have a solicitor present.'

'I appreciate that, Mr Osbald, but any help you can give me now may stop whoever did kill Clemency from getting away with it.'

Ned considered this for a moment. 'Clemmie leaves her personal laptop here. She has a box of stuff in the cupboard over there.' Ned moved over to the cupboard, took out the box and put it on the table.

'Her laptop?'

'Yeah. She had a separate, private one for her art, secret probably. Galleries are quiet. You only need to make a few sales a month to stay afloat, so it's a glorified security guard job. All those girls you see in galleries beavering away on perspex desks are reading the *Guardian* or doing their own projects most of the time.'

'Why did she leave it here?'

'Evelyn Bore doesn't take her seriously. Those awful videos she makes don't help of course – but they weren't done in earnest, they were tongue-in-cheek. She's much smarter than that. Always has a book on her.'

'Does the laptop have a password?'

'I don't know.'

'Can I take it with me? And the box with her other stuff in?'

'Sure,' Ned said. He had hesitated briefly.

'How did she get the job?'

Ned paused and considered his response. 'It was a friend of a friend of my wife's situation, I think. Not sure though. That's what it's like round here.'

'Mr Osbald, I will need you to come down to the station to make a formal statement.' Caius put on a pair of latex gloves to pick up the box. He always kept a pair in his back pocket. He quickly nosed through what else was in there: a box of paracetamol, an exhibition guide to a show on at the British Museum last year, a camera, a nail file, a lip balm, a notebook with a cutesy panda on the front and an unopened box of tampons.

As Ned walked him through the gallery, Caius stopped at a painting of a mauve splodge. 'Do you like the art you sell?'

'No, but people buy it. It's just business.' Ned went to shake Caius's free hand and Caius noticed the expensive timepiece on his wrist.

'Nice watch.'

'Thanks. It's a Rolex Submariner from the seventies. It was my father's.'

'Thank you again, Mr Osbald. Feel free to bring your solicitor tomorrow,' Caius said as he left the gallery with the box under his arm.

17

DS Amy Noakes's computer screen

Matt had 'forewarned' Amy about the YouTube channel. She'd overheard Matt and Caius joking about charcoal cleanses and vampire facials earlier that day. If Clemmie had written a blog about Arsenal, VAR, transfer windows or something else that most young women find asinine, she doubted they'd be sneering. They just didn't get it. And they didn't see the irony; they didn't see the money. There were links to this product and that product – if enough people bought enough recommended merchandise, then she'd make a few bob. Perhaps Clemmie was taking advantage of our bottomless desire to watch more and more videos to make a fast buck. She put her headphones in and collated the subjects of the videos in the spreadsheet she was working on. They included:

- The wonders of colonic irrigation
- Her opinion on Gwyneth Paltrow ('the greatest thinker of our generation')
- Her bedtime routine (including organic essential oils made only by blind Tibetan monks under a full moon)
- Her thoughts on land tax reform (this was uncharacteristic frivolity, and the experiment had never been repeated)
- Reviews of chai lattes from cafes arranged by London borough (she hadn't made it out further east than Canonbury)
- How to get an even tan (go outside when it's sunny, wear as little as possible and don't move)

- Her recipe for the best lemonade (add tequila)
- How she treats a cold with ginger and hope (Lemsip isn't enough, apparently)
- Her favourite brand of pink kettlebells (ranked by how rubbery the handles smell)

It struck Amy that this all might be an act. Maybe it was a piece of performance art? She worked in a gallery. Maybe it was going to be an installation – videos projected onto white walls. Perhaps it was a canny attempt at pastiching their generation's enslavement to pointless 'lifestyle content'? The deception was so good that everyone took it for what it appeared to be – or she might have been sincere. Either way, Amy thought Clemmie was much cleverer than Caius and Matt had been giving her credit for.

18

The King's Road

Clemmie's gym was in a sunlit loft space with polished wood floors and exposed brickwork. Everything was white and grey, and smelled like no gym that Caius had ever been in. There was a juice bar selling spirulina and optimism, and a perky young man with the teeth of an American actor positioned at a welcome desk. Portraits of the instructors hung on the walls in neat little frames. They were like old black-and-white portraits of film stars from the fifties – the trainers were probably all out-of-work actors. One of the squares was blank. Caius had never been to a gym before that had orchids, or branded Egyptian cotton towels in a delightful shade of dusky pink, or smelled welcomingly clean and pure and not of mildewy showers.

'DI Caius Beauchamp. I want to talk to whoever is in charge?'

'Of course. Please take a seat.' The receptionist gestured to some chairs on the side, Danish mid-century design, as he dialled a number. He sounded posh. He was muscular; Caius decided that he must be a West End dancer sort. His badge declared that his name was Tim.

Caius felt like he spent half of his life being asked to sit by young people. Young people . . . he was thirty-four, although he had never really felt truly young. Disappointed yes, disaffected sometimes and definitely disheartened, but never young. There was a low table arranged on a purposely distressed, soft-blush oriental rug. On it were various healthy living magazines. Each one had a label on the front saying *Property of Herculean Gyms*. Yoga, homeopathy, weightlifting – all possible variations of the health and fitness industrial complex were present.

'Do you have to put labels on your magazines so people don't pinch them?' Caius asked over his shoulder towards the receptionist.

'Oh, you'd be surprised at what wealthy people try to steal,' came the reply from an unknown voice. 'Hi, I'm Kamal, the manager. How can I help?' Kamal was dressed smartly in a light pink button-down shirt, rather than as a glorified PE teacher. Caius, like most of the country, had been traumatised by the sadism of school sport. He could not think of a more hateful, despicable group of people than PE teachers.

'DI Caius Beauchamp. I have a few questions about one of your members. Let's go somewhere private,' Caius said, standing up to shake hands with Kamal.

'Yes, if you wouldn't mind. Our members very much appreciate the privacy they get here,' Kamal said pointedly, handing Caius a guest pass.

'Lead on.' Caius followed Kamal towards the back office. He walked past a glowing young woman who looked rather familiar. Kamal showed him down a corridor that led to a series of studios. Caius peeked through one door and saw flexible women on fluorescent mats with their arses in the air. Another was full of beauties panting and grunting on spinning bikes. Oh, to be one of those saddles, Caius sighed to himself. He wondered if that was one of those thoughts he wasn't supposed to have. At least he hadn't said it out loud.

They arrived at the bottom of the corridor and Kamal used his pass to open a door with 'Private' across it. 'Sorry about that. We have a few models and the odd minor royal who get a bit paranoid. How can I help you?'

'A client of yours, Clemency O'Hara' – Caius showed Kamal

the photograph – 'may have been here on Saturday. I need to know when she was here and when she left.'

'Of course, I can look her up on the system,' Kamal said, typing on the computer. 'This is her, right?' On the screen was a mugshot of Clemmie. 'The barrier records when people scan themselves in and out. That's odd. She scanned in at 12.42 but didn't scan herself out.'

'How's that possible?'

'We can open the barrier manually at reception. She may have mislaid her card and whoever was on duty let her out. She booked in for yoga at 1 p.m. but didn't go – the instructor has an iPad that records attendance.'

'How hi-tech.' Caius wondered if his own regime would be improved if he were yelled at by a person with impressive muscle definition and a tablet for not turning up. The closest he had to a trainer was an ironic gnome who sulked in the corner of his garden.

'There's a huge demand for some classes. We use it to penalise those who book but don't turn up.'

'Do you have CCTV?'

'No, we don't. That's one part of our appeal. We're less stuffy than the Hurlingham, much more modern. This is a New York loft on the King's Road, but we're just as discreet as them.'

'Can I have a copy of the information you have on Clemency?'

'Well, we pride ourselves on—'

Caius interrupted him. 'Before you mention data protection, this is a murder inquiry, and I'd appreciate it if you didn't slow the investigation down because you insist on a warrant. We might make a bit of a scene when we come back. I'm not sure your clientele will like that. They might all start going to the Hurlingham instead.'

Kamal blinked slowly. 'That won't be a problem, detective.'

'Thank you, I appreciate your co-operation.'

'So she's dead then? The girl?'

'Yes. Did you know her?'

'Not personally. I'm usually out here doing paperwork, dealing with blocked showers and ordering more powdered hemp for the smoothie bar, but I recognise her. One of those girls who gets taken to all the best places around town, so doesn't eat carbs, and goes to classes five times a week. Not much to do.' The printer started whirring as Kamal read Clemmie's record. 'Oh, that's interesting. She used to train with Yan.'

'Who's Yan?'

'He was a trainer here. He was really popular but he quit before I started. I think he had some family trouble and went back home. Beauchamp is an unusual name. Are you French?'

'I'm half Jamaican.'

'Oh, I didn't realise . . .' Kamal made the face that people made whenever Caius had this conversation. The printer finished and Kamal handed over a copy of Clemmie's attendance record.

'My mum's family are Irish and my dad is pretty fair so . . . Don't feel weird about it. Honestly. Happens all the time.'

Kamal laughed. 'Actually, I thought you might be Turkish too. You look Turkish. Do you want to have a look around while you're here?'

'Yes, please. How expensive is it to join?'

'You wouldn't believe how much people pay.'

'Are you the owner?'

'Oh no, just the manager. I used to work at a Fitness First, so this is a bit of a step up. I'm still on probation.'

As they were leaving, Caius noticed a purple charity collection box shoved into a corner behind a packet of till roll. 'What's that?'

'Oh, a charity thing. The owners asked me to put it out on the smoothie bar last week, but I didn't think it worked with the aesthetic, so I never did. I didn't want to disrupt the ambiance.'

It was the third one he'd seen on this case, after the ones in the hairdresser's and the pub.

Kamal gave Caius a whistle-stop tour of the gym, eventually returning him to reception where he noticed a sign advertising the gym's optional extras: unlimited smoothies, private lockers, sports massages . . .

'Tim, wasn't it?' Caius asked.

'Yes. Can I help you?' Tim asked, looking between Caius and Kamal. Caius detected a small nod from Kamal out of the corner of his eye.

'Were you working on Saturday afternoon?' Caius asked.

'I was, sir,' he replied.

Caius pulled out Clemmie's photograph. 'Did you see this woman leave?'

'Yes, I buzzed her out. She'd misplaced her card in the studio but couldn't retrieve it because another class was happening. I have her card here in the drawer.'

'I'll take that. What time was it roughly that you let her out?'

'I can tell you precisely,' Tim said, rifling through a clipboard of delivery records. 'It was when we had the protein powder delivered. I buzzed them out together. 13.17, that's what I wrote here.'

'Thank you, Tim. Very helpful. I'm just going to take that sheet, if you don't mind, Kamal.'

'Of course,' Kamal said, anxious for Caius to leave before making a spectacle in front of a broad-shouldered man Caius recognised from the telly. 'Do you want to continue this conversation in my office perhaps?'

'Oh no, it's all right, I'm leaving now,' Caius said, smiling at Kamal before continuing. 'What was she wearing, Tim?'

'A pinkish hoodie and leggings, I think.'

'Did she have a bag with her?'

'I don't remember.'

'Thank you both. You've been very accommodating, and I hope I haven't spooked any of your clients.'

★   ★   ★

Caius was in his car outside Rupert's house, drinking a mediocre cappuccino. He felt smug that he'd remembered his reusable cup. He'd saved himself ten pence, and probably the planet, plus he'd had a little flirt with the barista. He'd needed an ego boost. He looked up at the house and doubted that Rupert had a reusable coffee cup. He doubted that Rupert cared about the environment at all – he'd probably purchased a remote Scottish island where he could ride out any one of the imminent apocalypses. A rap on the window let him know that Matt had arrived.

'Biscotti, buddy?' Caius asked, offering Matt one as he got out of the car. Perhaps the barista had merely been trying to up-sell to a gullible moron.

'No, you're all right. They hurt my teeth,' Matt said, running his tongue over a filling that he worried was coming loose.

'What are you thinking?'

'An affair is a pretty good motive for either of them. Would explain the mutilation as an act of punishment.'

'I think it's bigger than that. I don't know what yet.' Caius got out of the car. 'I've seen three Help for Hippos charity donation boxes on this case. I just googled them. I found a website, but it feels dodgy.'

'You think it's a scam?'

'Maybe. I don't know.'

'What are we looking for in the house?'

'Have a gander,' Caius said as he opened the boot. 'This is a box of Clemency's things from the Hesperides Gallery. Ned Osbald gave it to me, so he must think there's nothing here that would incriminate him. I think you can divide these items into two categories. The first one – practical things that women might need, like the nail file; and secondly – items belonging to an aspiring photographer, like the camera and the laptop. I've flicked through the notebook, and it looks like it's just her shopping wish lists. Things she's seen in magazines.'

'What about the art book? Do you file it under photographer?'

'Clemmie was no classicist, and she wasn't an art historian. She's a good time girl who spent an inordinate amount of her time Instagramming her breakfast, bending over in tight leggings and pretending to be Diane Arbus. This book isn't really hers.'

'Why do you hate these poshos so much?'

'You and me, we're both third generation immigrants. We're from the colonies. You get it, right? The lack of accountability? Where's the retribution? When the British government ended the slave trade, they borrowed £20 million to compensate the slavers for their losses, not us. Beauchamp was probably the name of the plantation owners that owned my ancestors, hence why I have it. I don't want you to think my judgement is clouded. If anything, this proves my innate sense of justice. I can hold on to something for two hundred years.' Caius looked up at the ill-gotten house. 'I'm jealous of you. You know what your name is, you come from a noble line of Cheungs. I don't have that. It's hard to carry the burden of someone else's name, not to know where you came from, and for people to then think you're bloody Turkish all the time.'

'What's wrong with the Turkish?'

'Nothing, absolutely nothing. Nice people.' Every time Caius tried to ask his paternal grandfather about his childhood in Jamaica, the normally talkative man clammed up. He remembered telling his father and grandfather that he was joining the police and how disappointed they'd been with him. They didn't seem to understand that after everything they'd been through, everything that had happened to his sister Lydia, he felt compelled to. That if someone like him was doing the job then it wouldn't happen again. His father said he could join his property company (his father had made more than a living buying houses and doing them up – he had made Caius learn to plaster as a teenager), while his grandfather had tried to insist that Caius use his degree to go into a more gentlemanly profession, not the thuggery of the police. His grandfather had always been deeply concerned with being a gentleman – he always wore a hat and a pocket square wherever he went.

'There's a bar by my parents' house called The Opium Den . . . Makes me livid every time I walk past,' Matt said, puffing his cheeks out. 'My offer from the other day still stands. Do you want to go for a drink soon?'

'Yeah. Yeah, I do.'

'Good, cause you're getting a bit messy, babe,' Matt said, looking at the box of Clemmie's effects in the boot and refocusing his attention. 'We're looking for cognitive dissonance?'

'Perfectly put. Who is Clemmie O'Hara? Is she an airhead or an aesthete? Is somewhere between the two possible?'

'Why are they a couple? He has a library in the house, she has an extensive collection of inspirational Gandhi quotes taken out of context on her social media.'

★　★　★

'No phone still, and all I really learned was that she spent a lot of money on shoes,' Matt said.

'Did you notice the bookshelf?' Caius asked. 'I got a closer look. I didn't want to prod too much yesterday.'

'I did. There was another copy of that exhibition guide on the shelf in the living room. It could be a coincidence? Beauchamp studied Ancient History at Oxford so I would expect him to have books like that. Maybe they went to the exhibition together?'

'Why buy two copies of the same museum guide when you live together? There are too many coincidences. There are hints of symbolism. The books, the flower crown and the posthumous mutilation, that has to have a greater meaning to whoever killed Clemmie,' Caius said, getting his phone out and checking for messages. There were none. Héloise hadn't texted him. Probably for the best.

'Help for Hippos could be a simple scam. People donate to a made-up charity,' Matt said, chewing on a fingernail.

Caius took out his phone and looked through the Help for Hippos website. There were pictures of the beast along with a few rudimentary facts about their loss of habitat. There were fundraising packs, downloadable posters for primary schools to use for their zoo animal projects, pictures of charity runs, cake sales and bike rides. It was enough to convince someone if they glanced at the website casually, but it didn't have a registered charity number.

'Yeah, it looks like they're trying to get drunks to drop their spare change in the pub.'

'Still up for that drink?'

'Yeah, sure. I bought myself a copy of that art book on Amazon,' Caius said.

'Really, but they're so evil!'

'I know, but it's so convenient.'

'So were the Nazis, buddy.'

'No, they weren't. No one would describe the Nazis as convenient. Well, unless you were blue-eyed, I suppose. Horribly
efficient.'

19

Nell's flat

Nell was sprawled across her sofa as she stared at the ceiling, waiting for her Deliveroo to arrive. She'd ordered a pizza – sourdough, of course, with extra burrata – and a tiramisu, and some garlic bread. She flipped between being a girl who felt like she shouldn't eat and a girl who ate her feelings, and that evening she was ravenous. Nell had put a documentary on wage poverty and zero-hour contracts on the television – another exposé of socialism for the rich and capitalism for the poor – but she wasn't paying attention to it. Her doorbell rang and she opened the door to find Alex holding her food.

'I bumped into the delivery guy on my way in,' Alex said, apologetically offering up Nell's carbohydrate hoard. 'Look, I know you said you didn't want to see me tonight, but we need to talk.'

'I should complain to Deliveroo. You could have been anyone.' Nell stood with her arms outstretched across the door frame, blocking his entrance.

'May I come in?' he asked.

'That depends.'

'On what?'

'What you're going to say.'

'What I have to say isn't about this, about us. Whatever *this* is, because you're rather a done deal for me.' Alex looked at Nell, who was looking not at him but through him. 'I think you need to hear the truth about Rupert.'

'Fine,' Nell said, slinking back into the flat.

'I need to apologise for today.' Alex closed the door behind himself and put the food on the table next to the vase with the flowers he had bought her. He walked over to the window, looked into the street and closed the curtains.

'What are you apologising for? For leaving me to fend off Rupert on my own? He was very nearly sleeping here tonight. He wanted to watch *Troy* and whinge about the historical inaccuracies.' Nell flung herself onto the sofa and muted the television, which was now showing scenes of food banks squirrelling tins of tomatoes for the working poor.

'I take it you've heard about Clemmie then.'

'Yeah.' Nell stared at the floor. 'Where do you begin with news like that?'

'It's awful. I had lunch with Teddie today. Loads of people from the party were pulled in for questioning by the police. They were asking about Rupert's whereabouts. I think you know why.'

'No, I don't know why, Alex.'

'Statistically it's likely to be—'

'I don't believe you.'

'You should.'

'Fuck.'

'You know he is dangerous, deep down. Nell, come on. There were all those rumours about him being rough with that fresher, remember? You know that Rupert is capable of violence.'

20

Caius's garden

Reggaeton played over the speakers as Caius and Matt were eating pizza on the patio in the garden. Quietly – it was midweek, and he was a considerate neighbour. Caius's garden was a classic green square with the judgy gnome standing in a corner with his back to them in disgust. Matt had stopped off at the craft beer 'curatorial space' that had opened up near the police station on the way to Caius's, and they were both sipping ales with psychedelic tins and ironic names.

'I really wanted to hate this, but it's delicious,' Caius said, reading the wackaging on the back of his beer: 'White's American IPA – smooth like Barry, sparkling like Betty.'

'You can't judge a craft beer by its obnoxious can,' Matt said, reaching for another slice of quattro formaggi. 'So, how are you?'

'I'm fine.' Caius leaned back into his stripy deckchair and watched the wisp of a cloud float past in the blooming twilight.

'No, you're not. Break-ups are shit, aren't they?'

'Real shit.' Caius nodded in assent.

'Particularly when you still want to be in that relationship . . .'

'I'd booked a train ticket for Paris the afternoon I found the body. I hadn't told Héloise that I was coming. I was just going to turn up and wing it. Come up with some grand gesture en route.'

'Sounds romantic.'

'Sounds romantic, but it's a dick move. A big public gesture would only soothe my wounded ego at being cheated on and put her under pressure to have me back. I need to get my shit together, I'm too old to act like that. In the beginning, things between Héloise and me were like something from myth, you know. I'd swim the Hellespont like Leander. Sorry, I've been reading Ovid. But . . .' Caius trailed off. The judgy garden gnome weighed on his conscience. Héloise had bought it for him for his birthday as a joke. They don't have gnomes in France.

'But?'

'I've never been good at anger; I don't like to be furious in front of anyone. I'm a bottler and she's a bottler. It was like a Coke that gets shaken up, dropped and then propels itself across the Co-op, leaving a sticky mess.' He wanted to ring Héloise. He was glad Matt was there.

'You're both conflict avoiders and it affected the level of intimacy between the two of you. She tried to find intimacy elsewhere because she loves you so much that she didn't want to risk losing you by voicing conflict. It paradoxically felt safer.'

'What a nice theory.' Caius wanted desperately to believe Matt. 'It's that or she's just a coward who was too petrified to break up with me. I'm so confused. I have no idea what I want. I'm not sure I even want to get back with her. I just don't like being alone. I think I might have only been going to Paris so she'd yell at me for being boring again, so I could download Tinder without any guilt.'

'Trust me – I did Psychology, didn't I? I started on a counselling course but then changed my mind and joined the police. It comes in handy for de-escalating conflict . . .'

'I don't know what to do next. I think I just need to get laid.'

'If I were you, as admirable as all the books and runs are – and to be fair, you found that poor girl that way – what you really need to do is talk with Héloise about what's really wrong and work out whether you want to get back together. I'd even go as far as to say that you've got a good chance of patching it up.'

'Do you think?'

'Give her a call,' Matt said, swigging from his beer.

'How are things going with your Swedish friend?'

'I'm meeting Freja's parents next week. They're flying over to do some sightseeing.'

'What does she do?'

'She works in design. I'll introduce you sometime soon when there are no dead girls on Hampstead Heath. So, you're reading Ovid?'

'Yeah, I went to a dodgy comp. I've never read these colossal works, these pillars of civilisation. I don't like feeling deficient. I want to be able to hold my own in conversation.'

'I had a lecturer who used to use Greek myths as the basis for Jungian archetypes. Read *The Iliad*. It's the start of the whole nasty business. Western literature begins with a massive sulk over an enslaved girl.'

'Sulking, sulking, sulking.' Caius took a sip of his beer. 'I still think the boyfriend did it. I think Rupert Beauchamp murdered Clemmie.'

'Socialite or sociopath?'

'Sociopath.'

WEDNESDAY

21

The Police Station

Today did not feel like it was going to be good for Caius. Sleep had not been forthcoming. He'd rung Héloise after Matt had left and she'd picked up. She was at a bar, there was Latin music in the background, and she sounded so blissfully joyful. She said a few rum-infused bon mots that he hadn't quite understood, but she promised that she'd ring him back in twenty minutes and then failed to do so. After his alarm howled at him at 5 a.m. he checked his messages – nothing from *la belle femme* – and then his work emails. One of these requested that he be standing outside the Chief Superintendent's office at 8 a.m., and here he was, sipping a cup of green tea and feeling really fucking terrible. That might have been because he'd tried and failed again to run up Parliament Hill at 6 a.m. He'd managed two thirds of it, so it was progress at least. The grand poohbahh was on the phone. Caius could hear the occasional chortle come through the door. Typical. The email had asked him to be prompt, and Caius was bloody prompt and yet he was kept waiting outside his office like a delinquent sixth-former who'd been caught bunking off chemistry to smoke cigarettes with the previously virginal Head Girl. The Chief Superintendent was probably organising his weekend bridge tournament or something else awfully Home Counties.

Silence.

'Come in,' the Chief Superintendent called.

'Good morning, sir,' Caius said, closing the door behind him. Caius looked around the room and noticed he'd had a bit of a reshuffle of his desk. Made it less personal. The family photographs had been replaced by an 'executive toy'. Plink plonk, plink plonk. Caius thought that those strung-up silver balls were the model of middle-management complacency unless they were ironic. Caius wasn't sure he was capable of that level of self-awareness.

'I was wondering how the O'Hara case is going. Nasty business.'

'We're progressing. We're waiting on forensics.'

'What's your main line of inquiry?'

'It has been suggested that Clemmie was having an affair with her boss, Ned Osbald. We haven't got anything more than hearsay, but if it is true then we might be able to prove it with either the semen sample or the paternity of the foetus.'

'So Rupert Beauchamp isn't your man?' the Superintendent asked. Caius noticed that he pronounced Rupert's surname 'correctly'.

'As it stands, sir, he has an alibi for the whole afternoon and evening. He's been very willing to allow us access to his property without a warrant, which suggests he has nothing to hide.' Or he's just very good at hiding it, Caius thought to himself. 'At this stage I think myself and DS Cheung have all but written him off as the perpetrator for lack of material evidence.'

'Right, good to know that you are no longer pursuing that line of inquiry. We don't want to inconvenience important individuals like Mr Beauchamp for the sake of it.' He straightened his cufflinks. He smiled knowingly at Caius with his lips pursed and his eyebrows raised, as if Caius needed the subtext of what he was saying spelled out to him. 'You have a promising career ahead of you. I know that you had some trouble the other year, but I'm glad that has all passed.'

'Thank you, sir. I want to do a good job.' Caius stopped himself from snorting – only just.

'Good, good. Beauchamp, Beauchamp, Beauchamp. Are you any relation? I know you pronounce it differently.'

'It's merely a coincidence, sir.' Caius left his office.

22

The Police Station

Amy had completed a comprehensive data analysis on Clemmie's dietary habits, with herbal tea being the most frequently posted about. Caius remembered all the boxes of concoctions he had seen piled up at the gallery, each of them promising some intangible benefit that cannot be found in hot drinks: balance; calm; telekinesis . . . Then he remembered all the miraculous powdered berries and plant protein powders that Clemmie talked about on her blog. His phone rang.

'Beauchamp, it's Barry.'

'Barry, just the man,' Caius said, as Matt walked in. He signalled for him to come and listen to the call as he put it on speakerphone.

'The O'Hara case, it was digoxin poisoning. It's a compound derived from digitalis. It's a pretty common heart medication. It can cause nausea and vomiting; people can get confused, dizzy and have visual disturbances. It can be fatal, but it's extremely rare.'

'Digoxin poisoning, that's a new one for me. So it wasn't supposed to kill her, only incapacitate.'

'You're looking for someone with a dodgy ticker. We started checking cups in the rubbish bins in the park when it became apparent it was a poisoning. We've not yet found a cup with the victim's fingerprints on amongst the rubbish, but we'll keep looking now we know what the poison is. Also, we failed to find any vomit at the scene other than that on her clothing, which suggests she died elsewhere.'

'Thanks, Barry,' Caius said, hanging up.

'Very Miss Marple,' Matt said, leaning against the desk. He was holding a travel mug of tea, the little white label poked out. He was eyeing it strangely – he'd taken a loose leaf out of Caius's book and was drinking something herbal and disagreeable.

'Rupert's too young for a heart problem. Ned might have one though.' Caius got up from his desk and picked up his mug. 'Would you like a coffee?'

'No, I'm all right.'

Caius looked around the incident room to see if anyone was paying attention to them. There were a couple of uniformed officers loitering in the corner going through all the crackpot reports from the public that had come in. 'I think you'd like a coffee, and you should come and make it with me.'

Matt twigged. 'Oh, yes, I would like a cup of coffee. I'll come with you,' he said. Matt followed Caius down the corridor and then into the empty break room, where Caius explained the meeting he'd had with the Chief Superintendent that morning.

'We need to be quieter about what we're doing until we can prove without a doubt who the murderer is. The grand pooh-bahh is a snob and won't be partial about it. His middle name is probably Hyacinth,' Caius said, heaving his shoulders in fake hilarity. He smiled as the Superintendent walked past the room. 'Pretend I'm funny.'

'That'll be hard.' Matt did a comically large shrug. 'Why is he so interested?'

'I've had a look at the names of the partygoers who came to corroborate Rupert Beauchamp's alibi and I think one of them is his daughter's fiancé. It's quite a common surname so I didn't clock it before. He normally has a picture of her graduating from Exeter on his desk so I checked her Facebook – she moves in those circles a bit. He mentioned the fiancé to me at the Christmas party – he's some posho and he's proud of the connection. Besides, he was a bit of a dick over the whole thing between me and that racist prick at the time . . .'

'Mate, I know I joked about there being some sort of conspiracy, but—'

'If Clemmie did die elsewhere and the body was dumped on the Heath, you'd have to do it at night not to be noticed, which rules out Rupert Beauchamp. I feel like I'm being played. My gut said Beauchamp did it. Today. God, today. What do we need to do today? We need to crack Ned Osbald. You go through Clemmie's laptop and I'll go through the camera. Osbald is coming in to give a statement. I'll try to make a bit of a show of him being here. It'll buy us some breathing room from the grand pooh-bahh.'

★ ★ ★

Staring at blurry images of a penis was not how Caius had thought he'd spend his morning. He was sifting through the photographs from Clemmie's camera. Individual parts of a man. Dissected. The same man, he would guess, by the skin tone. A finger: flexed, curled, pointing. A hairy big toe, bits of torso here and there, a hairy arse. Was this what passed for art? He was looking for a distinguishing feature: a birthmark, a tattoo, a scar from a shark bite. How many angles could you photograph a dick from? He had 672 of these to go through. Caius picked up the book from the exhibition and flicked through it:

The nude, not democracy, is the only ideological constant between our time and the ancient world. The nude survived Christianity's prudishness and aversion to the pleasures of

the body and remains the defining visual feature of Western
civilisation.

Caius hadn't ever considered the philosophical importance
of getting your boobs out. Evidently it was what made you a
European.

Mary Richardson is a name that is unlikely to mean
much to you, but in her day she committed an infamous,
sensational crime: the suffragette slashed Velázquez's
masterpiece, known popularly as the Rokeby Venus. *In our*
culture we are acclimatised to the nude being the preserve
of the female body. We are all familiar with the work of the
*Guerrilla Girls (*Do Women Have To Be Naked To Get Into
the Met. Museum? *1989). However, to the Ancient Greeks*
the young male body was the one they lusted after, not the
malformed female. Misogyny is a Greek word, after all.

Caius picked up the camera and started flicking through the
rest of the pictures. Even more penis shots. A wrist. More wrist.
The other wrist, with a 1970s Rolex Submariner watch on it.

★ ★ ★

Matt was looking through Amy's travel section folder and had
failed to find any pictures of Clemmie's last holiday. She hadn't
posted any blogs or Instagram photos about it. There was a folder
on her laptop called 'Holiday' and in it were pictures of what
Matt thought was Athens. Why would someone who was trying
to make money out of their mere existence not share the pictures or write a piece about some out-of-the-way restaurant that

served the most divine tzatziki or sublime stuffed vine leaves? Especially as Clemmie was supposed to be trying to be a serious intellectual. Where better to take a bikini shot and caption it with Aristotle? The first few photos were quite clearly of Athens and the Parthenon. Shots of Clemmie being impossibly beautiful next to a piece of fallen column of almost unfathomable scale. When the Saxons had conquered the remains of Londinium, they thought the city had been built by giants. More shots of Clemmie (in different outfits) next to more scenic ruins. The pictures all had the same date on the time stamp. She must have changed throughout the day to get material for her blog, which made sense because some of the shoes looked impossible to sightsee in. It was a curious mixture of intellectual and corporeal vanity: I've read Homer and I do my squats every day; I look like a Victoria's Secret Angel, but I think like Plato.

She must have wheeled a suitcase around with her to pull this off. So much effort. More pictures of Clemmie and columns; Clemmie and various other chunks of architectural debris; Clemmie and a pomegranate tree. An accidental shot of the floor with three pairs of feet – two male, one female whose lacklustre, practical, navy-blue plimsolls had yet to make an appearance on Clemmie's feet. Clemmie and Rupert were on a group holiday. Ah, a selfie with Clemmie and Rupert, whose outstretched arm showed that he was the photographer for the day. That made sense. Matt had glanced over his shoulder at the photographs that poor Caius was trawling through, and these were of a different quality. Rupert had a sense of perspective and propor-tion, while Clemmie had had a half-thought of subverting the patriarchy with a shaky grasp of camera angles and her married lover's penis. Perhaps he was being uncharitable? Cruel, even: here he was, critiquing the artistic aspirations of a corpse. He carried on looking through the pictures and found a group shot of the four of them. Matt didn't recognise the other couple. They hadn't given statements backing Rupert's alibi. Funny, you'd expect someone who went on holiday with you to come to your birthday party.

Matt took himself for a walk around the office to cleanse the sickly taste of cynicism from his mouth. It clung to his back teeth like a rancid toffee. It was Janet on the front desk's birthday and there were blondies in the breakout room to celebrate. Obligatory singing and asking about celebratory evening plans occurred before he carried on looking at the pictures through a kinder lens. He'd moved on to a different day. Pictures of breakfast. A few views. Quiet streets. An olive tree. Clemmie browsing through tourist stalls selling tat. Clemmie buying a miniature statue of Athena from an old woman. Pictures you'd use to pepper a blog with. They were all from the morning. Matt continued scrolling through photos of lunchtime spanakopita, and of churches and orthodox saints. The afternoon's pictures were different. Less theatrical. Clemmie wasn't in a single one, but the other girl was. If the early images were works of drudgery, then these pictures were declarations of love. No, not of love. This was lust. It was aggressive in its discreetness. A lingering shot of exposed thigh in the Hellenic dry heat; a close-up of a bitten lip; a neck tickled by a stray dark curl liberated by the breeze. Raging, furious, silent Eros. The other girl isn't present in the pictures although they are of her form. She doesn't know he's taking them. Voyeuristic. The girl is quite lovely in that English way: charming in, and because of, her obliviousness. Reading Jane Austen perched on a shady piece of dry wall and chewing on a fingernail. There were no more photos taken after that day.

23

Bloomsbury

An acoustic version of a rap song poured through Nell's head-phones. She had pretty much completed her work for the day before lunch. Being gainfully underemployed is a funny thing – £30,000 per annum to shuffle paper and send do-not-reply emails. She wasn't sure how the company made money, how they could afford to pay her anything at all, but she wasn't brave enough to ask. Nell put timers on her emails and spaced them out throughout the day, so it looked like she was busier than she really was. She had wondered if she should get a job at a more ambitious publishing house, but this gave her time to think, time to read and time to write. Her 'official' last task for the day was to read through a series of haiku from a navel-gazing twenty-something. They weren't as terrible as she'd expected them to be, or rather they were universal in their terribleness, but other twentysomethings would buy copies.

Keira/Ciara (I don't know how to spell your name, but I've heard it too often)

> *You kept her shampoo.*
> *Did you do it to spite me?*
> *Irrational thought . . .*

It wasn't Coleridge, but it was fashionable. She added it to the pile to take to her boss, Jonathan, on Friday morning. Friday was his slush pile day. He did whatever it actually was he did on the other days of the week – Nell strongly suspected that was mostly having lunch with obscure literary notables, bidding on eBay for first editions of T. S. Eliot (whom he tried very hard to emulate: the glasses, the suits, an over-fondness for felines – she hoped he wasn't an anti-Semite too), and complaining about Faber & Faber still not hiring him. She sort of fancied Jonathan – he was so comfortable in himself, so at peace with the level of arseholery that he'd already managed to achieve at thirty-six. That must be how stodgy MPs manage to have so many affairs.

Nell got her lunch out of her bag: a rather pedestrian salad – 5g protein, 8g fibre, vitamins A, C and E, trace amounts of manganese, an unknown quantity of antioxidants, 0g guilt. It wasn't going to be enough. She was ravenous. Rap-rap came a knock at the door to Nell's cupboard-like office.

'Nelly, darling' – it was Jonathan – 'are you there?'

'Jonny, darling, I'm in here.'

'There you are.' Jonathan popped his head round the door. 'May I come in?'

'You may.'

'Nelly,' he said. Nell hated being called that. In primary school a mean little creature called William used to call her Nelly the elephant. He'd puff his cheeks out and stomp around after her in the playground. Hideous boy.

'It's come to my attention that, um, you might be having a bit of a difficult time, and I just wanted to make sure that you're fine?'

'Oh Jonny, that's very sweet of you. Of course I'm fine.'

'You are my favourite colleague after all.'

'More than Deb in accounts?'

'Don't be a silly goose, no one likes Deb.'

Nell laughed. 'Oh, I don't know. Someone will, somewhere. Her mother?'

'What are you doing tonight?'

'I was planning on going to crochet club with Deb.'

'I've got tickets for a play. My friend wrote it. It's going to be a shitshow, and I would quite like someone else to witness it with. Come with me?'

'All right, but you have to stop calling me Nelly.'

'All right, Helena.'

'This isn't a date by the way. I'm sort of seeing someone.'

'I know. You're just my work-wife.' He did a cheery little wave as he left her office.

Nell finished her salad. She was, unsurprisingly, still hungry. She had a small pot of plain Greek yoghurt (it was good for the skin to eat full-fat dairy, or at least that's what she fervently believed) in the fridge that she was not allowed to eat until at least half past three. No one was enforcing this rule but herself. Alex hadn't texted her all day, so she was delighted to have other plans. Got to keep him on his toes. Nell kept a large A4 clothbound notebook covered in images of seaweed and coral in her desk drawer. She took it out and started to write. Flames flew from the tip of her pencil – this was it. This was how she'd quit her day job. This was how she'd leave London, retiring to a thatched cottage that had uneven floors and low beams that guests would hit their heads on. She'd leave as fiery Gloriana, triumphant in her literary endeavours. She reviewed the three sentences she'd just written and crossed them all out. They were shit. The muse had deserted her. If the muse had ever been with her at all.

24

The Police Station

The Chief Superintendent and Matt were on the other side of the two-way mirror watching Caius interview Ned Osbald. Thus far it was the standard sort of questioning, nothing eventful, traipsing over the same ground as yesterday. Matt thought Caius looked a little stiff. Ned kept still, as if any sudden movements might reveal a hidden truth. He was confident in his innocence, but a touch of shame lingered about his shirt collar. Something dogged him. Matt doubted that he knew he'd incriminated himself by handing over Clemmie's camera.

'Do you have a heart condition, Mr Osbald?'

'No.'

'Where were you on Saturday evening?' Caius asked, sitting rigidly on the squeaky plastic chair. None of the furniture in the station was dignified, but the least he could do was try to correct his posture.

'My wife and I went for dinner at The Court House in Marylebone. We had a reservation for 7.30 p.m. I'm sure the staff there can verify that.' Ned glanced at his solicitor who was hovering at his elbow, primed to interject. The solicitor looked pricey.

'And after dinner?'

'We went home to bed.'

'We?'

'My wife and I.'

'And your wife was with you the whole evening?'

'Yes.'

'Belsize Park is such a lovely part of London. So close to the

Heath.' Caius slid Clemmie's holiday pictures across the desk. 'Do you know who this young woman is?'

'Yes, she's a friend of Clemmie's. Well, no. What's the word? Frenemy. She's a frenemy of Clemmie's.'

'Clemmie didn't like her very much then?'

'No, not at all, although she never went into much detail. I think the girl, Helena – Clemmie always put the emphasis on the "Hel" – was at university with Rupert. Clemmie always thought she was a bit in love with him.'

'Why is he asking that? Who's the girl?' the Chief Superintendent asked, turning to Matt.

'She's an acquaintance of Clemency's. It's not a controversial question. Caius's trying to make him feel comfortable, that he can deal with everything coming his way,' Matt said.

'Do you think that's true? Is this Helena in love with Rupert?' Caius continued.

'I don't know much about their friendship circle. I don't pay attention to Clemmie when she talks about such things. It's a bit like having Radio 4 on in the background.'

'I doubt Jenni Murray licks your balls though.' Caius handed him another picture. 'Can you confirm that that is your penis?'

'It could be anyone's cock.'

'But this is your watch, isn't it?' Caius held up another picture. Ned grasped his wrist in an act of confirmation. 'This is where you start telling me what's really going on here.'

Ned's solicitor was one of the greyest human beings Caius had ever seen. Grey hair, grey suit, grey tie, grey shirt, grey face. He looked almost ill with greyness, like an overripe rain cloud: lumpen and angry with it. Caius handed over the warrant for a sample of Ned's DNA to him as one of the forensics team got swabbing the inside of Ned's cheek.

Ned and his solicitor were talking together in private as Caius and the grand pooh-bahh were having a huddle in his office, like a half-time team talk but without the Lucozade or orange slices or sense of camaraderie.

'Are we close to closing the case?' the Chief asked.

'We could be close to finding out who the father of Clemency's baby was,' Caius replied.

'Isn't that the same thing?'

'Could well be.'

The Chief leaned back against his plush executive chair with its fancy headrest. 'We're going to be on the front page tomorrow. We need to make sure that all our ducks are lined up with this one. I've given a statement on your behalf. We've been very fortunate that things have been so quiet thus far.' A knock at the door. 'Come in.'

'Sir, DI Beauchamp. Forensics have just sent over the DNA analysis. Neither the semen nor the foetus were a match for Rupert Beauchamp. They have also failed to find a cup with Clemmie's fingerprints on it from the Heath,' Amy said.

'Thanks, Amy,' Caius said.

'DS Cheung asked me to say that TfL have finally sent through the CCTV footage. Also Ned Osbald's wife has arrived and is downstairs.'

'Great, thank you,' Caius said to Amy as she closed the door. 'Better hop to it. She's a very capable officer. I'd like her to continue supporting us.' The Chief Superintendent nodded in agreement. 'I'm going to check on Mr Osbald. I'll let the wife stew downstairs, see if she gets upset and spills. Having an affair isn't a crime, but it is one hell of a motive.'

* * *

'Mr Osbald, would you like to take this opportunity to say anything pertinent?'

'I was having an affair with Clemmie . . .'

The ashen lawyer puckered. 'You don't have to say anything about that.'

'I was having an affair with Clemmie, but it wasn't me. I didn't kill her. I was with my wife the whole evening, she can verify that, and so can the restaurant. We didn't leave until 10 p.m. We were plastered. We got an Uber there and back. My wife paid for it. She'll have the receipt on her app.'

'Where were you from 1 p.m. on Saturday?'

'I was working from home in the afternoon.'

'Can anyone verify that?'

'My wife got home around 5.30 p.m.'

'Your wife is here waiting for me, so I'll check that myself.'

* * *

Fay Osbald was a monumental woman. She cut through a room like the prow of a ship. She was tall and willow-limbed. There was something quietly thunderous about how she was looking down at the table. Caius could understand the sense of humiliation for a woman like that. An immaculate Burberry trench was draped over the back of the chair. She wore a black slip dress, tailored, but not (heaven forfend) secretarial, and pearl earrings – not the grandmotherly sort but elegant droplet-like tears. Her glasses were large round ones seen on members of the European intelligentsia that cost far too much for something so utilitarian. Fay wore a shade of orange-red lipstick

142

like a 1950s pin-up poster of a cheeky housewife. An academic who cared about her image – she was an art historian, and she painted you a picture. Her curated image told you that she was better than you but in such a way that you couldn't articulate it fully. She was a mood, a feeling of inadequacy gnarling up Caius's stomach.

'Mrs Osbald – Fay, if I may – this must all be quite distressing for you. Would you like a glass of water, a cup of tea?' Caius asked. Sympathy from a young and not too ill-looking detective might get her to betray her husband, just a little bit.

'No, thank you,' she said with a certain controlled harshness. Caius thought that was a no both to the water and calling her by her first name. Caius took her statement, which collaborated her husband's alibi – to be expected. It would be too easy if she contradicted him.

'Were you aware of your husband's sexual relationship with Ms O'Hara?'

'I was.' Direct – looked Caius straight in the eye and froze his corneas off. Caius thought she was angry with him – he was the closest thing to her husband in the room.

'Did it bother you?'

'No, we have an open arrangement.'

'I understand that Ms O'Hara got the job through an acquaintance of yours?'

'Yes, I think so. I can't remember through whom exactly. It was a while ago.' She waved the question away with her manicured hand.

'Are you sure I can't jog your memory?'

'It was probably through one of my students, but as I said I can't be sure. Might have mentioned Edward was hiring at a dinner party.'

'Where do you teach?'

'At the Courtauld Institute.'

'How interesting,' Caius said, as he jotted a note. 'Did you know Ms O'Hara well?'

'Not hugely. I'm not involved in my husband's affairs, business or otherwise. She was a pleasant girl from what I saw. Bookish but pretty. Such a shame. So young.'

'I see, so you wouldn't know if she had any enmity towards anyone?'

'No.'

'What was Clemmie's relationship with Rupert Beauchamp like?'

'I don't know.'

'Have you met her partner, Rupert?'

'Yes, he's a writer, I think. They came to a public lecture I gave last year. A well-mannered young man, quite charming.' Caius wanted to ask more of her but something about the taut arch of her eyebrow being pulled back like a bow killed his curiosity. She looked like a Rembrandt portrait of a Dutch merchant's wife. Dressed in black with a certain Protestant severity and an innate belief in the greatness of her destiny.

'Do you have a heart condition?'

'No, I don't. Just a touch of insomnia.'

'Where were you Saturday afternoon?'

'I was having lunch with old school friends until about 3 p.m.'

'Where?'

'Some mediocre Italian in Mayfair. I forget the name.'

'And after that?'

'I pottered around Bond Street for a while, I have receipts, then I went home. Edward was back before me.'

'What time was that?'

'I don't know, five thirty-ish. We were together for the rest of the day, then we went out for dinner.'

'So there's two and a half hours where no one can vouch for your movements.'

'What are you implying?'

'That you have a motive and no alibi for murder.'

'Don't be ridiculous, you stupid boy. Of course I didn't do it.' The mask slipped.

'Do you have any questions for me, Mrs Osbald?'

'I have none. I would, however, like to say that my husband lacks the imagination to be a murderer.'

'Then let us end the interview there,' he said, turning off the recorder and standing up. 'May I show you out, madam?' Caius held the interview room door open for her as she walked out and down the corridor. 'What sort of art do you teach?'

'Is this part of your questioning?'

'No. I'm just curious.'

'I teach feminist art theory.'

'Do you give public lectures often?'

'Fairly frequently. It's a requirement of my job.'

'I see.' He held the door to the station's reception open for her. Ned was crumpled on a plastic blue chair. He looked like a dirty shirt awaiting laundry day. 'Thank you both for your time.'

'Not at all,' Tay said, smoothing out non-existent creases in her trench coat. Ned got up and helped her put it on. Silence. Not a word was uttered between them. Caius watched them leave the building.

★   ★   ★

It had gone 8 p.m. and Caius, Matt and Amy were in the break room gorging on gourmet burgers after being glued to their screens for the last three hours. Caius dripped aioli on his notebook. He was looking at his notes from interviewing Fay Osbald while googling her. And trying to eat a cheeseburger, sans bun. He was failing abysmally at all three.

'Eat the burger first, you dirty boy,' Matt said. Amy looked mildly shocked. 'Don't worry' – Matt turned to her – 'despite the reputation he has somehow developed, old Beauchamp can take a joke.'

'Only if there is some truth in it. I don't know how I got that reputation.'

'You yelled at all the racist white people.'

'Oh yeah,' Caius said, putting the dripping burger down. He skimmed through the Courtauld's event page and found a talk on feminist art theory tomorrow night as part of their public lecture programme. He clicked the link and quickly scanned through, spotting an action shot of Fay mid-lecture nestled amidst the description. He booked two tickets. 'Matt, Amy, are either of you free tomorrow evening?'

'It's my mum's birthday, but I'd be more than happy to be your date. I'll take you for dinner afterwards. I will have earned at least a kiss for that,' Matt said.

'Amy, please?' Caius asked. 'I don't want to put Matt on a register.'

'I'm supposed to be playing netball, it's my first match back after, well . . . actually I can cancel it. No problem,' she said.

'You have the pleasure of coming with me to a lecture.'

'On what?' she asked.

'Art history. Fay Osbald is giving a talk tomorrow and I want to go.' Caius licked runaway ketchup off the side of his hand. Fay intrigued him. 'Amy?'

'Yes.'

'Your first match back after what? Were you injured?'

'No, I um . . . well, there was an incident, but I can't talk about it. It was settled out of court.'

'What?' Matt asked, his eyes wide.

'Say no more.' Caius thought it was best to change the subject. He remembered the mean girls in high school who played netball for county. 'How are you getting on with the TfL CCTV, Matt?'

'Amy's looked through South Ken to no avail. I've been going through the Kentish Town footage. So far, no Clemmie. A surprising number of BAFTA winners live around here though. I've got to about 6 p.m.'

'Could you cross-reference the partygoers' arrivals with the footage? It's the closest tube to the McDonald's. See if the couple from the Greek holiday pictures you found turn up.' Caius looked at the ketchup-smeared burger mess on his plate and fetched some cutlery. 'IT tracked Clemmie's iPhone and the last known place was at her gym, which doesn't help with the timeline. I've also been having fun with *Burke's Peerage*. Rupert is set to inherit a baronetcy.'

'What's that?' Amy asked.

'It's an inherited title, although technically he's a commoner like the rest of us, not an aristocrat. He'll be a knight once his grandfather dies. He was a Tory politician of little note – although he may have just got on with the job and kept his nose clean. I found an obituary in the *Telegraph* for Rupert's father from eleven years ago, and his mother died when he was a small child in a car crash. He has no siblings. The Beauchamps historically owned a significant amount of property in London. Rupert's father used a loophole to get around inheritance tax by setting up a private limited company for their properties that Rupert now owns. It's legal, if unsavoury. Rupert is listed as the sole director. It's big money. Looks like he owns bars and restaurants too.' Caius wondered if his dad had made similar arrangements.

'That's the mystery of how a writer who has never written a thing can afford bespoke shirts solved. It was keeping me up last night,' Matt said, looking down at the plain white M&S cotton twill he was wearing.

25

The Princess Caroline Public House

The charm of The Princess was that it was in such an odd hiding place in the city that not a single tourist would ever find it by accident. Down an alley and up another, crouching between two Georgian buildings, twisting among the remnants of medieval London's street plan, it remained one of the grottiest old man pubs you could find. You stuck to the carpets, they definitely didn't do food other than pork scratchings and Frazzles and the men's loos stank. You wouldn't ever bring a respectable young lady there unless that respectability was questionable. It was glorious. It was also discreet enough that if Rupert tried anything it wouldn't be embarrassing. Alex was tucked away in a corner – the corner furthest from the repugnant bogs – trying to build up the courage to tell Rupert never to speak to Nell again. The wall next to him was crowded with sketches of obscure boxers from the turn of the nineteenth century. He was nursing a pint of ale and had another waiting for Rupert who was, *quelle surprise*, late. Well, to be fair to the man, his girlfriend had just been murdered . . .

Fifteen minutes had passed and still no Rupert. Alex had drunk a third of his pint but had switched to Frazzles. Didn't want to be down one when Rupert got there – he needed his wits. Alex started looking at the cricket scores in a discarded copy of the *Telegraph*. Would he turn up at all? His phone buzzed. Rupert was stuck on a bus. Did Rupert already know about him and Nell? What would Rupert try and do about it? He clearly still had intentions towards Nell, and he wasn't a man to give up something like that, something close to love. There would be some bravado, a trick, perhaps even a duel for her honour.

'You never get the bus,' Alex said to Rupert, as he finally arrived and threw himself onto an uncomfortable-looking stool opposite Alex. 'I've got you one in already.'

'Thanks, Al.' Alex hated that he looked so damn sharp. Rupert was wearing an old-fashioned pair of wide-legged linen trousers – that somehow hadn't creased – with a light blue, broad-collared shirt and a pair of brown brogues. He looked like Cary Grant between takes. 'Had some business in the city, hence the bus. I hate catching the peasant wagon if I can avoid it but sometimes it is quicker.'

'How are you?'

'I don't really know.'

'I can't imagine what you're going through. Can I help at all?'

'No, no. It's all in hand. Clemmie's parents are flying back. The funeral is next week if you're still in the country.'

'I'll still be here; they've extended the project I'm working on.' Alex saw Rupert's jaw tense at that news. 'I just can't believe what's happened. The whole thing is so weird. Honestly, mate, if you need anything at all just give me a call.'

'The police have rifled through the entirety of my possessions. I suffered the indignity of having my cheek swabbed for a DNA sample by a man called Barry. Barry! Clemmie was apparently pregnant, and I got a call today to say that it wasn't mine, which is a relief. I can't imagine Clemmie as a mother. She'd have been awful at it. No compassion. Children need that in a mother, that and whimsy.' Rupert's eyes misted over before he snapped back. 'You can't imagine the week that I've had. Everyone is ringing me. It's constant. There were journalists, filthy vermin, outside my front gate this morning. I had to make a few calls to make them go away.' Rupert took a sip from his pint. 'Have you seen Nell recently? I think she's mad with me, but I don't know why.'

'She hasn't said anything to me, but I've not seen her since Saturday evening. Why would she be mad with you?'

'I haven't a clue.' The pair fell into silence.

'Do the police know who killed Clemmie? It clearly wasn't you. Not your style.'

'God knows. I'd have staged a yachting accident if I'd done it. No body that way.' Rupert played with a beer mat. 'I was going to dump her this week and she wouldn't have taken it well.'

'Are you going to miss her at all?'

'Yes, you know, I think I will.' Rupert stared at a stain on the carpet that could have been either red wine or blood. 'I almost loved her once.'

'I've known you for what, twelve years, and I still can't tell when you're joking. I think you're still in shock. It'll hit you in ever bigger waves.'

'How's work?'

'Rubbish. I've got a couple of interviews set up, otherwise I'm thinking about maybe setting up my own consultancy firm. You know, freelance for a bit. I'm just weighing up whether it's feasible without a formal pension scheme and whatnot.'

'I can help you out with the set-up,' Rupert said, leaning in towards Alex conspiratorially. 'I know people, I can get you the start-up cost. They'll have their own terms. You'll have to do the odd favour to help them out, if you know what I mean, but I also have a condition, of course.'

'And what would that be?'

'That you never go anywhere near Nell again.'

26

The garden of a Clapham theatre pub

'One half of chocolate stout,' Jonathan said, placing the miniature glass tankard in front of Nell, 'and a tub of luxury seaweed peanuts. Luxury . . . How can peanuts be a luxury item?'

'Oh, dinner, thank you,' Nell said, putting her cardigan on. The sun had set and it felt chilly and ever so slightly romantic. The walled pub garden was dotted with fairy lights and flame-orange poppies, creamy roses and couples canoodling in cosy corners. 'I really enjoyed the show. I didn't think a one-woman performance of *The Tenant of Wildfell Hall* would work so well. I'm thrilled to be very wrong.'

'Yeah, she's been working on it for a while.' Jonathan opened the tub of snacks. 'Ali said there was a blond guy lingering at the office for you yesterday. It's not your friend from Oxford, is it?'

'Bingo.'

'That was a weird lunch you sent me on last year.'

'I thought you said you had a good time with Rupert?'

'I did. I was blotto. He got me plastered on gin and tonics, and brandy, then insisted on paying.'

'He's obscenely rich so I wouldn't worry about that.'

'I just don't know what he wanted from me. I offered to look at his work. I mean, he talked a good talk, but he never sent it over.'

'He's a funny one. I read a short story of his years ago at college. He's prodigiously talented and wants to be published, but somehow can't bring himself to try. Fear of rejection perhaps?'

'At lunch it felt like he was interviewing me rather than me doing him a good turn. He kept talking about setting up an indie publisher. I thought he might make me a job offer.'

'I can imagine him setting up a small imprint as a hobby one day. Something quirky and financially unviable – selling only stream of consciousness novellas or Victoriana about consumptives residing in spa towns. Something commendable but ultimately pointless.' Nell sipped on her stout. 'Rupert and I aren't friends any more. Former friends. What's the term? An ex-friend. We have consciously defriended. No, we're in a state of post-friendship.' She helped herself to some of the nuts. 'Oh no, this one's wasabi. Talking of friends, yours is very talented. How do you know her?'

Jonathan shuffled closer to her on the bench, his leg pressing into hers. 'Yes, well, she's actually my ex.'

'That's nice that you guys are still on speaking terms. Very civilised.' Nell saw the actress enter the garden from the pub and gave her a warm smile.

'Well . . .' He fumbled.

'Jonny, darling, what are you not telling me?' Nell was sick of this.

'We're not on speaking terms.' He put his arm around her shoulder and the other hand on her knee.

'I see. Well, she's on her way over here so that's about to change,' Nell said, watching the actress brace herself for a conversation with her cheating ex – who had had the nerve to sit in the middle of the front row – and his new, younger, hot girlfriend.

'God, Helena. I'm so sorry. I don't know what I was thinking.'

'Things like this happen to me with a wearying frequency. I don't want to be your work-wife any more. I want a work-divorce. Tomorrow, Jonathan.' Nell got up from the bench and walked past the somewhat shell-shocked actress, stopping to say,

'Well done. Really excellent work. So honest. I'm Jonathan's lesbian colleague. Goodbye.'

Nell walked back into the pub and into the ladies' loo – there was a queue, of course – some girl was violently crying in one of the stalls with the sort of raging self-pity that usually brought down city walls. The two other women in the queue were sharing the concerned look of sorority.

'Darling, he isn't worth it,' said the first.

'Might not be a he? We don't know,' said the second as the other loo freed up. 'We should be more inclusive.'

They heard the lock come undone and the crying girl came out. 'Oh thank God, I didn't want to pee myself,' said the second girl as she rushed in, banging the door behind her. 'It'll get better, sweetheart.'

'Minty?' Nell said.

'Oh God, you heard that, didn't you?'

'Um, yeah. I heard that.' Nell opened her bag and pulled out a packet of make-up wipes and her red lipstick. 'I'm bursting. You fix yourself up and then we'll go and get some chips. OK?'

★ ★ ★

Minty licked the salt off her finger as they sat on a bench next to the church where William Wilberforce had preached. The Common was awash with twilight joggers and juvenile stockbrokers taking an evening stroll. 'You just yelled "lesbian colleague" at your boss's ex-girlfriend who'd just performed a solo show based on a Brontë novel, after he lied to you to get you to go to make himself look better.'

'Yep.'

'Fuck, that's messed up. But that was a fucking cool exit.'

'I'm not cool. Was that homophobic? I must have "take advantage of me" written across my tits, because shit keeps on happening.'

'That was also quite an exit on Saturday night. I saw you throw that milkshake.'

'I didn't think anyone had paid much attention to that. Cocaine makes people selfish.'

'Rupert says that you're a force of nature,' Minty said. She wistfully watched a couple of gulls fight over the remains of a discarded Pret tuna baguette.

'No one uses the phrase "force of nature" in a positive way. It's meant for floods, and volcanoes, and hurricanes. I'm a woman, not a geographical phenomenon,' Nell said, eating a chip covered in garlic mayonnaise and cheap rubbery mild cheddar. 'I'm so glad I plumped for the extra cheese.'

'Are you going to ask me about what happened?'

'I assumed you'd tell me if you wanted me to know. But that assumption appears to have been wrong, so what happened, Minty?'

'Bad date.'

'Why was it bad? Are you all right? Were you attacked?'

'No, I'm just horribly in love with someone else.'

'Do they know how you feel?'

'Oh yeah, they know.'

'Then fuck 'em. It's not your problem any more. Best thing you can do right now is get your hair cut, listen to a few hours of Beyoncé's angriest songs and get twatted on Friday. Maybe make out with someone that you'll never have to see again in a dodgy nightclub where you lose a pair of good shoes to the sticky carpet.'

They were engulfed by silence as Nell ate her chips and

happy-wiggled from the hit of salt, fat and sugar. A couple of lycra-clad young men started doing press-ups not so far away that they couldn't be appreciated. 'I can't believe Clemmie is dead,' Nell said, putting the remainder (most) of the chips in the bin next to the bench.

'Yeah, it's crazy.'

'What an obscene world we live in.'

'Are you seeing someone? I heard that you broke up with that artist.'

'Yeah, me and Casper ended a while ago now. I've just started seeing a guy recently. We've been friends for a really long time. It's delicate. I'm treading lightly for now, but it might go somewhere. I'm aware that I've gone over that invisible line in your late twenties where you go from "you're pregnant eek" to "you're pregnant yay". I should grow up. Breed. Get a mortgage. Have you got Bumble?'

'Yeah, I do.'

'Can I have a go on yours?' Minty gave Nell her phone. 'What's your type?'

THURSDAY

27

The Police Station

'Amy, what do you think of Clemmie's social media? You've been through it all. What do you think? Who did she want us to think she was?' Caius asked, dunking his little tea-brewing doodad in and out of his mug. 'Besides the basic silly posh-girl starter kit of pricey yoga pants, swishy hair and long vowels.'

'First and foremost, I think Clemmie was bloody clever.' Amy peered down her nose at Caius and raised her eyebrows.

'What? Is there something between my teeth?' Caius ran his tongue over his incisors, checking for stray chia seeds.

'No, I just wanted to subtly hint to you that your attitude towards Clemmie keeps crossing the border into misogynistic territory.' Amy, having put Caius in his place, continued with her analysis. 'She knew how to position herself. I'd hate-follow her on Instagram. All those green juices and core workouts. This perfect existence that I couldn't ever have. Cosseted in a fantasy world. She's aspirational and I'd say she was in it for the money. She wants you to know that she's richer than you, that her shoes cost more than a family of four might pay for food and electricity combined for a month. She wants me to know that she doesn't have to work like I do, she can have a job that she is passionate about rather than to pay the rent. She posted pictures of books with cups of herbal tea and pretty little jam jars of flowers to make her look genteel. It's all about the vanity of virtue – but of the body and the mind, not the spirit. People buy the idea of her and then spend money on her affiliate links. Did she really read that Jane Austen, or did she just google the plot and buy a pretty clothbound copy because it photographed well and worked for her brand? Either way, she was making a few thousand quid a month.'

'Do you know who does read Jane Austen? Our mysterious Helena. She was reading *Persuasion* in that photo from their Greek holiday,' Matt chimed in from across the incident room. Amy noticed that his cheeks were a little flushed – she'd intended for him to hear her speech too.

'Clemmie copied her, competed with her even,' Caius said, twiddling with his sterling silver cufflinks as he stared at his computer. He'd taken Amy's words on the chin. 'Clemmie was probably jealous. Rupert and therefore probably Helena went to Oxford proper, while Clemmie went to Oxford Brookes. Clemmie might have had a chip on her shoulder about that.'

'A reasonable assertion,' Matt said.

Caius tried searching for Helenas at Oxford University on LinkedIn but returned too many results. 'Matt, give me the name of one of the hoorays you interviewed. Maybe they are connections.'

'Tabitha de la Croix.'

Caius found Tabitha's profile and scrolled through her connections. 'Got her! Her name is Helena Waddingham, and she works at Antigone Publishing.'

'I've got her here too,' Matt said. Amy and Caius crowded behind him to watch the TfL footage. 'She came out of the tube and turned right, which is the wrong direction for the restaurant, plus she's rather early.'

'Pre-drinks?' Amy asked.

'There are a couple of decent pubs that way,' Matt said, as he stared at the screen, 'and boom, five minutes later. Hello, tall mystery man. They must have gone to the pub together beforehand.'

'Why weren't they on the list that Rupert gave to us? Why did he miss them out?' Caius asked as he loomed over Matt's shoulder.

'Maybe they left early? It sounds like an awful party. I wouldn't want to have been there,' Matt said.

'Perhaps if Rupert really is in love with this Helena, then he'd want to keep her out of the investigation in case it shows him in a bad light? He could use the situation to his advantage, play up the lonely grief-stricken boyfriend to get close to her,' Amy said.

'I could imagine him doing that,' Caius said, considering the implications this idea would have if found true as he scrolled through the website for Antigone Publishing. 'How could any man be so concerned with manipulating another woman less than twenty-four hours after his girlfriend's corpse is found pulled through a hedge?'

'The party started at 7.30 p.m. If you didn't want to go, but felt like you had to show up at least, you'd be what, thirty minutes to an hour late? You'd hang around for another hour or so, then piss off out of there,' Amy said.

Matt sped through the footage. 'And . . . found them. They entered Kentish Town station at 9.17 p.m. Amy, you are on fire today.' They watched Nell and Alex kissing violently against a ticket machine. An impatient queue of silently horrified Londoners formed behind them. A scandalised granny eventually tapped Alex out of the way so she could buy a ticket.

'It's a love triangle,' Amy said.

'It used to be a square.' Caius picked up his desk phone and dialled the number for Antigone Publishing. 'I'll put her on speakerphone.'

'Good afternoon, Antigone Publishing,' came an Antipodean voice.

'Hello there, can I please speak to a Ms Helena Waddingham?'

'Who may I say is calling?'

'Beauchamp. DI Caius Beauchamp.'

'All right, I'll just pop you through.' Caius heard a clicking noise and then a voicemail message. Bleeeep . . .

Caius dialled the number again.

'Good afternoon, Antigone Publishing.'

'Hi there, I just rang a moment ago to speak to Helena Waddingham. It's very urgent, could you please tell me when she will next be in the office?'

'Listen, Mr Beauchamp, I've been warned about you. Pretending to be a police officer now, are you? I'm pretty sure that's a crime and I should report you to the authorities,' she said before hanging up on him.

Matt had stopped what he was doing a while ago and was listening wide-eyed. 'Your telephone manner is adorable, that little posh voice you put on.'

28

Bloomsbury

Antigone Publishing was based inside a pristine, clotted cream-coloured Georgian town house. Railings shaped like spears formed an imaginary moat around the building, a genteel defence against the great unread. Caius walked up the stairs and entered the reception. A neat woman with a headset on was behind the shabby-chic marble desk typing. Caius glanced tentatively around and was relieved to see that there was an absence of charity donation boxes.

'Good afternoon. How can I help you?' the woman asked with a soft Australian accent.

'Hello, we spoke on the phone earlier,' Caius said, pulling out his badge. 'DI Caius Beauchamp. I would like to speak to Helena Waddingham, please.'

'Oh my god, I'm sorry. I thought you were someone else.'

'It's an uncommon surname.'

'I'll just call her. Bear with me. I'm really sorry,' she said, fumbling with her headset.

'Rupert Beauchamp? Is he harassing Helena?' Caius asked once she was finished.

'He waited outside for Nell at lunchtime on Tuesday. She wasn't very happy about it.'

'I see. Is that the first time you've seen him here?'

'Yeah. Nell is a lovely girl. She has a lot of admirers.'

'What do you publish here?'

'Mostly contemporary poetry, and a few short story anthologies a year.'

'Interesting.'

'Some people enjoy that sort of thing.'

'Each to their own, I guess.'

* * *

'Would you like a cup of tea?' Nell asked as she showed Caius into her tiny office.

'No, thank you. May I?' He gestured towards a spare chair leaning against the corner.

'Oh God, yes of course,' Nell said, rushing to pick up the chair and move it over to the desk. A volume slid off the seat and Caius picked it up from the floor. 'Sorry, I don't get many visitors to my cupboard.'

'*Persuasion*. I've not read that one yet.'

'It's the best of Austen's work. People rave about *Pride and Prejudice*, partly because of the Colin Firth wet shirt scene, and it is wonderful – the book, that is. The lake scene was made up. But *Persuasion* is my favourite. It's about finding love again after a grave error of judgement the first time round.'

'I'll add it to my list.' Caius understood it now, Rupert's infatuation with her. He might have been a little in lust at first sight. 'Why does *Persuasion* resonate with you?'

'Who doesn't have regrets?'

'Who doesn't want a second chance at love?'

'How can I help you?' Nell asked.

'I have a few questions for you. What were you doing on Saturday afternoon?'

'I went to my hairdresser's for a 3 p.m. appointment.'

'Until when?'

'Until five thirty-ish. I got my hair done and then my nails and things. I wanted to look my best for the party. Then I went home, got changed and headed straight back out to meet Alex beforehand.'

'Can anyone vouch for any of that?'

'My hairdresser?' Nell said, as she pulled out the appointment card from her purse and gave it to Caius. 'You think I'm a suspect?'

The salon was in Hackney. It would be tricky for Helena to get back across to Hampstead with those timings.

'When was the last time you saw Clemency O'Hara, Helena?'

'Call me Nell. Last month. The three of us went to visit Alex in Athens. He was posted out there by his firm.'

Caius pulled out the photograph of the four of them and handed it to her. 'Is this Alex?'

'Yes, I've never seen that photo,' she said, barely glancing at it.

'Alexander what?'

'Alexandros actually, his dad is Greek Cypriot. Alexandros Adonis.'

'Great name.'

'He hates it. He got teased for it relentlessly at school. It would've been worse if he didn't have a face like that. I can give you his number?'

'Thank you.'

'There aren't many Beauchamps in the world, detective.'

'Indeed.'

'Are you related to Rupert?' Nell asked, although she already knew that he wasn't.

'Not that I'm aware of. What did you think of Clemmie?'

'She was very beautiful. It's a very sad business,' Nell trailed off.

'Oh, come on, what do you really think?' Caius stared at Nell as she stayed silent. Caius got out more of the photos. 'No? Are you sure you can't elaborate any further? All right, I'm going to tell you what I think with the help of a few handy visual aids.' He pulled out more pictures and fanned them across the desk. 'Here's Clemmie posing in six different outfits in one day. On that first day there were four of you, but on the second day Alex wasn't there. Must have put you in a spot?' Still nothing. He pulled out the other set of pictures. Nell wouldn't look at them. 'No? All right then. Rupert's bored of Clemmie and wants a serious girlfriend. He's in love with you. It's intense. He takes these pictures of you without your consent, but you can feel his searing gaze. There's a level of emotional intimacy between you that's inappropriate, perhaps. Something left over from your student days. Clemmie realises the full extent of Rupert's feelings for you on that holiday, gets angry. She sees the photographs, perhaps? It is her camera, after all. Caught him touching your knee under the dinner table? Hence why you haven't seen her, and presumably him, in over a month before the party. Is that correct?'

'I have a knack for attracting upper-class arseholes.'

'Rupert is obsessed with you, and since Clemmie died it's been turned up a notch. He's been turning up uninvited to your work. Does he follow you around London? Maybe waits outside your house? His affections are either reciprocated or they're not. If they're reciprocated that's a motive for murder, Nell. Getting rid of the competition? I'm assuming they're not, considering that you arrived late and then left his birthday party much, much earlier than everyone else. You're scared. I would be if I were you.'

'I had a crush on Rupert back when I still had a "teen" at the end of my age. It fizzled out from childish, unrequited love to nostalgic affection quite some time ago. I moved on. Went out with other people, but we remained firm friends.' Nell stared at a crack in the plaster, her cheeks burning, so as not to look at Caius. Her cheeks burning as this man who she'd never met before articulated everything uncomfortable she felt. 'Alex, Rupert and I, we were all in the same Mycenaean History class in our first year. Most students in our department were a bit too *Time Team* and not enough tequila, so we started hanging out, a lot. The boys rowed together as well.'

Caius didn't believe her that she'd moved on. He could see it when she said his name. 'Can you think of anyone else who'd want to harm Clemmie?'

'No. She could be difficult, but I can't imagine anyone would want her dead.'

A handsome, millionaire baronet-to-be who she's in love with would be motive enough for some. If it was mutual, then why didn't Rupert just leave Clemmie for her? 'I've watched enough of Clemmie's YouTube channel to guess what a young woman with a double first in Classics might think of a six-minute video on the virtues of incorporating sprouted bread into your diet.' Caius could hear Amy admonishing him for sexism, but it seemed to be working.

'Have you read *Mansfield Park*?'

'No.'

'You should. I've always felt like Fanny Price to Clemmie's Maria Bertram. It's a gentle novel. Quiet moral fortitude, but not enough overt criticism of the slave trade for my liking. I went to a grammar school. Only way a girl like me could study Latin. Whereas Clemmie is an international school brat. All that opportunity, the connections, and in the end she just wasn't very clever. Well, clever enough to get a rich boyfriend . . .'

'Did Clemmie ever mention her work?'

'A little. I think it was a bit dull. She was angling for a photography exhibit there. Those girls who work in galleries in West London, and the auction houses for that matter, are sitting there waiting for someone to marry them. They're poorly paid status jobs. Treading water until they can pass their Norman genes on.'

'Clemmie wanted to marry Rupert?'

'Oh, God yes. Her second cousin got married at some castle in Italy last year and it was all she talked about on the flight over to Athens. The flowers. The dress. It was insufferable. Rupert was so embarrassed.'

'How embarrassed?' Caius wondered how far someone would go to avoid a messy break-up.

'You can never quite tell with Rupert. Boarding school brutalised emotional displays out of him.'

'Would Clemmie do something stupid to get the ring?'

'For the ring? For the title! You think Clemmie forgot to take her pill to force Rupert's hand? Rupert told me that she was pregnant and that you were running tests. That girl would have suffered anything to be a lady. I can't help you with Rupert's alibi. You appear to already know that I left the party early.'

'Did Clemmie have any problems? Debt, maybe? She had a lot of expensive things for a "poorly paid" gallery assistant.'

'Rupert is as rich as Croesus and her father sends her a stipend every month. He works in big pharma out in Singapore. I think their relationship was purely monetary. They weren't a close family – workaholic father, alcoholic mother. Expats . . . Rupert did say that Clemmie had a drug problem once, but honestly I don't know how reliable that report is. They live in Kensington; of course she must dabble. Even the pigeons in that end of town have a small habit.'

'Were they faithful to each other?'

'Historically no. I don't know about her, but Rupert was always a bit of a blackguard. Clemmie studied at Oxford Brookes, other end of town, so he'd usually have a girl or three back at college as well. "For fun." Clemmie was always the constant though.'

'Rupert have any side pieces more recently?'

'He wouldn't want me to know that.'

'Why?'

'Rupert and I aren't close like we were once. He wouldn't want me to hear about it. He just wouldn't. It's improper. I went to Greece with them because I missed Alex, I'm broke, and Rupert insisted on paying for the villa we stayed in on the Apollo Coast. Over the last year Clemmie went through a phase of being friendlier towards me, but that tailed off after Valentine's Day. I heard from Tabs that Rupert had said something silly after she yelled at him for not proposing.'

Caius considered her tone for a moment. Perhaps she had been telling the truth, and she wasn't in love with him any more? 'Always smart to put in writing that you don't want to see him again. Keep a diary of all the times he tries to get in touch. Screenshot messages. If you decide to report him for harassment you have a sympathetic ear.'

'Thank you, detective.'

'What was the party like?'

'Awful. Right Hons chugging champagne and chewing chicken nuggets.'

'Do you have any pictures of it?'

'No, we were expressly told no photography in the invitation.' Nell played with a small statue on her desk of an armless woman. 'I'm not a damsel in distress.'

'Oh, I know. The others at the party, "the Right Hons", what are they like?'

'Patrician Tories, owners of swathes of Scottish moorland. The smarter ones are in finance or law, but really most of them have failed upwards, you know?'

'No, elaborate.'

'Alex and I are pretty much the only people that Rupert knows who have had the semblance of an average childhood, even though Alex's father is a heart surgeon, and they are rather comfortable. He grew up in the wealthy part of Essex that pretends it's Cambridgeshire. I hate it when politicians talk about social mobility on television. The problem is, for someone to go up the ladder someone else has to slip down a snake. To go back to Jane Austen, imagine your father was a wealthy landowner in the nineteenth century and you have two older brothers: primogeniture means that the eldest inherits all your father's property, your other brother is lucky that a maiden aunt has left him a small fortune that he can just about manage on, but what of you? You have to become a lawyer, a merchant selling tea or people, buy a commission in the household cavalry or preach dreary sermons as a vicar. You gain a profession and then you're left to your own devices. That doesn't happen anymore in the same way. The clever ones go into finance, but the idiot children who don't inherit significant fortunes work for a family friend for a few years, set up a consultancy firm for luxury face creams, nightclub PR, they have an obnoxious fashion brand or some other upper-class bullshit status profession that depends on their social connections rather than their innate competence. I guarantee one of those "Right Hons" will be a backbencher within the next five years. It's cushty being an MP.'

'Why did you go to the party?'

'It was the last hurrah. The end of it, the end of our friendship.

Alex and I agreed that beforehand. I wasn't going to go at all, but he twisted my arm.'

'Who do you think killed Clemmie?'

'I don't know.'

'Do you think Rupert is capable of it?'

'I doubt a normal man would kill his girlfriend rather than just dump her. Rupert is Teflon-coated from years of familial neglect – he doesn't think like a normal human being. He has high-flown thoughts and literary aspirations but no real understanding of the physical world. He believes he has some God-given right to do what he likes. This is off the record, right?'

'I merely wanted to introduce myself, although I may need a formal statement at some point.'

'How very polite. When you do get me in properly, don't make a show of it. I'm sure he's watching me, and I don't want to deal with the USSR nuclear-grade fallout.' Nell picked up the copy of *Persuasion* again and handed it to Caius. 'You should read this, detective.'

'Thank you.' Caius took the book from her. No one he'd ever questioned, even informally, had lent him a book before. He wondered what that meant. 'Here's my card. Call me if Rupert gets out of hand, or if you remember anything else.'

'Rupert thinks he's Zeus. Not in a psychological disorder way. The world is his to survey from the top of Mount Olympus. He can throw lightning bolts and smite us mortals. The nymphs . . .'

'I do hope he's not a shape-shifting serial rapist. I've just read Ovid – in translation. I went to a dodgy comp and we didn't get taught Latin.'

Nell laughed gently, turning in on herself, and Caius stood up to leave.

'I didn't hate Clemmie,' Nell blurted out as Caius reached for the door handle. 'I wanted to, I pretended to for fun. I feel absolutely terrible. I made jokes at her expense. But I didn't hate her. I felt sorry for her, I suppose, but mostly I was just confused by Clemmie. Confused by the power that she could hold over Rupert. Rupert shouldn't be beholden like that, it's against his nature, against the very laws of physics. I was confounded that he just couldn't leave her. Some people are magnetic, aren't they? They have their own force. Others stick to them like paperclips through their own innate strength of being.'

★   ★   ★

Caius got back to his car. He felt like he'd learned something, but he wasn't entirely sure what. He'd left his phone in the glove compartment and was now fumbling around for it amongst the stray mints that had fled their wrapper. Three missed calls from Matt in the last twenty minutes.

'Matteo, what's up? Have you found Clemmie on the TfL footage? Listen, I need you to send uniform out to check Nell Waddingham's alibi.'

'There you bloody are. Ned's come in to confess.'

'We already know he was having an affair with Clemmie.'

'No, he's confessed to the murder.'

★   ★   ★

Nell stared out of the tiny window in her office and into the paved courtyard below. Deb from accounts was having her hourly cigarette break. Alex had texted her. She texted him back. Rupert had called. She deleted his voicemail.

172

29

The Police Station

'What did I miss?' Caius asked, holding the door open for Amy. Caius was watching Ned as he waited for Matt to take his confession. He was staring at a corner of the room as if he was waiting for a door to appear for him to flee through.

'Ned Osbald claims to have killed Clemency O'Hara,' Amy said, walking into the side room with a tray of tea.

'No, I know that, Amy.' Caius took a mug from the tray. 'Thank you for the tea. I meant what did I miss about Ned? I'd have bet my first born on it being Beauchamp.'

'Clemmie's pregnancy gave both Rupert and Ned a motive. Osbald is married, he's knocked up his young assistant. I know you said he and his wife had an open arrangement, and I had like two girlfriends at one point last year, but there's a difference between fooling around and impregnating someone.'

'Yeah,' Caius said, opening a share-size packet of Wotsits. He'd not had lunch. He'd bought a Snickers for afters. He'd do an extra set of reps to make up for it tonight.

'Did you see the *Daily Mail* today?' Amy asked.

'I actively avoid it. What did it say?' Caius asked Amy as she handed him her phone with the article on. '"Cops confused by corpse in the copse: Socialite stunner brutally murdered in London beauty spot." God, look at all the pictures they've pulled from Clemmie's social media.' Caius gave Amy her phone back.

'Do you still want to go to Fay Osbald's lecture tonight?'

'Yes, although I think you're going to be needed here.'

Matt opened the door. 'Are you sure you don't want to do this instead, petal?'

'No, bambino, I've spoken to him twice already. Besides, you need to get the practice in if you want to be promoted,' Caius said.

★ ★ ★

'What happened to your alibi, Ned? Did your wife casually perjure herself for you?' Matt asked as he leaned nonchalantly against his chair.

'She takes sleeping pills. Fay thought what she said was the truth. I went back out after she had fallen asleep. Fay has nothing to do with any of this sordidness.'

'So you're saying what?'

'That I went back out in the night and I, I . . .' Ned trailed off and stared into the middle distance.

'You did what?'

'I slit Clemmie's throat.'

'What did you do earlier in the day?'

'I lied when I spoke to you before. I was at the gallery on Saturday. Clem came over after going to the gym in the afternoon and I drove her to my house. We had made plans to see each other after her yoga class. I knew Fay was out all day. I took her for a walk on the Heath under the pretence of having sex outdoors before she went to Rupert's party. I drugged Clemmie. It took a while to kick in. I bound her up. I was back before Fay – she didn't know. I went back that evening and slit her throat. Just to be sure. The baby was going to ruin my marriage.'

★ ★ ★

'How am I doing?' Matt asked Caius as he came into the side room.

'Cracking opening, mate,' Caius said, before pausing for a moment. 'Matt, prod him for specific times. Ask where her gym clothes are – she changed out of them after she left the gym. That phone is still a problem, isn't it?'

'Hard to imagine Clemmie putting it down anywhere for very long,' Amy said.

'Amy, go back to TfL and ask for traffic camera footage through the congestion zone. I want to see a picture of them in that car together. Yell at them if you must. I want that picture now.'

'Sure, no problem,' she said, leaving the room.

'Fuck, it's really not Rupert.'

'You don't sound sure,' Matt said.

'Do you believe him?' Caius asked.

'The story fits. We've yet to find any physical evidence that detracts from it. The results just came back: Ned Osbald's semen and his baby. I know that Dorian Gray gives you the heebies, but a confession is a confession.'

'I'll put in the request for a search warrant. Pooh-bahh will push it through. He wants this closed. The clothes, the knife and the phone may all be at his house. It's 5 p.m. Fay Osbald is supposed to be delivering a lecture at 6 p.m. at the Courtauld Institute. I need to catch her. There's more to Fay, I can feel it. Ask Osbald about the route they took to the Heath. Specific road names. I'm sorry, you're going to be late for your mum's birthday.'

'She's my least favourite parent.'

'Never mind then.'

30

The Courtauld Institute

Caius stuffed into the packed auditorium behind a group of students with wonky haircuts. He had forgotten to bring a printout of his ticket and had to flash his badge at an overly officious events co-ordinator. Caius was glad he'd worn a plain white button-down shirt today. He had left his tie and jacket in the car and rolled up his sleeves. He blended in at the back a little more than if he were wearing a boxy grey suit. The audience was filing in, a mix of determined young women, a few beautiful young men and a charming collection of retirees who sat at the front. Fay Osbald was talking to what looked like an IT guy who kept gesturing towards the screen. Caius looked around the auditorium. Héloïse would have loved this, lived for it. Why do the English hate cleverness? Every classroom has a child despised by their peers for being a modicum quicker than the rest of the dullards. This was a room full to the rafters with Hermione Grangers. The double doors to the auditorium swung open and there appeared a face that Caius had been daydreaming about all afternoon. Nell had changed costumes between scenes and had gone from charmingly owlish librarian who philosophises about class warfare through Jane Austen to sexy librarian who would really let you have it for your overdue library books. Caius felt guilty for having that thought, and then he felt a little foolish when he realised that trailing behind her was a tall, broad-shouldered man he recognised as the mythical Alex, true to his surname. He had soft curls that caressed his forehead and an almost hungry look in his eye. These people, they're all so connected. Can it be a coincidence? Caius wondered. This was the sort of thing he could picture Nell going to, but there are never coincidences in unsolved murders.

★　★　★

Alex held the door open for Nell – he wanted to watch her walk. She gambolled over to two spare seats and he followed her, enthralled. Nell sat down and then turned to Alex.

'This should be interesting. I love Millais,' she said, peering up at him from under her eyelashes.

'You had that poster in your room in first year,' he said, leaning in and kissing her neck.

Nell bit her lip. 'Did I tell you that I bumped into Minty last night? She was sobbing in a pub loo in Clapham. The poor thing is in love with some arsehole who doesn't love her back . . .' Nell was interrupted by Fay coughing lightly and a hush fell over the audience.

★　★　★

'There, on the pendent boughs her coronet weeds
Clambering to hang, an envious sliver broke;
When down her weedy trophies and herself
Fell in the weeping brook. Her clothes spread wide,
And, mermaid-like, awhile they bore her up;
Which time she chanted snatches of old tunes,
As one incapable of her own distress,
Or like a creature native and indued
Unto that element; but long it could not be*

Till that her garments, heavy with their drink,
Pull'd the poor wretch from her melodious lay
To muddy death.'

'Millais's depiction is the most vivid image in our collect-ive cultural psyche that we have of this scene. It's on fridge magnets and postcards, jigsaw puzzles and tea towels. The Pre-Raphaelite Brotherhood is thought of as prosaic in some circles, but the beauty is undeniable. To the contemporary feminist it is, however, problematic. Ophelia is a woman who lacks agency – is entirely dependent on her father and brother, and emotion-ally abused by a disturbed suitor. She's a plot device. Some have found the pose in the painting with her hands outstretched, lips gently apart, erotic. I personally think that men will find women erotic no matter what they do. The pose to others has suggested martyrdom. There is an interesting contrast in the way that men display women as martyrs and the way that women do. Take, for example, Artemisia Gentileschi's self-portrait as Saint Catherine depicted here, which is a rather more self-possessed work.

'The other strand to the current feminist criticism of this painting comes with a refocusing on the woman who posed for the picture. We all know the story of Elizabeth Siddal catching a cold after lying in a cold bath for hours for Millais. Siddal went on to marry the notorious bounder and fellow member of the Pre-Raphaelite Brotherhood, Dante Rossetti. When she died, probably by suicide, Rossetti buried the only copy of his poetry with her. He later realised the financial error and dug her up to retrieve it . . .'

★   ★   ★

Caius stayed in his seat at the back of the auditorium as everyone else started tussling towards the double doors. He watched as Nell and Alex left the hall – no look of acknowledgement fell between either of them and Fay. It could have been a coincidence that they were there. Could. Fledgling cognoscenti milled around chatting to Fay. Light heroine worship, a queen holding court. He got it. He understood the power she held over them – she was whip smart, statuesque, charismatic. The whole room was eating out of her palm like a feral pack of malnourished pugs. He waited for the crowd to disperse before making his approach. 'Mrs Osbald.'

'It's Dr Bruce,' Fay replied.

'I'm sorry?'

'I use my maiden name professionally. I failed to correct you the other day. You seemed to enjoy calling me Mrs Osbald, like *The Graduate* or something. Why are you here?'

'I need you to come to the station.'

'I have no desire to see the inside of that building ever again,' Fay said as she packed up her things from the lectern.

'I must insist, Dr Bruce.'

'Are you arresting me?'

'Why would I arrest you?'

'I don't know, hence the tone of alarm in my voice.'

'We need to have more of a chat.'

'All right, but I need to change my shoes. These aren't for outside. My trainers are in my office.'

'Let's go there then.' Caius held the door open for her as they walked out into the building's foyer. There was a queue for the women's loo, and he spotted the back of Nell's glorious head amongst them.

Caius and Fay got out of the lift on the second floor. This level

179

was far less exciting than the polished floors of the auditorium. The institution's donors clearly only cared about the public areas where their names hung on gracious glass plates announcing their generous tax breaks. They walked down a long thin corridor. The name of a lecturer and their office hours was plastered to each door.

'Lecturing, even somewhere like this, doesn't pay much. How do you afford Burberry trench coats and Mulberry handbags?'

'I'm also a curator and I write in the odd magazine. You'd know that if you had bothered to google me. Besides, my husband does well for himself. He wouldn't want me walking around looking shabby.'

'You curated the exhibit on nudes at the British Museum last year, didn't you?' Caius wondered whether Fay had written the art book that both Clemmie and Rupert owned. Perhaps Clemmie had been gifted a copy after they had already purchased one at the show.

'I did,' she said, sighing. 'What aren't you telling me?' Fay stopped at her office, took out her key, jingled it around the lock and gently opened the door a sliver.

'We'll talk more at the station.'

'You arrested Edward, didn't you?' Caius didn't respond. 'I'll take your silence as confirmation.' A strip light above their heads blinked as Caius stared at Fay, who in turn was staring at a small section of chipped paint on the door frame.

'Someone should fix the light,' he said.

'I won't be a moment,' Fay said, going into the room and leaving the door a fraction ajar behind her. She quickly exchanged her heels for a crisp pair of white Miu Miu leather sneakers from under her desk. 'Your colleagues are tearing through my house right now, aren't they?'

'They will be later on this evening.'

'You seemed to be so sure that it was her boyfriend who'd killed her yesterday.'

'Material evidence sticks.'

'But what about the motive? I've told you: we have an open arrangement. This wouldn't have ended our marriage.'

'We'll get into it all at the station if you wouldn't mind, Mrs Osbald.'

She looked at him pointedly.

'Aren't you going to lock the door, Dr Bruce?' Caius asked, correcting himself.

'I have nothing worth stealing.'

31

The Police Station

It was 8.30 p.m., and a family support officer was attempting and failing to comfort an ice-cold Fay. Cups of weak tea, orange squash and cheap biscuits made with synthetic butter had been offered. Mascara did not run down her cheek; there was no hair pulling and no wailing, just quiet dignity. She couldn't explain why Clemmie and Rupert both had a copy of the exhibition guide for the show that she had curated. She couldn't remember how Clemmie had got the job at her husband's gallery. She repeated that Clemmie and Rupert had come to a lecture of hers and spoken to her afterwards. She hadn't recognised photographs of Nell or Alex. She said again that she was at a boozy lunch with school friends for most of Saturday afternoon. She hadn't known that Clemmie was pregnant. Caius believed her.

Caius was doing squats while waiting for the kettle to boil and his toast to pop. His quadriceps were as weak as his intuition. Amy had come in with a still of Ned and Clemmie in Ned's car on Tottenham Court Road as they left the congestion zone. Clemmie was smiling.

'Add it to the pile of damning physical evidence,' Caius said, pouring hot water into his and Amy's mugs.

Matt put his head through the door. 'We've got the warrants to search the gallery and the house. How do you want to split it?'

'You take the gallery and I'll take the house. Have tomorrow off, Matt, it's going to be a long week. I'll finish up the paperwork. Amy, would you come in for the morning on overtime?' Caius asked, buttering his toast.

'Only if you give me a piece,' Amy said, before helping herself.

* * *

The Bruce-Osbalds lived in a four-storey Victorian stucco house. One of those large white villas that have a wine cellar and tiny attic bedrooms. It was a house that yearned once again to have servants running up and down its staircases. There was a small garden to the front – palm trees and gravel, too modern for foxgloves. If the house was outwardly a staid and formal dowager duchess, the inside was like the very worst excesses of the Tate Modern. Everything was painted grey. The banisters, the ceiling and the walls. The floors, the windowpanes and the kitchen cabinets all grey. Every wall had a piece of art. Caius was staring at a canvas painted blue in the hallway. Nothing else, just the same shade of blue. Barry was already there and rifling through kitchen drawers, looking for the offending knife. He'd already bagged two with potential. Caius opened the fridge. The Bruce-Osbalds were clients of an organic vegetable delivery service as evidenced by the abundance of globe artichokes, rarefied micro-salad leaves and branded brown paper bags of new potatoes. There was no kombucha in sight, but there were a lot of stinking cheeses and raw steak. They were 'proper' people who ate 'proper' food. The cupboards yielded an array of delicate spices and fascinating, obscure pasta shapes. Waitrose. The bastard bought his staples at Waitrose.

He checked the bathroom next for Fay's sleeping pills, which he found unopened at the back of the medicine cabinet, but he did not find any heart drugs. He did, however, find some very pricey-looking hand soap from Jo Malone. His snooping

183

was interrupted by forensics, who wanted to rifle through the laundry hamper for dirty sheets and bloodstained shirts.

Caius wandered back downstairs and opened the living room door. The bookcases were heaving. They'd had custom shelves built to accommodate their collection. Asimov to Zola. Every litany of literary sin and sainthood was accounted for. A little statue of a naked woman lounged languorously on the mantelpiece. Caius walked through the living room and into the dining room. He opened the French doors that led to the garden. It was full of dark green fronds with a smattering of dull purple from alliums and lavender. Violet-grey slate abounded. A Japanese-style water feature rhythmically clunked away in the corner. There was an incongruous, gaudy digitalis (commonly known as a foxglove) in a pot next to the kitchen window. There was also what must have originally been an outhouse attached to the back of the building. It wasn't locked. Caius opened the door and found a blood-covered knife on a shelf next to a trowel and a ball of gardening twine about the same thickness as the marks on Clemmie's wrists.

FRIDAY

32

Cafe 42, Bloomsbury

Nell stood in front of the cashier and sobbed. She'd ordered three almond croissants and a hot chocolate, and when the cashier had asked whether she wanted cream on top she couldn't decide. This had first set her off, only to be exacerbated by a kindly woman in the queue behind her who asked her if she was all right. She wasn't all right. A mob of caffeine-deprived commuters were beginning to tut at her. The cashier gave her a wodge of napkins, and she purchased a copy of the *Telegraph* out of embarrassment.

★　★　★

Nell had read through the interview with the Poet Laureate in the paper and had sifted through the few emails in her inbox. She had an ignored pile of submissions on her desk, most of them drivel. Morbidity had captured her that morning as she flicked through the newspaper for the obituaries. A prominent civil servant, an aristocratic old bird who'd been chums with Cecil Beaton, an ancient general, a renowned historian of Napoleon's erotic life, and Rupert's grandfather, Sir Edgar Beauchamp. The pipe-smoking old boy had been in a home for the last three years. He had sympathised with Enoch Powell and called Alex a 'wog' at their graduation ceremony. Curiously, Sir Edgar had had a soft spot for Nell. Rupert was always astounded that he was still going and claimed it as proof of his superior genes. She should say 'Sir Rupert' now, she supposed.

'Knock, knock,' Ali said, coming through the door bum first.

'Morning, morning. Hullo, what have we here?'

'What's happened to you this week?' Ali had a bouquet of flowers in her arms.

'As flies to wanton boys . . .' Nell took the flowers from Ali, who was lingering. Ali had decided on her first day that she was going to be friends with Nell, but the English are so prickly. 'Thank you, Alison. Exceedingly kind of you to bring them all the way up the stairs,' Nell said, dismissing her with her full name.

'No worries.' Ali skulked off back to reception, her morning's entertainment scuppered.

Nell opened the card:

Dinner tomorrow at 8 p.m., The Bohemian. I want to apologise properly Rx

A push notification came through on her phone from the *Guardian*: *Met arrest man for Hampstead Heath murder*. She scrolled through the article: the man, who had yet to be identified, was known to the victim and in his fifties. Rupert was off the hook – for that crime. She took her notebook out from its place between the hole punch and the spare staples and began to write.

33

The Police Station

Caius had had his second croissant in a week. Shame. No, he wouldn't feel shame. He shouldn't. He felt shame. He also felt tired, really bloody tired. It was late when he got home, too late to do YouTube yoga, and boy could he feel all that pent-up tension in his shoulders. His morning had been filled with paperwork now that Ned had been charged. There were still holes in the investigation – they hadn't found Clemmie's clothes or her phone, and forensics had failed to find proof that she had died at Osbald's house. Caius had gone through the full transcript of Matt's interrogation of Ned, but he had been vague as to the route they had taken to the park. There was so much CCTV in this city that it was close to impossible not to have been captured at some point by a camera outside a fancy organic olive oil shop. Caius had printed multiple copies of a map of Belsize Park and Hampstead Heath and had plotted the six most logical routes from Osbald's house to where the body was found. Every single one of them went past the HSBC bank at the bottom of Ned's road.

'Morning, Amy,' Caius said, as she entered the room. 'I have a small mountain of random paperwork and a CCTV request for a bank,' he said, watching her take her trainers off and put on a pair of black leather shoes that lived under her desk. 'Amy, is that a normal thing to do?'

'Huh?'

'Changing shoes like that. Fay did it when I picked her up after her lecture.'

'Yeah. I mean, particularly if you've got heels. You don't want to ruin them, plus they may not be that comfortable if you're going far. I've got a pair of heels in my car boot in case I have to go somewhere nice and don't feel smart enough.'

'In that picture from TfL, Clemmie was wearing a hoodie. She was still in her gym clothes.'

'She changed at the Osbalds' house?'

'We didn't find any evidence of the gym kit – I find it hard to imagine that he'd keep the knife and the foxglove but get rid of her leggings. I read over the transcript of Matt's interview and there's nothing about the clothes. He couldn't get anything out of him. Osbald refused to comment. The question is, Amy, why would you change into a filthily expensive ball gown to go have sex in a park? You'd get it dirty or you'd tear it. You'd get stains on it. You couldn't wear it to a fancy party that evening. Who'd go for a nice walk on a sunny afternoon in a pair of heels that high? The body was found on the other side of Hampstead Heath. That would've been uncomfortable, right?'

'She might've got a kick from that?'

'Appearances were too important to Clemmie.'

Amy walked over to the whiteboard and looked at the picture of Clemmie's body from the crime scene. 'Well then, I don't think Clemmie would pair those shoes with that dress and definitely not with that handbag – it's too hefty. It's a daytime bag.'

'Clemmie didn't dress herself, the killer did. Put your trainers back on. I want to check something. We'll need to get a warrant.'

★ ★ ★

Caius charged up the stairs to Clemmie's gym with a pair of bolt cutters in hand. Amy followed behind him at a pace – in her

190

trainers, thankfully. They barrelled past a young woman with brown ringlets leaving. Amy did a double take. Barry and some of his team came up the stairs at a more leisurely pace.

'Did you see her?' Amy asked Caius.

'Who? Is she famous?'

'Yes, so famous. Huge. So huge. She was in that band.'

They reached the desk at reception; the ever cheerful and toothy Tim was standing sentry. 'Hello, officer. Back again? Should I get Kamal for you?'

'Yes, please,' Caius said, as Tim called his boss. 'Did Clemency O'Hara have a private locker?'

'Yes, she had locker number nine. She paid for it in cash, whereas her membership was paid for by an R. A. de Courcy Beauchamp.'

Kamal came through the door to the studios.

'Kamal, nice to see you again. My colleagues DC Noakes and Dr Barry James from forensics.'

'Nice to meet you. Would you like to come through to my office again?'

'Not this time. We need to look through the women's locker room.'

'That's impossible. There are members using it right now.'

'It's not impossible when you have a warrant.'

★ ★ ★

Barry was staring at the ground; his cheeks were purple. A rather beautiful woman had huffed at Caius when he asked her if she wouldn't mind waiting outside for a moment. Amy tugged at his sleeve to let him know that she was also someone famous, but he wasn't in the mood for ogling sweaty actresses. He had a case

191

to solve, and he could always google her later for an airbrushed image. Amy was wandering around the shower cubicles, picking up the complimentary bottles of Jo Malone shower gel and sniffing them.

'Barry, would it be possible to lift prints from the door of the locker?' Caius asked.

'I'll give it a go.'

'Are you going to be here long?' Kamal asked.

'We could take the door with us?' Barry suggested, trying to be helpful.

'Amy, you had some further questions for Kamal, didn't you?' Caius asked, pulling on a pair of gloves and giving her a knowing look.

'I do indeed,' she said, bounding out of the shower block. 'Have you had any creepy men hanging about outside, inside, anywhere really? Any stalker types?'

'Not that I can recall. We've definitely not had any complaints about that.'

'How does the smoothie bar work? Is it part of the membership?' Amy continued.

'Members pay cash for them.'

'Barry, remember the necklace Clemmie was wearing?' Caius asked as Amy distracted Kamal.

'No, I don't remember. What was on it?'

Caius pulled out the plastic-wrapped key that Clemmie had had around her neck on a chain from his leather bag. 'I thought it was ornamental, but then I remembered that this is a ridiculous place that may well give you a sterling silver key to your own private locker for an exorbitant fee.' Caius opened the locker using the key as one of Barry's team took pictures of Clemmie's belongings.

34

The Police Station

Caius was in the Chief Superintendent's office, staring out of the smudgy window. No one had cleaned the station's windows in a while because of the cost. The portrait of his daughter was back in pride of place.

'I'm not saying that we've arrested the wrong man. We have physical evidence: the knife, the string that was used to tie her up, a foxglove from his garden which had a few leaves removed (which suggests that the digoxin was administered not as a pill but as tea straight from a cutting), and he was the last person we can prove the victim was with. The man came to us to confess. Plus the semen and foetus are both Ned Osbald's. We have the motive. What I'm saying is that there is more to this case than we thought. Any jury would convict him with what we have already – it's just that there are quite a few loose ends that I need to tie up.'

'You think this is some sort of conspiracy?' the Chief Superintendent asked.

'Conspiracy is a word for crazy people.'

'What then?'

'Clemmie paid for the locker herself in cash. I doubt Rupert knew it existed. She took it out the week before she died. He paid for her membership – why not just alter the direct debit to include the locker?'

'She was using it to hide something?'

'Exactly. In the locker we found a small carry-on suitcase with her iPhone, plus a cheap burner, her passport, €5,000 in cash, a

Eurostar ticket to Paris for last Saturday at 6.30 p.m. and about a week's worth of lightweight summer clothes. There's some jewellery in the lining of the case, all of it precious – it's easy to carry large amounts of money in your earlobes.'

'She was running away. Why?'

'It's who she was running away from that I'm interested in. Osbald is the obvious answer. Besides, Beauchamp is in love with someone else. Clemmie had been putting unwanted pressure on Beauchamp for at least the last few months to get married. Her running away would be a boon for him. Gets to play the sad puppy dog with the other girl.'

'Who's the other girl?'

'A young woman called Helena Waddingham. Goes by Nell. She's a university friend of Rupert's. She's the girl in the photos from the Greece holiday. I don't think she had anything to do with it.' Caius paused for a moment. 'I know why you're interested in this case so much. Your daughter was there at the party.'

'Her fiancé is loosely associated with that group. He won a scholarship to boarding school.'

'I get it, it's a bit too close to home, but your daughter being there is mere happenstance. Do you not think that we should find out the full truth? We've got a pregnant young woman who was hated so much by her murderer that they went back and slit her throat when she was already dead. We owe Clemmie justice.'

'I don't think the party has much to do with it all.'

'Me neither. It was a distraction, an opportunity for Clemmie to escape. Based on the evidence we found at the gym, we've got a new theory. The Eurostar ticket was for a train an hour before the start of Rupert Beauchamp's birthday party. Clemmie just needed to say that she was running late, and she'd be in

Paris before anyone noticed that she was gone. No one may have known that she was bolting – she might not have told Osbald that his little problem was about to flee to France. Her going to the house might have been one last kiss, a grand finale to the affair. I need to tie up the loose ends. A half-decent barrister could sow just enough doubt on the investigation for there to be a chance that Osbald could get off.'

'All right. Where are you starting? What's your strategy?'

'Forensics have the suitcase and are going through it right now. There were some drugs at the bottom of the locker too, and IT are unlocking the phone. Amy is reviewing all of Clemency's social media and the laptop contents again in case we missed anything. Trying to work out if she had a friend she might have confided in. I think I also owe Mr Beauchamp a social call.'

'He's a baronet now. Grandfather died two days ago, saw it in the papers. For the record, my daughter can't stand Rupert Beauchamp. She said she can't put her finger on it but he "creeps her out".'

'That makes two of us.'

'Have Amy do the bulk of it, if you must. Sounds like the loose ends are mostly computer research. I'm not sure why you're still bothering; it's an open and shut case if you ask me. Besides, there's a lot of pressure coming from above that we proceed with the charges against Osbald. A confession is a confession, after all. I will put you and Matthew on the next new case that comes in. Focus on that and forget about Osbald; he's at the mercy of a jury now.'

35

Thurstone

Caius stood on the doorstep of Rupert's house and rapped on the door. He turned around and admired the garden: roses, lavender and a plethora of other plants that Caius couldn't name, but no foxgloves. Rupert opened the door.

'Detective, good afternoon. Come in,' Rupert said, wearing a pair of pyjamas like John Darling in *Peter Pan*. Pale blue stripes in the middle of the day. Caius remembered his grampy owning a pair for when he had to stay overnight in hospital.

'I was sorry to hear about your grandfather.'

'Thank you. It was a relief, actually. He was rather infirm in his last days.' Rupert showed him into the sitting room opposite the 'library'. All traces of Clemmie – as small as they had been – had been purged from the house.

'My nan went senile in the end; it was difficult for everyone. Care homes are very expensive.' Caius couldn't help himself from needling him. That was wrong. He'd been bereaved twice in one week.

'No, it was more that he wasn't compos mentis. He couldn't tell you what year it was. Would you like a cup of tea?' Rupert asked. He clearly didn't want to make Caius one.

'No, thanks.'

'How can I help you?' Rupert asked. A bang was heard from the first floor. 'Minty is here, she's been very supportive. She's helping me box up the rest of Clemmie's things for her parents. They're flying over on Monday.'

'I know the support team have been in touch, but I thought I'd come personally.'

'That's very kind of you.'

Caius's phone started ringing. 'I'm so sorry. I need to take this. Excuse me.' He got up and walked into the hallway. 'Hi Barry, what's up?' he asked. He was aware of a presence at the top of the stairs eavesdropping on him. 'You're sure that's the shape stamped on them? All right. Thanks, Barry.' Caius walked back into the living room. 'I'm so sorry. I really am.'

'I think I'm still in shock, you know. I'm not good at expressing my emotions at the best of times,' Rupert said, sighing exaggeratedly.

'I hate to ask any more questions, especially as you've been so very accommodating throughout this investigation, but I have a couple more for you. Did Clemmie have a drug problem?'

'I don't know if problem is the right word. She once was a bit of a party girl, but she stopped all that last year. Took up yoga properly, became evangelical about the benefits of turmeric. But then again, addicts lie.'

'Ned Osbald, was Clemmie scared of him?'

'Scared? He had a bit of temper, I think. Yelled at her once for buying the wrong type of rosehip tea on a run to Waitrose. Something silly like that. She came home upset that day.'

'Rosehip tea, wow. Thank you for your time. And again, I'm sorry for both your losses.' As Caius turned to leave, he spotted a photo on the piano of a young Rupert with his arm around Nell's shoulders. It hadn't been there before. His smile was wolfish and wide enough to eat a girl. He really was painfully handsome. Caius understood why all these girls kept falling for him. 'You look young there. Who's this? She's rather beautiful.'

'A friend. If you need to ask any other questions then please call me,' Rupert said, walking Caius to the door. Rupert was tight, wound up. His amenable facade slipped away for a moment when Caius mentioned Nell.

'Of course,' Caius said. He walked slowly back to his car.' He got in, wound down the window, put the radio on and started audibly singing along to Earth, Wind & Fire before driving off. He needed Rupert to relax and think it was all over, that he wouldn't be questioned any more. That he, Caius, was an idiot. He shouldn't have mentioned Nell at all, but he was curious. The tension was palpable – like a fox that would fight you for a chicken bone carcass from a tipped-over bin.

★ ★ ★

'Must everyone disturb me when I'm trying to write?' Rupert yelled at Minty as she tiptoed to the foot of the stairs. He stood peeking through the porthole window next to the door at that idiot policeman until he drove off.

'I'm sorry,' said Minty.

'Sorry? Sorry for what?' Rupert turned and gave her a look that bored through her.

'I don't know . . . Um, well, I . . .' Minty tripped over her words.

Rupert huffed and looked at the empty cardboard boxes in the hallway. He picked one up, marched into the library and started packing up his books. He had nearly stuffed a box full when he came across a slim volume. He picked it up and read the inscription in the front. He started to breathe fast and quick. Minty was pressing against the door frame.

'Rupert, I . . . I . . .'

'I've got to make it right, Minty, I have to.'

* * *

Caius had plugged his phone into the hands-free and dialled the number of an old friend while stuck in traffic near Sloane Square.

'Errol, mate, how are you?' Caius asked.

'Not bad. You?'

'I've been better. I'm working on the Hampstead murder.'

'The hottie on the Heath, eh?'

'God, I hate the tabloids – what an awful phrase. I stumbled across her when I was out jogging.'

'You don't jog.'

'I do now. Mate, can I ask you a question?'

'Yeah, sure.'

'Have you guys come across any purple pills with a hippo stamped on them? Or a bogus charity called Help for Hippos?'

'Are you free tonight?'

'Yeah, I am.'

'I'll come to you, all right? You still in your grandparents' old place?'

'Yeah, I'll see you later.'

'I'll be at yours about 7 p.m. Keep it low key, OK? It's sensitive.'

'Loose lips sink ships and all that, mate.' What else had he stumbled on when he stumbled across Clemmie?

36

Valhalla, Camden

The barman was at least six foot three, heavily tattooed, and his arms bulged – not in an 'I do weights so I look like a monument in a V-neck T-shirt' way, although he really did look amazing, but in an 'I might burn down a monastery, kidnap you and take you to Iceland' way. Nell was nursing a ginger ale – a fancy organic one that cost £4.95 because even when you're in a Viking-themed bar, you are still ultimately in Camden, and someone is taking you for a mug. Minty was late. Who better to feel glum with than miserable Minty? Who better to throw axes with than Minty, sad sad Minty, whom she had found sobbing in a Clapham toilet? Poor fucking Minty, to be nearly thirty and in thrall to a prick. The ginger ale was more than a penny per millilitre – she must have been paying for the label design. She poured the rest of the ginger ale into her glass and considered taking the bottom-heavy, curvy bottle home with her to use as a tiny vase on her silly little dining room table. She could put a tacky gerbera in it. Cut flowers are inherently tragic. A life so vibrant and so vital decapitated in its prime to look pretty on your sideboard. Used to say, 'I'm sorry your mother died, but here are some roses.' To say, 'I'm sorry for throwing up in your room in college after some boat club party that I said I'd take you to but then changed my mind, and for sleeping in your bed that night, and for holding you against me and for pressing an erection into your back, and for breathing sick into your hair, and for telling you that I loved you but couldn't be with you right now because your father is a sales manager for a company that makes fans for electronic systems and not a peer, and you know, I don't want my grandfather to disown me, not yet, I haven't made my own money, and I want the house first, but one day I would inherit and then you'd marry me,' and to say, 'I'm sorry for knowing that I said something like that, something quite awful, but the tequila stops me from remembering exactly and I stopped myself from asking what, but I know it's bad because you won't talk to me, haven't talked to me in a week.' To say, 'I'm sorry for, oh God, for everything. I'm sorry for everything you ever let me do to you.'

'This place is so weird,' Minty said as she surprised Nell from behind, making her jump and knock over the empty ginger ale bottle.

'Oh, hullo. Crumbs, you just scared the living ghost out of me.'

'Sorry. Have you been waiting long? Am I late?'

'No, no, not at all. Our time slot is not for another five minutes. We're not allowed to drink beforehand though.'

'I signed the waiver. This is very exciting. I love your outfit. How do you dress like that?'

'Like what?'

'I don't know.'

'Like a ghost that haunts a drapery shop? I make my own clothes. I'm tall, and I like to know that the sweat involved in the manufacture is purely my own. Are you ready to release your inner Valkyrie?'

'Yes. I need to throw an axe at something, someone.'

'The only time you're allowed to talk about men is now. Once we pick up an axe then that is that. No more men. They won't ruin our Friday evening.'

'You know what, I don't want to talk about men ever again.'

'They're exhausting,' Nell said, as Ragnor the barman gestured towards her to let them know their turn was up. Nell stood up from her chair and gave him that look that arrogant teenage boys with floppy hair practise in the mirror: direct eye contact, look away, laugh to yourself and picture something obscene. Nell had added a little gambol to her bit as Minty trailed after her. Full-grown adult males, or 'men' as they insist on being called, should be treated with the callousness with which teenage boys treat plain girls whose chemistry notes they need to borrow for a passing grade.

★ ★ ★

A silky breeze flew through Camden's polluted evening air as Nell and Minty walked up the high street to a pub that used to be a dive two years ago but now pretended it was in the Cotswolds. Nell walked with the buoyancy of a woman who'd just spent an hour dismembering her enemies. She had pictured the face of nearly every person she had ever mildly despised and every man she had ever violently loved when aiming her axe at the target.

'That was satisfying,' Minty said, as she dodged a tourist with an Amy Winehouse T-shirt on.

'Wasn't it just.'

'Did that barman give you his number?'

'He did.'

'Are you going to call him?'

'No, of course not. I wouldn't think of it.'

'Liar.'

'I am not an inveterate maniser – maniser, that doesn't scan, you know what I mean. No, I'm not going to call him. You just broke the no-men rule, so you have to buy me a packet of crisps at the pub. I'd say a shot, but I've taken up running. Got a 10k coming up. Did you like the mead they gave you as your prize at the end?'

'No, it was vile.'

'I quite liked it when I tried it before,' Nell said as they arrived at the pub. Disappointingly it was under new management again and they'd tarted the old girl up, given her a trim, an unsuitable shade of lipstick and a push-up bra, but it wasn't too busy, and it still had the bijou secret garden that sparkled like a little emerald out the back.

'These places are the best,' Minty said, patting a purple hippo on top of a charity donation box. 'So, a packet of crisps and what? Have a proper drink, go on.'

'A whisky, then. I'll have a whisky. Nothing American, and nothing expensive, but not so shit that it burns.' Nell's gaze wandered, taking in the latest renovation works. The cornicing had gone, and the walls had been painted a cool shade of 'equinox moss'. The botanical prints on the wall had all been replaced with black-and-white shots of London landmarks.

'I can probably do that for you,' the barman said, laughing at the funny girl with sarcastic eyes. 'And what can I get you, red?'

'I'll have a shot of tequila and a large glass of the Picpoul.'

'No problem.'

Minty leaned in so that Nell couldn't hear and quietly asked, 'And can we get a half-pint of Coke each?'

'Is Pepsi all right?'

'No, no it's not. Coca-Cola, please. I'd like to donate my change to charity.'

'Of course. I'll bring your drinks over to you if you like? You need to pay in cash.'

'Thank you,' Minty said, as she paid the barman in twenties, 'we'll be out back.' Nell grabbed her bags and frolicked at a pace past Minty as she fumbled with her change. Minty trailed after her into the small walled garden and found Nell squashed up on a bench next to two men that she was ignoring.

'What did you spend your pocket money on when you were a child?' Nell asked, patting the seat next to her as Minty came over.

'I didn't really have pocket money growing up. I had money for tuck, of course . . .'

'I used to buy this magazine called *I Love Horses*. I was obsessed. Do you remember the theme song? *I love horses, best of all the animals. I love horses, they're my friends.*'

Minty laughed. 'So you ride?'

'No, never. I'd be dreadful at it.'

'It's not that hard. You'd look very handsome on a horse. You should come to my parents' house for a long weekend. I'll teach you.'

'Cheers, mate. Freud had this theory that young girls are obsessed with horses because they've realised that they don't have penises and want to feel something powerful between their legs.'

'Sounds like bollocks to me.'

It was creeping up to 9 p.m. Sensible people with partners or Labradoodles had started to make their way home, and the garden was slowly emptying. The barman lingered and told the pair that he had brought them some pistachios on the house.

'Thank you,' Minty said to the barman as he left.

'My favourite type of snacks are ones that get brought to me in tiny little silver trays like these,' Nell said, taking a nut.

'There's a little something extra in there.'

Nell moved some pistachios out of the way to find a small clear plastic bag with three small purple pills in. 'I have to go to this brunch thing for my cousin Marina's birthday early tomorrow morning, but thank you. Don't hold back on my account.'

Minty waved off Nell's politeness. 'Pills aren't fun when you pop them on your own. So, what is your weird obsession now?'

'I love novels about and by Americans living in Paris in the twentieth century.'

'That's niche. Like what?'

'Gertrude Stein et al. At one end of the spectrum you have *Giovanni's Room* and on the other you've got *The Dud Avocado*. Read the latter on a terrible day and the former when you're blissfully happy. Life is about balance, after all. What about you?'

'I'm quite dull.'

'That's not true, Minty. Don't let him tell you that,' Nell said, eyeing the tequila that Minty had failed to drink. 'May I propose a toast?'

'Of course,' Minty said, picking up her shot.

'Here's to Clemmie. May she be doing hot yoga and drinking green juices in Elysium.' Minty downed her drink while Nell slyly chucked half her whisky into a poorly sculpted topiary and fell into silence. She felt guilty for all the times she'd called Clemmie 'Phlegm', and she reasoned that Minty was one of the few other people who'd understand what it was like to hate Clemmie when really it was Rupert you were angry with. Nell looked around the garden. Fairy lights twinkled and she could smell the lavender. In London there are no stars in the sky, only the odd satellite. 'You guys were pretty close, right?'

'I suppose.'

'I understand that "suppose".' Nell picked up her whisky and pretended to drink it. 'It's so bizarre to think she's so very dead.

You expect to grow old and apart from people like Clemmie. To somehow hear that they've died of cancer in their fifties or in a car crash in some part of the world that I couldn't find on a map.'

'I only knew Clemmie because of Rupert, which never endeared me to her. Still, it's quite awful.' Minty stared into the bottom of her glass, searching for something, anything.

'Same. She'd be lovely to me and then a gorgon, with no in-between.'

'I think I was privy to a bit too much for her liking.'

'Privy to what?'

'I don't need to tell you.'

'You were Rupert's creature and not hers?'

'Exactly. But we aren't supposed to be talking about men, are we?'

'We can talk about that one particular man. He looms over this friendship. I heard about Rupert's twenty-fifth the other day . . .'

Minty interjected before Nell said the word 'pond'. 'Are we friends?'

'Yeah, why not? How's Rupert taking it all?' Nell asked. Minty frowned at Nell's question, but Nell didn't notice as a man in a pair of shorts, ones that could almost be deemed formal owing to the virtue of being from Uniqlo's chino range, slithered over to the pair, interrupting their conversation.

'My friend thinks you're cute,' he said to Minty, 'but I like you best,' he said to Nell, giving her his business card – well, half of a business card. It had been ripped asunder, his company's logo obliterated but his phone number intact.

'We're both married, but thank you. We're extremely flattered.'

'Well, if either of you fancy cheating on the little men at home, then we're in the corner over there. Unless you're married to each other?'

'Thank you. We'll bear that in mind,' Nell said to his back. Turning to Minty: 'On the friendship thing, I resolutely cannot be friends with anyone who has a "Pop the Prosecco" plaque on display in their home.'

'I would never own one of those. They're so naff.'

'Do you think that drinking gin is a suitable replacement for a personality?'

'No, I drink it because the drunkenness to calorie ratio is low.'

'Spoken like a true scientist.'

'You can take the botany nerd out of a lab and give her stilettos and eyeliner, but I still love a good ratio.'

'How's your business going?'

'Good, yeah.'

'It's so cool that you're an artist. I'd love to work for myself. So, you do these botanical sculptures, right?' Her phone vibrated.

'Yes, I've been doing a lot of weddings recently. Ultimately, I want to be a proper garden designer and exhibit at Chelsea. I breed a few varieties of plants too.'

'Minty, darling. I think I'm going to have to dash. That whisky hasn't agreed with me,' Nell said, standing up to kiss her on the cheek. 'This was so much fun. We should do it again. Let's go for dinner next week.' Nell said the words over her shoulder as she dashed out of the pub.

★   ★   ★

Nell practically fell on top of Alex, who was pacing up and down the pavement. 'Crashing girls' night?'

207

'Let's catch the Overground back to yours.' Alex took her by the hand and turned up the high street away from the tube at a pace.

'There's a vegan place back on Jamestown Road that does this amazing fake chicken. Fancy it?'

'I fancy going back to yours.' Alex hadn't been the only interloper that evening, but he was the one who hadn't got lost coming out of Camden Town station. He'd seen Rupert floundering at the ticket barrier and had legged it to the pub, getting there before him.

'OK,' Nell said, trotting after him. They crossed over the bridge and turned down Castlehaven Road.

'How hot was this Viking barman then?'

'A solid nine and a half,' Nell said as the Overground station came into view.

'Do you remember the ball at the end of our final year?'

'Best ball I never went to,' Nell said as she started the ascent up to the platform.

'You spent the whole evening in A&E with me because I trapped my finger in a fire door and it was pointing in the wrong direction. You were wearing cream and I bled all over your dress.'

'And then when we got back, we had sex on top of a pile of laundry in my room. You were jacked up on morphine and adrenaline. It was quite exciting. Like the filler sexy scene in an action movie.'

The train pulled into the platform. The doors opened with a beep, beep, beep as tipsy hipsters poured out of the carriage, and they got on.

'I handed my notice in today.'

'Are you moving back to London?'

'Yes, and I mean this, I've never stopped feeling about you the way I felt that night when I cried as the nurse gave me a tetanus shot, and you held my good hand and told me that everything would be all right.' Alex put his arm around Nell's shoulder as they stood holding on to an orange pole. 'I adore you, and I'm sorry about what happened in Athens. I should have stopped Rupert from kissing you like that. I should've been there.'

'No, it's my fault for thinking you can treat a wolf like a Labrador, that it would sit in front of the fire like a good boy. I always knew what he was. I was just naive to think that it wouldn't be me that got bitten.'

37

Caius's garden

Smoke from the barbecue wafted through Caius's house as he flapped about in the kitchen. He was wearing a light blue apron as he tried to solve the conundrum of how to get at the seeds from a pomegranate without becoming violently saturated in juice. He had a YouTube tutorial up on his phone that had promised a miraculous outcome. He was making a salad to go along with the lamb and mint burgers on the grill. Pine nuts and feta had been whizzed around, and a few fistfuls of baby spinach were draining in a colander in the sink.

'I'm going to flip the burgers,' Errol yelled from the garden.

'Go for it, mate,' Caius said. He'd managed to deseed a third of the pomegranate and was thoroughly done with the exercise. He threw all the ingredients into a pretty ceramic salad bowl that was actually Héloise's. He took a picture of it and sent it to her – told her that he missed her. Caius took the salad outside and placed it next to the tzatziki he'd made.

'If ten years ago you would've told me that Caius Beauchamp knew what tzatziki was, I would've been surprised.'

'I am a sophisticated man now, Errol,' Caius said as the door-bell rang. 'Back in one second.' He opened the door to Matt.

'Darling, I'm home,' Matt said, acknowledging Caius's apron.

'Hey, thanks for coming over, I thought it would be good for you to hear this too. I know it's your day off.'

'You're feeding me, right? Dinner nearly ready?' Matt asked, before handing Caius a six-pack of their favourite IPA and heading through to the garden.

'Errol, meet Matt; Matt, this is my old buddy Errol.' The two of them exchanged 'mates', shook hands and stared approvingly at the barbecue together. 'Errol and I were at Hendon together.'

'Mate, have you put pomegranate seeds in a salad?' Errol asked.

'Yep, and extra virgin olive oil grown by monks in Thessaloniki. I bought it from the farmers' market.'

'You've changed,' Errol laughed as he inspected the grill. 'I think these burgers are done.'

The three of them sat down to convivially eat, and when they were done Errol said, 'Help for Hippos, then?'

'Help for Hippos,' Matt echoed.

'It's a great name, isn't it?' Errol said, shaking his head. 'It could almost be real.'

'So it is definitely a sham charity?' Caius asked.

'Yeah, although it isn't a regular fraud thing. The charity collection boxes are an advertisement. If they have one, then they're selling the pills.'

'We have some of the pills. They're with the lab now.'

'It's mostly MDMA. Help for Hippos is one of the smartest drug operations I have ever seen. It's been going for at least five years. We've never managed to get to grips with it fully because it creates so little drama. It caters to dinner party drug users, not homeless addicts. There haven't been any known overdoses, there are no gangland murders, teenagers aren't fighting each other for pitches on street corners. The product itself is good quality. It's not that strong. They sell it in small quantities only. Users don't get into trouble with it. It's the most bourgeois drug operation you can imagine; it's discreet and convenient. The people running it must be making a killing, and there's little appetite at the NCA to go after it. Between us,

I think there's something fishy, bribery maybe. That or just basic double standards. How does it connect to your case?'

'We identified the dead girl on the Heath by an appointment card from her hairdresser's. We go down and there's one of the collection boxes at the till. The next day I go to her work, it's closed, I pop to the loo in the pub a few doors down, and I see one. I go to the gym that she went to the day she went missing, I'm in the manager's office and there's another. He didn't put it out because he thought it was tacky, although he got told to by management. He's pretty new there, might not have been initiated into it yet,' Caius said.

'This is between just us. MI6 took over the investigation into Help for Hippos two months ago. They're working with Interpol. They're probably already watching you, but I'll call it in with my contact that there's a tenuous connection between the drugs and your murder.'

'We've arrested someone for the murder already. This is merely a loose end for us,' Matt added.

'Yeah, I saw on the news. Who have you booked?'

'Ned Osbald. He was Clemency O'Hara's boss and father of her unborn child,' Caius said.

'So it was a crime of passion, but you still think there's a connection to drugs?'

'We found the pills – enough for us to think she may be dealing – amongst some of her belongings that she'd hidden at her gym. She was planning to flee the country the evening she was murdered.'

'Your victim, what was she like?'

'The reductive take is that she was a West London trophy girlfriend who liked to take pictures of herself in expensive bars.'

'It's too circumstantial. Your vic is the target user living in their patch. I can't stress strongly enough the scale of the Help for Hippos operation. Like I said, it's posh, it's white. Black kids aren't getting killed because of it. The newspapers don't care, the BBC hasn't picked up on it. Hell, half of the journalists in this city probably indulge. I mean, fuck, you're good at your job, Caius, and you stumbled across it by providence. Honestly, best thing to do is for me to call it in, then you might get a quiet tap on the shoulder and you have to hand the evidence over.'

'All right, call it in,' Caius said.

'Beer, anyone?' Matt asked as he started to rise from his chair. 'I bought wacky ones again.'

'I nearly forgot, I bought a trifle from M&S. I'll get the beers too,' Caius said, getting up and going into the flat.

'Has he been replaced by a pod person?' Errol asked Matt.

'Héloise dumped him a few weeks ago, but I like trifle so I'm not going to say anything about the fifties housewife apron thing he's got going on. It's a new vibe for him, but it's working.'

★ ★ ★

Guests departed and washing up done, Caius sprawled across his sofa musing on *Persuasion*. Nell had written her name on the inside of the front cover as a teenager. It had what he presumed was her parents' address written on the flyleaf. They had a Coventry postcode. She'd shaken that accent. If it weren't for the investigation and the Greek god she was already shagging, he'd ask her out. If only he'd met her in a bar. His phone rang. It was Héloise. He sent her to voicemail. He didn't want to talk to her any more.

SATURDAY

38

Islington

A pair of sphinxes guarded the path up to the flat where the body was. Caius liked Islington. It was the little bistros and homeware shops that did it for him. Bento boxes and novelty egg timers. Monochrome menswear boutiques and gluten-free bakeries. You never knew when you might come across a *Guardian* columnist. Caius saw Matt puffing up the road after he got spat out by his bus a stop too early. Matt wheezed closer into view.

'Welcome to your next case!' Caius said as Matt clasped at the stitch in his side. Caius had finally run up the top of the damned hill that morning. 'You should start jogging too, chubby wubby work-hubby.'

'Smugness doesn't suit your bone structure. You don't have the cheekbones for it,' Matt said, slowing down as he reached Caius. 'What have we got, amigo?'

'It's not pretty,' Caius said, walking up the steps past the sphinxes.

'I had an omelette for breakfast, was that a bad call?' Matt asked, following him.

'Yeah, it smells putrid in there. The house has been turned into a duplex. Our victim had the top half of the building.'

'God, there's stairs as well?'

'Downstairs got back early this morning from a three-week trip to New Zealand to the smell. It's been hot this week.' Caius opened the door to the flat. They were smacked with the stench of human sludge.

'Morning, Barry,' Caius said, cheerfully.

'Morning, gentlemen. Is he all right?' Barry gestured to Matt, who was leaning aghast against the wall opposite.

'No, he had an omelette for breakfast.'

'Oh, tough luck. Lots of vitamin D and folic acid in an omelette, Matt, not great for repeating on you at crime scenes though,' Barry said, returning to his work.

'What do you think happened, Barry?' Caius continued.

'The victim, Caucasian male early to mid-sixties, has had his neck broken.'

'Was it an accident? Did he fall?' Caius asked, acknowledging the ladder in the middle of the room and next to the body. There was a lightbulb on the top rung of the ladder.

'No, I would say that someone has wrapped their arm over his head from behind and broken his neck. With some considerable force, I might add.' Barry did a rather graphic twisting motion.

'It was definitely murder then,' Matt piped up before collapsing again. 'Why are the grim ones never natural causes?'

'The facial structure of the victim suggests it is the owner of the flat. There's a picture on the mantelpiece. He's wearing the same fetching bow tie. There are also some fibres of what appears to be rope underneath the chair over there near the bookshelf. I've taken a sample.'

'The murderer tied him up and then broke his neck. They then removed the rope and put the ladder up to make it look like a fall.'

'Yes, although anyone doing the post-mortem would notice that the injury isn't commensurate with the scenario of a fall from a ladder. There's no obvious damage to the forearms or wrists, which you would expect. People put their arms out to catch themselves. You might break your neck, but you wouldn't break it like that.'

'So we have an amateurish murderer. Other than the rope, any more signs of torture?'

'He's missing a fingernail, which we found near the chair. I'll be able to give you more once I've done the post-mortem.'

'How long has he been dead?' Caius asked as he inspected the chair.

'At a guess, around seven days.'

'Thanks, Barry,' Caius said, before walking up the stairs into the bedroom.

Matt slowly edged into the living room and then crept up the stairs after Caius.

'Where are the guy's things?' Matt asked as he looked around the bedroom. There was barely any furniture in the flat. Only the bare essentials.

'According to downstairs, he retired at Christmas from one of the auction houses,' Caius said, moving back down the stairs, through the living room and into the kitchen. 'He'd bought a villa in Crete and was planning on moving out there properly at the end of the summer. The flat was going to be let out, and he'd passed them the details of the agency in case the tenants were a problem. The empty bookshelves and the lack of super-fluous furniture would suggest that the victim, whose name is Hereward Trollope-Bagshott by the way, had already started downsizing in anticipation of leaving the country.'

'Hereward Trollope-Bagshott is the most English name I have ever heard, and I grew up in Surrey,' Matt said.

'I'm going to call him HTB in my notes for ease. The couple downstairs also very helpfully gave me the phone number of his sister. He gave it to them in case of emergencies.'

'He sounds like too cautious a man to be involved in anything dodgy enough to be tortured and then murdered for.'

'Evidently not. The neighbourhood is being canvassed in case anyone saw anything suspicious over the last two weeks. Are you all right to go to the auction house where he worked?' Caius asked.

'I'm sure it'll smell better than here,' Matt said, moving down the stairs and towards the kitchen and an open window.

'I'm going to ring the sister. She's out in Chichester. Local constabulary have been dispatched to tell her the news,' Caius said, opening the fridge. 'There's some heavily reduced prosciutto from Waitrose with a sell-by date of 21 June.'

'He died sometime after Saturday mid-afternoon, that's when Waitrose starts to reduce everything. I go on yellow sticker rampages on my days off.'

'Such a waste of fancy ham.' Caius leaned against the kitchen counter and stared at a tacky magnet from Athens on the fridge.

'Do you know what he did at the auction house?'

'No. Just turn up and demand to speak to HR. That sort hate a scene. They'll be very obliging.'

'I bet they have good biscuits.'

'You'll be lucky if you get a glass of water,' Caius said, scanning the room. 'Why would someone torture a retired, bow tie wearing bachelor? It's not going to be drugs, could be a gambling debt. A love affair gone wrong? That feels off, but you never know. Matt, you're a pensioner in a young body. Imagine you know you're in trouble with some scary bastards and you wanted to hide whatever you have of value – and by value, I mean anything, not necessarily money – where would you put it?'

'I wouldn't put it in a drawer in the bedroom, that's too obvious. If it was small, then I would put it in the bits and bobs drawer with the foil packets of ketchup and takeaway menus in the kitchen. There's too much stuff in there and no one would have the patience to search for it. Anything bigger I'd hide some-where else in the kitchen, somewhere domestic. Particularly if I'm scared of a man, and let's be honest! Statistically, how many women have the strength to break someone's neck like that? Under the sink?' Matt got on his knees and started rummaging amongst the half-used bottles of bleach and glass cleaner.

Caius opened the door to a long thin cupboard behind the fridge. There was a shelf at the top with a few tins of beans and a tin of condensed milk. There was a mop in a bucket and a mangy blue-and-white J-cloth, that had definitely lived through its glory days, hung over the top of the bucket.

'I've found an iPad behind a bottle of floor cleaner,' Matt said.

Caius dropped the J-cloth on the floor and let out a shriek. 'I've found a head in a mop bucket.'

39

The Police Station

Caius walked into the station, having stopped off at Lidl on the way back from Hereward's flat. Caius had bought himself a bag of apples, a salad and a cheese twist from the bakery. Matt was lying across the back seat of Caius's parked car, taking a moment to recover from the crime scene. Much to Matt's relief, the head that Caius had found wasn't a real human head, only a weird painted stone one like a garden gnome. Caius went to find Amy and found her looking ashen at her computer.

'Would you like an apple? They're packed with vitamin C and pectin,' Caius asked.

'No, thanks,' Amy said.

'They're Pink Ladies?'

'No, I'm fine. The CCTV request for the bank in Belsize Park has been escalated to their corporate legal team. They said it would be a couple of days.'

'Are you all right?'

'Yeah, I'm fine. I went through Clemmie's Instagram posts by month and sorted them into who she tagged in each one of the pictures or the description of the post.'

'What did you learn?'

'I put it all into a bar graph to see it more clearly,' she said, handing Caius a colourful chart. 'It's by month and the number of instances where that individual has been tagged. I've done the last three years – Clemmie was a prolific poster, we've got quite a large data set. There are a few women who are consistently tagged throughout that time period. It looks like they're friends from her university days, but you'll see she tends to have bursts of intense friendships and then she drops that person.'

'She dropped Nell Waddingham recently,' Caius said, looking at the chart.

'Yeah, well we can see that she had a thing about Nell Waddingham, she copies what she reads. I cross-referenced all of Clemmie's book posts over the last five years with what Nell has posted. Clemmie read every single one of them between two weeks and six months after Nell did. Clemmie posted a picture of *The Dud Avocado* with an avocado-based green smoothie six weeks ago, which is one of Nell's favourites, but she stopped copying her after that.'

'She gave up on trying to compete with Nell. Why?' Caius asked.

'Nell has been consistently featured over the whole period, usually three or four a year. Empty pro-feminist slogans: #slay. Always on large nights out. Rupert is always there too. Nell has a distinct way of dressing. It's bold and attention-grabbing, and it always gets extra comments for Clemmie. There was an uptick near Christmas lasting up to a month or so ago. They went for brunch together, an art gallery opening and a slam poetry night, but then it fell off a cliff.'

'Which coincides with the Greece trip. Nell was having an affair with Rupert?' Caius thought that was disappointingly likely after Nell's comments. He didn't want to imagine it.

'No, she wasn't. Clemmie might have suspected that because Rupert is in love with Nell. He's been in love with her for years, that's why the book thing has been going on for so long. That whole time Clemmie knew that Rupert wasn't in love with her, and still she stayed. Why do that to yourself? I went through the file of pictures again from Greece and I found a video in the folder. Matt must have missed it accidentally. The program he was using to view them didn't recognise the video format or something . . . Clemmie left her camera on a table to try and catch Rupert and Nell at it. She turns it on at the beginning of the video, so it looks like it was on purpose.'

'What's on the video, Amy?'

'I can't watch it again today. I watched it to the end, and I wish I hadn't.'

'Amy, do you want to take the afternoon off? Do you want a lie-down? Matt is still strewn across my back seat right now because the body in our next case was oozing. There's no shame in needing to take a moment to make sure you're all right. We see the worst of it.'

'Nah, I'm a big girl. I can handle it. The tickets were purchased on 15 June in cash from the Eurostar terminal; her last video was the day before that. She hadn't posted anything since. I think Clemmie had been loosely planning her escape since they got back from Greece. Something changed. Maybe she'd only just found out that she was expecting two weeks ago and it spurred her into booking the ticket. Just watch the video. It'll make sense. Your gut was totally right about him. I'm going to go through Clemmie's vlogs again in case I missed anything else. Men like Rupert are habitual abusers. It won't have been a one-off.' Amy stood up from her desk so Caius could watch the video. 'I'm going to get a cuppa. Want one? One of your special teas?'

'Regular's fine.'

'16:36 is where it begins. Brace yourself.'

40

Transcript of the video recording that Clemmie made
of Rupert Beauchamp raping Helena Waddingham as it
was seen on Detective Constable Amy Noakes's desktop

[It's dark. A door leading into a white building
is visible to the left of the frame. Light pours
through it. There are two figures partially lit
by the light from the building and a fire pit
burning to the right of the frame. One is clearly
RUPERT; the other, a woman, is less visible. They
are sitting close together on a bench, talking
and drinking in what appears to be a courtyard
garden. A bottle of wine is on the floor next to
the leg of RUPERT'S chair.]

HELENA: I'm so jealous of Alex. I never want to
leave.

RUPERT: Greece?

HELENA: Yes, it's had so much of my imagination,
so much of my energy. Imagine if Christianity
hadn't happened. Think of where the world would
be right now. Bacchanalia rather than, I don't
know . . . Easter. Eleusinian Mysteries and paeans
to Apollo, not 'Jerusalem' or 'All Creatures
Great and Small'. I would've been a priestess

to some obstinate goddess. Offering the fatty bits of pork chops wrapped around the bones as a sacrifice. Athena maybe, or Hera. I'm not cut out for Aphrodite.

RUPERT: You are a dreadful romantic.

HELENA: It's the worst possible vice imaginable.

RUPERT: It's charming.

[A crashing noise is heard elsewhere, and what sounds like muffled sobbing.]

HELENA: Is Clemmie all right? She was really off this morning and now, well, this.

RUPERT: No, she's furious with me, again, and swallowed a fist of pills. God knows how she got them through customs. The clattering. Such drama. Always one for a scene is Clemency. She's so high she thinks she's a bird. A raptor.

HELENA: Like problem high?

RUPERT: Yes, problem high.

HELENA: Oh, Rupert. I'm sorry. That must be difficult to live with. Are you going to send her to rehab?

RUPERT: I'm going to send her packing.

[An audible 'Fuck you, you utter bastard, how could you do that to me' is heard off camera.]

HELENA: I should go and check on her. She doesn't

sound OK.

[HELENA starts to rise.]

RUPERT: Don't, Nell. Just leave her. You'll only get caught in that harpy's talons.

[RUPERT stops her with a hand on her hand. He holds firm.]

HELENA: But what if she hurts herself?

RUPERT: It would be convenient for me.

HELENA: Rupert. Don't be awful. You owe her that. Just be kind when you break up with her.

RUPERT: If only it were that simple.

HELENA: I know, I know. The flat is full of Casper's detritus. How do you untangle two threads woven together? Without fraying the edges of the twine?

[RUPERT leans in and kisses her.]

Don't mock me. We're not eighteen any more. You can't do that and there be no repercussions.

[He kisses her again.]

RUPERT: Nell, I fucked it.

HELENA: Fucked what?

RUPERT: Everything.

[He kisses her again and she kisses him back. His

hand wanders, unbuttoning her shirt.]

When we get back to London, I'm taking you to dinner.

HELENA: Rupert, look . . . This isn't right. We can talk about whatever this could be back in London when you've done the right thing, but not now, not now. Not like this. Maybe I'll let you take me to dinner. Maybe. That's a lot of pride for me to swallow. It's cruel to both of us and I won't let you treat me like that anymore.

[HELENA stands up and tries to go back into the house, but RUPERT holds on to her arm and pulls her in to him, kissing her neck as she tries to break free. She fails. His grip on her arm tightens as he loses his grip on her heart. She asks him to stop. He doesn't. She pleads with him to stop. He doesn't. She begs him to stop. Of course, he doesn't. She pounds on his chest but that has the opposite effect. Defeated, she freezes, paralysed. RUPERT acts like the stories of old where gods begot heroes: he rapes her.]

[CLEMMIE stands at the door having heard the wounded pleas and watches it happen. Unflinching. Offering nothing but silent 'I told you so's and 'You can have him now's.]

41

Nell's flat

Nell picked up an exquisite, dusty orange peony from the blue-and-white vase on her dining room table. It was one of the flowers that Rupert sent yesterday. She couldn't bear to bin them. It wasn't their fault that Rupert was the one who had sent them. The vase was next to her laptop as she typed up her letter of resignation from Antigone Publishing. She needed change. She couldn't be bothered to write a letter with any particular flair and had found a template online. It was American, so she was adding the 'u's back in. Alex was making pancakes for brunch.

'We never ate pancakes in my house unless it was Pancake Day,' Nell said absentmindedly. 'One of those funny things my mom used to insist on. She refused to make them the rest of the year.'

'My mum used to make them every Sunday. Bananas and Nutella,' he said, flipping one theatrically. 'I forget that you're practically a Brummie, until you say things like "mom".'

'I'm not a Brummie. I'm from Warwickshire.' Nell attached her resignation letter to an email and sent it to Jonathan. 'I've got bananas but no Nutella. There is, however, crème fraîche, strawberries and raspberries in the fridge, if you are so inclined.'

'I am so inclined.' Alex rooted around the fridge for the strawberries, which he proceeded to slice.

'I don't want to go.'

Alex was rinsing the raspberries in the sink. 'Then why are you going?'

'I need a clean break.'

'These are finished,' Alex said, bringing over a plate of pan-cakes. He'd put the berries in a little dish.

'This looks delicious.' Nell moved her laptop out of the way and got up to fetch plates and cutlery. Nell was inordinately proud of her dishes. She'd collected a hodgepodge assortment of granny china from charity shops, naff spoils from package holidays and Anthropologie homeware going cheap in the sale.

'I'm thinking of buying a place once I start my new job. Would you ever consider moving in with me once I'm settled?'

Before Nell could reply, the doorbell rang. Nell went to answer it and opened the door to a laden-down courier. 'Hello.'

'Hi, Miss H. Waddingham?' the courier asked.

'Yes, that's me. What have I done now?'

'I . . .' The courier looked confused. 'I have a delivery for you?'

'Thanks. Shall I sign for it then?'

'Yes, it's this box and these,' he said, handing her another bunch of flowers and putting a large box on the welcome mat.

'Cheers.' Nell looked at the flowers. She went and put them in the sink as Alex picked up the substantial box and brought it into the room.

'How many bunches of flowers can one scrotum send?' Alex asked, looking over at the flowers. Both bunches were flashier than the ones he had bought her the other day.

'Has he sent the same bunch again? These are identical to yesterday's. They're pretty. Like a sunset.' Nell opened the card:

I'm very much looking forward to tonight.
A car will arrive at 7.15 p.m. Rx

'I wouldn't think too hard about it where he buys his flowers. What's in the box? It's not ticking, is it?'

Nell fetched a pair of scissors from a kitchen drawer and scored through the parcel tape to reveal a glut of gifts demonstrating Rupert's belief in his material entitlement to Nell. 'Geez, look at all this.' Nell pulled out a jewellery box with a diamond necklace in it. A smaller box contained the matching earrings. There was a bottle of perfume that he'd had made specifically for Nell, with her name on the bottle in Greek. There was an evening bag made from crocodile which she found repulsive. A pair of impossible heels. A tight Dior dress that she had seen in last month's *Vogue*. And worse. An accurately sized set of Agent Provocateur lingerie.

'He thinks you'll sleep with him.'

'Well, that's not going to happen.'

'Do expensive things make you happy?'

'No, of course not. I like wearing odd hats, buying cheap second-hand books and having pancakes made for me by very handsome men. Are you jealous?'

'Put the knickers on now. Then I'll take them straight off again.'

42

Farleigh's Auctioneers, Kensington

Matt was raging as he sat belligerently in the waiting area of Farleigh's Auctioneers. The ceiling was vaulted in that faux medieval style that attempts to lend modern buildings authority. The patterned carpet, the curtains and the ascot around the awful receptionist's neck were all Tyrian purple. He had walked in and shown her his badge and asked if he could please speak to whoever was in charge of Human Resources. She told him he needed to give her the name of the person he wanted to speak to for security reasons. He showed her his badge again. She said she needed a name. It went on like that for a good five minutes, and there he was sitting on a seat opposite her desk furiously googling the Head of HR so he could give the stupid cow a name as she was gabbling away on the phone.

'They're not talking any more because Frances was rude about people from Kent. And you know we all know that Kent is awful and all the people who live there are just awful, but that's where Sophia's boyfriend is from. He's quite awful.' She snorted at the end of her riveting anecdote.

'McIlroy, Roderick McIlroy. I want to speak to Roderick McIlroy.'

'I'm on the phone.'

'I'll charge you for obstruction of justice.'

'My uncle is a barrister.'

'My uncle is a dentist; I don't see how each of our uncles' professions is pertinent to this discussion.'

'He's on annual leave.'

'Someone else in his department then, please.'

'Give me a name.'

'Give me a break,' Matt said, pulling out a pair of handcuffs and slamming them on the reception desk.

'Security, security, help! This man is harassing me.' Two burly men who looked like ex-soldiers grimaced in solidarity with Matt as they slowly approached. 'Call the police.'

'I am the police,' Matt roared, showing the two security guards his badge.

'Excuse me, sir, so sorry. Is there a problem?' asked a man wearing tweed. Tweed. He was wearing all that heavy wool in June, and he was not perspiring. The awful receptionist rolled her eyes and went back to doing bugger all as the two security guards returned to their posts.

'Detective Sergeant Matthew Cheung. I want to speak to the most senior available person in your HR department. Would that be at all possible?' Matt showed him his badge.

'Roderick is in Amalfi so unfortunately I'm the best of the rest. Jeffrey Warde, how do you do? Would you like to come through?' Jeffrey shook Matt's hand. He was a tall man, ex-rugby player sort. His moustache was neat, and Matt admired his pocket square which complemented his tie perfectly – a sublime dissonance between colour and pattern.

'I would be delighted, thank you.'

'Let's play follow the leader,' Jeffrey said, taking Matt through a rabbit warren of industrial concrete passages that felt at odds with the reception's muted neo-Gothic form. 'It's quite ugly out back, isn't it? There's a certain brutal charm to its austere functionality, do you not think? You're lucky I'm in today. We're normally closed on Saturdays, but we have some hideous gala tonight, attendance at which is mandatory. Here we are,

welcome to Human Resources. I'll get us a pot of tea. Earl Grey?'
He pushed open the door to a small office with two desks in it.
Jeffrey ushered Matt to an empty seat in front of the first desk.

'Yes, please. Thank you for seeing me,' Matt said. The room
had a minuscule kitchenette with a kettle and microwave. One
wall was covered entirely in filing cabinets. There was a cricket
bat resting against the other desk, and he spotted a bottle of
whisky poking out from behind a leg.

'I cannot apologise profusely enough for Euphemia. Security
know to call me when she starts. That woman is wicked, and
I want her head on a spike. Her father is an earl, a drunk and
an inveterate gambler at that. Roderick hired that monster
because a higher up has had a tip-off that he's going to have
to sell the contents of the house to keep himself from jumping
off a multi-storey car park. The National Trust can't cover the
debt if they tried to buy the house outright, but a large Russian
hospitality conglomerate probably could – if His Grace can live
with the shame of losing the ancestral pile. They have a large
collection of Chinese ceramics and some exceptional paintings
from the Dutch Golden Age that, if sold, would tide him over for
a little while longer. It would only be putting off the inevitable
though.'

'You hired her so that you could sweep up the sale of her
father's estate.'

'Exactly. Milk?'

'No, thank you.'

'We shall have lemon instead,' Jeffrey said, bringing a tray
with a teapot and two cups and saucers over to the desk.

'As amusing as that was, why are you telling me this?'

'Because I need you to write a report of what just happened.
As soon as we get those Rembrandts in one of our auctions she's

fired. Did she say anything racist? Mime anything? I really need to build a compelling case. I cannot stress how much I hate that woman. She may be titled but she's not a lady.'

'Right, I will write that report for you, mostly because I am still thinking of arresting her.'

'Thank you. I'll get you a form to fill in. You can do it now if you like.'

'Can I scan it over? I am working on a pressing investigation right now.'

'Yes, of course, whenever is most convenient for you.' He reached over his desk and pulled out a business card. 'My email is here. I think the tea will be brewed by now. Tea tastes better from a cup than a mug. I'm sure of it. I'll be mother,' he said, peering into the teapot to judge the colour.

'May I ask you a few questions about a former colleague of yours?'

'Oh God, which one? Some of them are quite ghastly,' Jeffrey said, pouring Matt a cup of tea and then placing a thin slice of lemon on the saucer.

'Hereward Trollope-Bagshott.'

'Oh, HTB.'

'We've been calling him that at the station too.'

'What's he up to?'

'He's dead, I'm afraid.'

'Oh Lord, how?'

'We don't know exactly yet. What can you tell me about him?' Matt asked, picking up the cup. 'This is delicious. Where's it from?'

'Fortnum & Mason. HTB was old-school. A gentleman – could make small talk with a vase and the vase would leave thinking how charming it was.'

'He spoke to inanimate objects?'

'No. Maybe – everyone talks to things, don't they? I meant that he had what my mother would call "lovely manners". He made whomever he spoke to feel . . . wonderful, like you were the most thrilling person in the world. It's a talent.'

'How well did you know him?'

'Quite well. Loves his cricket. We'd go to the pub together with Roddy for the occasional snifter on a Friday. He'll be quite upset but I shan't ruin his holiday. It's so sad. HTB only just retired. He was moving out to Crete soon.'

'What did he do here?'

'He was in the Mediterranean Antiquities Department. I can see if they're free to come over and chat? They will all be attending the gala tonight too.'

'If you would be so kind.' Matt's mother was an Audrey Hepburn fan. Today he was feeling the benefit of having been made to watch that VHS of *My Fair Lady* so frequently in his childhood.

'Not at all. I will send a quick email now,' Jeffrey said, typing furiously.

'What was his role?'

'Oh, HTB was an expert, and Lord knows what they actually do.'

'I suppose they know things.'

'Sent. Indeed, ha.'

'Did he have any enemies?'

'No, of course not. He was one of those sorts who lived in his head. Loved a cryptic crossword and read Livy in the original for fun. Classicists are a funny breed. They live in a different age. He was always trekking up Cretan mountainsides hoping for a glimpse of the Minotaur on his holidays. That sort. Romantic in the non-sexual sense.'

'Did he have any problems outside work that he may have spoken to you of? Or any romantic attachments?'

'No, not at all, no problems. He has a sister out on the coast that he was a little fond of, but that was all of his personal life that I knew about. I would guess that he was one of those, gosh, I don't know how to explain this. He liked Oscar Wilde. He adored his mother, like Kenneth Williams, but never came to terms with it. One doesn't like to assume things about people, but I would guess that was the case.'

'I see. You think he was closeted?'

'Yes, that's the phrase. Different age. People couldn't be themselves like they can now. We have personnel files on everyone. I can photocopy his for you?' He went over to a filing cabinet and started looking through it.

'Yes, please.'

'I emailed D'Arville, De Courtnay and Bruin for you. I imagine they'll materialise at any time.' Jeffrey pulled a red folder out and took it over to the photocopier.

'Interesting names.'

'There are enough Normans in this building to recapture Hastings ten times over. I'm sorry if I haven't given you the information that you needed. From your line of questioning, am I to assume that HTB met an untimely end?'

'An official statement will be made in due course.'

'I understand.'

'Do you hire many classicists?'

'Yes, we do actually. Being frank, you have to go to the right sort of school to be taught Greek and it's easier to get into Oxbridge to read Classics than it is to do English, or History, or PPE. Although for antiquities we actually prefer archaeologists. Classicists will make speeches at you about Cicero – how long his sentences are and something about verbs – whereas archaeologists will point to a vase and give you an estimated date.'

'Those folders . . . how long do you keep them for?'

'Oh, these go back to the 1980s. That's probably not legal, thinking about it. I'll mention it to Roderick when he's back. Why do you ask?'

'Do you have folders on work experience students as well as full-time employees?'

'Yes, I should think so.'

Matt wrote down a list of names on a piece of paper. 'Could you tell me if any of these people have ever worked here?'

'Of course, I'll have a rummage,' Jeffrey said, taking the list from Matt's hand.

'This is a personal question, and you can not answer if you'd prefer, but why do you hate your job?'

'Ha, why do I hate my job? Is it that obvious? I must try harder. I took this job under duress thirty-odd years ago. My father made me; I used to be a bit of a champagne socialist. I went through a punk phase as a teenager and never really settled into anything after university. Scared the old boy. It has a good pension, that's reason enough to stick it out for another five years. The work isn't hard, and no one cares about HR because we aren't glamorous, so Roddy and I flap about listening to 5 Live, drinking tea and frequently something stronger after 4 p.m.'

There was a rap at the door. Jeffrey finished saying, 'Gird on your armour,' as three experts poured through the door like overly excitable spaniels. Two men: one late fifties and the other early thirties. The woman was in her late twenties.

'Jeffo. Our presence was requested,' said the petite, birdlike woman in a bright red dress and pearl earrings.

'Have you got any of the good biscuits left?' asked the ruddy-cheeked younger man wearing one of those fuddy, cream and blood-red check, country shooting shirts.

'Hello, I'm DS Matthew Cheung, I would like to ask you some questions about your former colleague Hereward Trollope-Bagshott,' Matt said, standing up and surveying them.

'Oh God, what's happened to the old blighter?' asked the older man.

'He's dead, Bert,' Jeffrey said, as he searched through the wall of filing cabinets.

'Such a shame. He had a terrible diet. He only really ate toast with strawberry jam. Heart attack? Bertram de Courtnay, how do you do. Head of the department. Here's my card.' Bertram shook hands with Matt vigorously. Weirdly strong grip.

'Daddy's friend karked it on the golf course the week after he left Standard Chartered. So sad, so sad. I'm Camilla Bruin. I was hired as his replacement. I only ever met him once, at my interview. May I leave?' she asked, or rather demanded. Not a shaker.

'Yes you may leave, Camilla,' Jeffrey said, dismissing her like a school master. She bounded out the room as she had bounded in.

'Hugo D'Arville,' said the third and final member of the Antiquities Department. 'That has made me melancholic.'

'Melancholic? You were fond of him?' Matt asked. The photocopier was whirring in the background.

'Very much. Used to lend me Cold War spy thrillers,' Hugo replied.

'He had a lot of books?'

'Oh, yes. Lived for them. Read everything and anything, didn't care for genre. Would have Dickens one day and *Bridget Jones's Diary* the next,' Bertram said. 'He read on his commute in all the way from the north. He used to get through three books a week.'

'Did he ever talk about his personal life to you?'

'No, not at all,' Hugo said, grimacing, 'it would've been rude to ask.'

'Do you know of any disagreements that he had with anyone?'

'No,' Bertram said.

'Romantic attachments?'

'Definitely not. None of that business. Wasn't that sort of gent.' Bertram shook his head from side to side.

'Is there anything else relevant that you can think of?'

'No,' Bertram said as Hugo chimed in with, 'Nothing at all.'

'Well, thank you, gentlemen, for your time,' Matt said.

'Righto. See you later, Jeffo.' Bertram left.

'Jeffo, can I take a biscuit with me?' Hugo asked.

'As you've had a shock you may, but may I remind you that these are not company biscuits. They are my biscuits and I pay for them out of my own pocket.' Jeffrey opened his desk drawer and took out a tin of shortbread. 'Just take one.'

'Thank you.' Hugo took a finger and ran away.

'Never marry your cousin. Would you like a biscuit, detective?'

'Yes, please.' Matt took a dainty finger from the tin. 'Is that lavender I can taste?'

'It is.'

'What a revelation.'

'Here's a copy of HTB's folder, and we have folders for two of the people on your list,' he said, handing over two extra sets of documents. 'I would like it on record that Farleigh's Auctioneers have been helpful in your investigation and, off the record, I hope that no undue attention is placed on the company.'

'Thank you for your co-operation.'

'And please, fill in that complaint form. Escalate the issue to your superior. Do you still want to arrest Euphemia? Anything you can do to help me get rid of that harpy.'

43

The Police Station

The gnomes in IT had unlocked Clemmie's phone that they had found at the gym and Caius was trawling through her conversations, not that he was supposed to be now that they were officially working on another case. He had entertained the idea that she had been blackmailing Rupert about the rape, but he couldn't find any evidence of it. Clemmie and Ned Osbald had carried out their affair the old-fashioned way, by calling each other. It probably helped that they were trapped together in a white cube for most of the week. No sexting, no blurry pictures sent at 3 a.m. After all that, the phone was useless. Caius had rung Hereward's sister and had a little chat with her. She hadn't said anything especially useful. Caius turned his attention to other murders over the last few years with the same cause of death. Only one came up, a young man called Yannis who had died under suspicious circumstances in his flat in Deptford very recently. Neck broken, a clumsily placed set of weights on top of the corpse as if he'd had an accident doing squats. Caius requested a copy of the case file. The officers investigating the death had closed it for a lack of leads. Yannis, Yannis. Why did that name feel familiar? It was the same MO as Hereward's murder. An inept contract killer perhaps?

Matt ran down the corridor yelling, 'Caius, Caius!'

Caius lifted his head. 'What have I done?'

'Thank God you're still here,' he said, wheezing.

'I don't have a personal life any more. This is my Saturday evening. I'm going to head off soon actually. Apparently I have

242

to take tomorrow off. An archaeologist from the British Museum is coming in at 10 a.m. to look at the head and I told her to ask for you. You should get checked out for asthma. You've wheezed a lot today. It's a serious condition and London is very polluted.'

'I'm just unfit. Fay Bruce. She lied to you.'

'What do you mean, she lied to me? About what?'

'She said she couldn't remember how Clemmie got the job. She lied by omission.'

'Can you prove it?'

'Oh yes. While I was interviewing Hereward's colleagues at the auctioneer's, the guy in HR photocopied his personnel file.' Matt pulled out photocopies of three personnel folders and put them on Caius's desk. 'The HR guy said that they had paper records going back to the 1980s on all staff in the cabinets and that they hire a lot of classicists because they're all posh and well connected.'

'Right, and?'

'I gave him the names of the three classicists and the one art historian involved, however loosely, in Clemmie's life – Nell, Alex, Rupert and Fay. Fay Bruce moonlights there as an outside expert if they need extra clarification on an item; dating mostly but sometimes provenance tracing. She's on a retainer. Clemmie and Hereward's murders might be connected.'

'We have a substantial connection between Fay and Hereward. But where does Rupert Beauchamp come into this?'

Matt opened Rupert's folder and put it in front of Caius. 'Rupert did three weeks' work experience in 2010 in the Mediterranean Antiquities Department with Hereward. He got the internship because his godmother, Fay Bruce, pulled some strings. She's known him his whole life. We have two murders that are connected through both Fay and Rupert.

Between them they could have set Ned up after Rupert killed Clemmie. It would suit them both. They'd both get rid of unwanted partners.'

'Fuck!' Caius fell back into his chair, having just remembered where he'd heard of a Yannis recently. He opened a folder on his desk and took out the record of Clemmie's gym attendance that Kamal had printed for him. 'We have three murders actually: Kamal, the manager at Clemmie's gym, said that she used to train with a guy called Yan. Same cause of death as Hereward – some weights he'd been lifting at home fell on him and unconvincingly broke his neck.'

'And another terrible attempt at hiding it.'

'Before we go into the Chief's office and have that conversation, we need to get as many facts straight about this as we can. What do we know?' Caius asked.

'Fay Bruce perverted the course of justice.'

'Yes, why?'

'Because she did it. She killed Clemmie.'

'Did she strike you as capable of the crime?'

'No, but people are surprising like that.'

'This is all supposition. What are the facts? Fay Bruce didn't admit to being Rupert's godmother. Rupert, fuck, I haven't told you. Amy had another look through the Greece pictures this afternoon and found a video at the end of the file. Rupert raped Nell Waddingham on the Greece holiday and Clemmie filmed it.'

'He raped her?'

'I've left a voicemail asking Nell to come in on Monday. I wanted to talk to her face to face before I do anything.'

'Did you get a call from Errol's contact at the NCA?'

'Not yet.' Caius stood up and started mapping his thoughts on the incident room whiteboard. 'We have three bodies: Rupert's girlfriend who filmed him raping a girl, the girlfriend's personal trainer who worked at a gym that is probably a drug front so big that the NCA had to hand it over to MI6 – which means there's a national security angle that we don't know about yet – and an old gent who worked with Rupert's godmother, who denies knowing her godson, and with whom Rupert did work experience a decade ago. The last two murders were by the same person. To make it weirder, the old gent kept the decapitated head of a statue in a bucket in his empty flat.'

'Don't forget that the girlfriend's middle-aged boss-slash-baby daddy is married to the godmother and claims to have killed her but is weirdly fuzzy about quite significant details like how they got to the Heath that day.'

'We haven't found Clemmie's gym clothes yet. They should've been at the house with the other evidence, which felt as planted as that fucking potted foxglove in the garden. Who would be stupid enough to buy a plant for that specific purpose and leave it there? This whole investigation is about wealth, isn't it? Ridiculous gyms, art galleries, auction houses. The damned Help for Hippos party drug. Where does all the money go? Matt, trawl through Ned Osbald's bank statements. Look into the gallery's finances. The whole lot. I am not arresting Rupert or Fay until I can prove to the grand pooh-bahh that Ned definitely didn't do it.'

★ ★ ★

Fay Bruce's website was grey. Helvetica. It was smooth and off-putting. Tasteful by virtue of its lack of boldness. No colours. She was clearly the one who'd decorated the house. Caius loved the internet. We give so much of ourselves to it that it's not difficult for someone to find out the minutiae of our lives – a list of every academic article that Fay had ever written, recordings of public lectures on the sublime and every exhibition that Fay had curated for the last twenty years. Including an exhibition at the National Museum of Contemporary Art in Athens exploring images of motherhood over the last three thousand years, which opened the same day that Rupert, Clemmie and Nell flew into Athens. Caius remembered the gimmicky magnet of the Parthenon on Hereward's fridge.

★ ★ ★

Caius was chewing on a slice of pizza and over the day's revelations. 'Rupert Beauchamp, unlike everyone else his age, doesn't have Facebook or Twitter. There's no blog, no Instagram and no LinkedIn any more as he's deleted it recently. He wants to be a ghost.'

Matt dipped his pizza crust in a pot of oily garlic dip. 'He's a topsy-turvy person – dinner parties in McDonald's . . . So, Fay was in Athens at the same time as the others?'

'Yeah. What if Rupert arranged the holiday as a pretence?' Caius asked, as he started googling recent art thefts. 'There's an article here in the *Guardian* from a couple of months ago about Roman ruins in war zones and how local militias are looting art from the sites to purchase arms.'

'That makes it a national security threat, I suppose,' Matt said, clicking on the link to the article that Caius had just sent to him.

'Exactly. It would have to be something big for MI6 to be sniffing around. It says here that London auction houses act, knowingly or not, as clearing houses.'

'That could explain Hereward's role, I guess.'

'What if historical sites all over the Mediterranean are being looted too? Not just ones in war zones. Lots of those pictures of Clemmie were at ancient ruins. The sightseeing was a cover.'

'And Fay's there at the same time doing the same thing. Giving Rupert a second opinion maybe?'

'I doubt Nell Waddingham was involved.' Caius wanted that to be true. 'I don't know how we can prove any of this without either an extensive paper trail, which I doubt exists, or either Fay or Rupert confessing. Tea?'

★ ★ ★

It had gone 9 p.m. and it was too late in the day for Caius to be drinking proper tea, and not something herbal, but he thought he was going to be in the incident room for a few more hours. He'd even added a cheeky teaspoon of sugar. He could feel it clinging to his teeth as Matt showed him what he'd found.

'I had a look through Companies House and Ned Osbald is listed as a Company Director of the Hesperides Gallery, but the owner is the Halcyon Age Corporation which is listed in Delaware in the US,' Matt said, showing Caius the webpage. 'The gym that Clemmie went to, and where Yan worked, is also listed to a shell company in Delaware, as are the pub near the gallery and the hairdresser's.'

'Delaware became the money-laundering capital of the western world after Cyprus cracked down on it after the 2008 crash. You can filter the money back into the City from there via the Caymans and no one would notice. Is there any more information on the Halcyon Age Corporation?'

'No, there's just a registered address, which is probably a post box. Not even a website.'

Matt had just returned from the twenty-four-hour Tesco round the corner with a bumper family packet of chocolate Hobnobs, a packet each of strawberry laces, a six-pack of Coke and the vague feeling that they were making progress. It was late enough that the only people in there other than the staff had been himself and a group of pissed students.

Caius flicked through the camera roll on his phone, searching for the splotched painting that was in the window of the Hesperides Gallery. 'What does this look like to you?' he asked, showing Matt the picture.

'Like a child did it, but that's contemporary art, right? I'm not supposed to understand it.'

The next picture was the description, artist's name, medium and year. 'Naomi Eve Tyson is the artist. Oh, piss off – "naivety". It's not a real person, just a dad joke.'

'What, like Banksy?'

'No, think about it. Art galleries can charge what they like for a piece of work. The value of which is determined not by the materials involved but by its perceived value. The gallery sets the price. The art isn't what's being sold.'

'It's a money-laundering exercise.'

'You could shift anything illegal under the guise of a terrible Jackson Pollock knock-off. Contemporary art can be anything. Kamal, the gym manager, told Amy that the smoothie bar was cash only. A gym could charge you ten pounds for a matcha shot or sixty pounds cash for a "massage" and no one would bat an eyelid.'

'It's another cover?'

'It's conveniently located for their posho clientele. Kamal felt like a straight shooter. I bet that the drugs are being sold through the smoothie bar or the personal trainers. They're probably all freelance and do private sessions for their most wealthy clients at home.'

'And the salon?'

'A salon could claim to have three more blow-dries a day that never happened. You get a cut on Friday afternoon, pay extra for "styling". How did I miss it? What's Ned Osbald's role?'

'He's on there as the Director. He's being paid a salary to be the public face. He's a pawn. Why was Clemmie working there?'

'It's a status job for her. Keeps her out of the house so Rupert can carry on as he likes with other women. It gives Clemmie the semblance of being independent of Rupert, but she had to be in on it. Or perhaps she wasn't? Perhaps she found out about the drugs and was going to blow the whistle, and that's why he killed her? But then again, she was going to that hairdresser's for some reason other than how well they did her highlights.' Caius played with the ring pull of his can of Coke Zero. 'Halcyon. I read about her in Ovid. Alcyone was an Ancient Greek queen who, along with her husband, angered Zeus for blasphemy. They were transformed into kingfishers. The gym was called Herculean Gyms, right? The pub was The Grapes, the symbol of Dionysus. Cythera – sounds Greek to me. The Hesperides Gallery . . .'

'What sort of person names their shady money-laundering operations after figures from Greek mythology?'

'A pretentious dick with an Ancient History degree: Rupert Beauchamp. It's got to be him. Drug trafficking goes hand in hand with art smuggling. They grow poppies next to Roman ruins in Syria. Help for Hippos is probably just the bougie end of the business. Yannis, who worked on the drug side, was murdered in the same way as Hereward . . .'

'Who works on the art-smuggling side.'

'He was probably putting through trafficked items as legitimate sales. Faking the authenticity checks the auction house must have. Even smuggling art himself?'

'His colleague said that he was always in Crete searching for the Minotaur,' Matt said, remembering the lavender biscuits that Jeffrey had. 'What about that statue head in the mop bucket? It's legit?'

'Is it reason enough to kill a man? It looks tacky to me. He might have been skimming off the top to save for his retirement – to buy that second home. There must be proof of his involvement somewhere. If you were moving to another country, what would you do with your belongings?'

'I'd donate them to charity and put some stuff in storage. He was letting out the flat, not selling it. He probably meant to come back at some point. Didn't want to be in a country where he didn't have family when his health started to fail?'

'IT said that they'd get the iPad to us tomorrow. Hereward would've been sent an email confirmation if he's rented a storage space, which could be why he hid the iPad. He didn't want them to find his stash. Check it out. See if you can find the rest of his things. Have a look at his financial records. I'm going to take tomorrow morning off, but I will come in after lunch. I need to sleep in.'

'If Ned didn't kill Clemmie, then who did?'

'Fay could've killed Clemmie because she ruined her marriage. Maybe the open relationship thing is true – it works perfectly for a lot of people, but maybe it didn't work out for her in the way she thought it would. Babies complicate things. Full of indignant fury like Hera. Righteous and riotous misplaced rage.'

'You've really taken to Ovid, haven't you?'

'I resent my state school education. Fay doesn't strike me as capable; she's a mannered, manicured art historian. Rupert, however. Rupert would kill Clemmie because he wants to be with Nell and Clemmie knows far too much about what he does. Imagine what he'd do if he knew that she had that footage.'

'I bet he could've bought her a villa in Ibiza and been done with her.'

'No, he couldn't shake her. She wanted the title and the manor house. Or even worse, she was in love with him. It must be him. Rupert probably told Ned that Fay did it. Then all Rupert had to do was plant the evidence at his house when Fay was out. Ned felt guilty and said he murdered Clemmie to spare his wife a prison sentence.'

'How gallant,' Matt said, yawning as both clock hands crept up to greet midnight and his bed beckoned.

44

A private hire car

Nell was in the back of an oversized Mercedes that smelled more delightful than any taxi she'd ever been driven in before. Vanilla, maybe. She was wearing all of the clothes that Rupert had purchased for her – she couldn't help herself. He knew her shoe size, her cup size. She smelled her wrist – perhaps it was her that smelled of vanilla. Vanilla and naivety. Or was that fear she could smell, sickly and cloying? Sticking to the back of her throat. It was strong. Eau de parfum, of course. Rupert would never buy eau de toilette. The vanilla would mask the stench of her dread. Her shoes cost more than three times the rent she paid to Casper every month. Damn Casper. Damn Rupert. Damn Jonathan. Damn Alex. Damn the driver. Damn them all. The car's windows were tinted, and people stared as it swam through Embankment like a tiger shark in the shallows. The box of perfume had had a sticker on the bottom with the day that the perfumery had been commissioned to make Ἑλένη. It was the day after Casper had dumped her. Rupert had ordered it months ago. What game was being played? For the rules were unbeknownst to her. She smelled her wrist. Vanilla. It was definitely her that smelled of vanilla.

★ ★ ★

Mycenaean History was where the three of them met, became the worst of friends and the best of enemies, and fell horribly in love with each other.

Nell always sat in the front row of her lectures. She needed to see the spittle flecks from the mouths of professors when they aspirated, to smell the instant coffee on their breath, for it to be real.

Alex sat next to her because she was the only real girl in the class – there were other girls, but they were afflicted with moustaches, unsightly ankles and the fatal disfigurement of not being Nell.

Rupert sat next to Nell because an aggressively mediocre gang of hungover fourth-rate Etonians always got there early so they could have the back row, like little boys on a school coach trip to a museum. Besides, Nell was a girl. A girl who kept immaculate notes that he could borrow and who smelled like vanilla. A girl whose skirt rode up when she wriggled in her seat and he could see the tops of her stockings. Nell wore stockings and suspenders like it was the fifties. Her handwriting was cursive. Nell quoted Sylvia Plath and smoked cigarettes, but only when she'd had a few. She smoked when she was drunk, because drinking made her think of death and when you think about death sometimes you want it, whether you know it or not. Nell drank Scotch. Nell drank port. Nell's family were the wrong sort, you know, and he couldn't go out with her. Not properly anyway, and that hurt him. It hurt that he was a coward.

Alex and Rupert were both tall. Over six foot. Pious College Boat Club never won a damned race. They were both drafted in to boost the Boat Club's chances by virtue of the lengths of their arms. Neither of them complained. The way they looked in lycra all-in-ones, what it did for their biceps, and how the girls admired them, made it worth it. The Boat Club continued not winning a damned thing. No one minded: the boathouse was for drinking more than anything. The boys competed with each other – romantically, athletically and in the bacchanals. They were a little in love and in hate with each other.

Rupert would be cruel to innocent girls. Good girls, with prospects and solid A Levels. Girls who had featured on the front page of the local newspaper jumping while holding their results only a few months before in August. Good girls whose mothers had cut that article out and put it on the fridge with pride. He'd never call them back. He'd leave them with little butterfly bruises and gaping holes in their chests where their hearts used to be. Or worse. He'd keep their underwear under his bed. Then once a month on the first night of the full moon he'd slyly throw them all into his metal wastepaper bin, go to the college car park on his own and burn them in honour of both Aphrodite and Artemis. He'd drink a Scotch in each of the goddesses' honour – one in triumph and the other in commiseration. He'd take Nell to dinner every Wednesday night. He'd insist that he paid. Every week would be a different restaurant. He said it was an anthropological study; she said it was delicious. They both agreed that the best restaurant in the city was the tiny Italian around the corner. He still hadn't kissed her. He couldn't. He didn't know why, but he couldn't. He couldn't take her to parties. He didn't know why, but he couldn't. He couldn't let anyone know that she existed. They too would want her, as he knew Alex did. Damn Alex and Mycenaean History. Rupert took Clemmie to their little Italian, and he didn't think Nell would ever forgive him for it. Clemmie would take his mind off Nell. She wasn't unattractive. She'd do, for now.

Alex's room was next to Nell's, and he knew that they were mirror images, and that were it not for the wall they could touch each other as they lay in bed. Alex would pace up and down every Wednesday in case he had to hear it, but he never did, and

254

he never understood why. Once he had the courage to ask Nell for a coffee. They went; she drank tea. Asking someone out for tea sounds tragic; asking them out for coffee is cosmopolitan, as sophisticated as an eighteen-year-old can be. Nell didn't get the subtext. Being taken for dinner once a week had ruined her. She thought that was just what Oxford boys did: they took you out, fed and watered you and then released you back into the wild with never a kiss. Alex considered knocking on Nell's door naked once. If it worked it worked, if it didn't in ten years' time it would be a good story, but Alex wasn't brave. He decided to continue just sitting next to Nell, whose hair smelled like vanilla, in Mycenaean History, and stare at the tops of her stockings like he'd caught Rupert doing. That first year was a cold war. The disastrous second year was like Napoleon invading Russia complete with snowstorms, cannon fire and cavalry charges. The third and final year was trench warfare. Alex narrowly edged it through the barbed wire of no-man's land.

★   ★   ★

Girls whose knickers were lost to the fires: Jessica P, Jessica H, Jessica L, Naomi, Nisha, Naia, Maya, Harriet, Henrietta, Hannah, Anna, Annie, Amelia, Alice, Alexa, Arabella, Aphra, Araminta, Isobel, Isabel, Isabella, Emily (twice, he'd forgot that they'd met before until she reminded him, reprimanded him), Elspeth, Elizabeth, Lizzie, Lexi, Leigh, Charlie, Charlotte, Cleo, Clara, Chloe, Florence, Flora, Nora, Pandora, Penelope, Jayne, Janey, Jennifer, Viktoria, Stella, Laura, Lara, Sara, Zara, Tara, Tamara, Natalia, Natasha, Zelda, Adelaide, Catherine, Katharine, Kathryn, Kate, Cate, Kat, Georgie, Georgia, Georgina, Georgiana, Ginny and Virginia (these were the ones Rupert could remember; there were more).

The Mercedes pulled up in front of a building that must once have been a tram shed. It was tucked away in a mews off the main road. It was private. There were no buses running past every five minutes. There was no corner shop opposite. The driver opened the door for Nell, and she got out. He hadn't said a word to her all the way from Hackney. She assumed that he had been told not to speak to her. The street was cobbled, and her ankle twisted as she walked up to the bright red, barn-like doors. The restaurant was empty. There had to be a hundred seats and only one of them was filled. There was a sign on the door that said: *Closed for a private function*. The walls were exposed brick, and the artwork was suitably forgettable. The maître d' greeted Nell and showed her to their table. Rupert got up, kissed her on the cheek and moved her chair for her. He was wearing a jacket that fitted him impossibly well. Nell caught a glimpse of the lining: azure silk with dragons woven into the pattern.

The wine waiter appeared with a bottle of Bollinger. 'Champagne, madame.'

'Yes, thank you,' Nell said pointlessly – he'd practically poured it before the words had left his mouth. He must have been under orders to get her drunk. The waiter poured a more restrained glass for Rupert.

'Thank you,' Rupert said as the waiter scuttled back into the kitchen. The maître d' had also disappeared, so that they'd be left together in a ghost ship of a restaurant. 'Cheers.'

'I suppose I should call you Sir Rupert now.'

'You know I'm not one for ceremony amongst friends.'

'We're not friends any more.'

'I want to be more than a friend to you.'

'I was sorry to hear about your grandfather.'

'I wasn't. Can't believe the old git took so long to go.'

'Clemmie's funeral is on Wednesday, right?'

'It is. It's at the Brompton Oratory at 11 a.m. I haven't got round to thinking of my grandfather's funeral yet.'

'I'll be there on Wednesday.'

'I don't know whether to go. I'll probably just sit at the back and join in on the chorus of "Jerusalem". I don't especially fancy developing a public reputation as a cuckold.'

'I suppose.'

'Clem really liked you, you know.'

'Phlegm despised me.'

'She was jealous, but it doesn't mean she didn't like you. She was a bit obsessed with you, actually. Used to stalk your Instagram. She'd buy anything if she thought you had it. She just knew, well, you know.'

'No. Knew what?'

'Clemmie was unnatural. A lot of unnecessary energy went into that artifice. Whereas you exist on your own terms. You're one of Plato's ideal forms. You're not real, you're from a novel, a dream. A woman made of cloud: an εἴδωλον. I was going to break up with her when we got back from Athens. I promise you I was.'

'It really doesn't matter.'

'It does matter.'

'You've been telling me that you were going to break up with her since 2010. I don't take anything you say seriously.'

'My intentions were honourable . . .'

'Your intentions? Rupert, fucking hell, you have never had an honest intention when it comes to me.' Nell stood up to leave, but sly shame made her stand still. Alex had asked her not to go, she'd sort of said she wouldn't, but not in such a way that

257

she'd felt like she'd lied to him. She sat back down, screwed her eyes tight for a moment to terrify any tears that had had the audacity to form, and picked up the menu in front of her. It was composed of all their favourite things from their Wednesday Oxford feasts. Nell had wondered how he'd managed to book an entire restaurant at such short notice, but then she realised that he must own it. He'd opened a restaurant that only sold her favourite food. 'Is there any point in me looking at this menu or have you ordered already?'

'It's just there for reference.'

Nell put the menu down on the table. 'Why couldn't you give me up? I've been giving you up constantly since that night in college when you threw up luminescent snakebite everywhere and ruined the rug in my room.'

'You've never given up on me,' Rupert said. Nell did not respond. 'You look beautiful.'

'Of course I do, Zeus fashioned me from a cloud.'

'My grandfather would've disinherited me.'

'No, he wouldn't, he quite liked me. That's a lie you've told yourself. You snob. You don't live in a Dickens novel, Rupert. Besides, judging by this restaurant that apparently you own, you seem to have done quite well for yourself over the last few years without access to the family Coutts account.'

'I've worked very hard to be independent, not to be haunted by the ghost of my ancestry. I'm sorry. I just, I just got stuck with Clemmie and I couldn't get rid of her in the end. God knows I tried; other men were interested in her. I even threw her in the path of my godmother's hound of a husband. I thought if she was in love with someone else that might do it. You know? If she thought she had options other than being the millstone around my neck, then she might finally fuck off. I said I'd buy her a villa in Ibiza if she'd go. I tried offering her a fucking pension like I was Charles II. We hadn't had sex in two years.'

'You coward.'

'That's not a totally unfair comment. I admit that I scared off your boyfriends every now and then when they got serious. I'm not proud of that, but in my defence, Casper was clearly in love with what's-his-name. I just had to pay him to go to Bristol for a year. I sent that other one backpacking across Australia. I'm telling you all this now, so we can start afresh. I don't want this to boomerang back on me.'

'My God. All of this is because you didn't have the nerve to veer ever so slightly from social convention when you were nineteen.'

'I'm not a coward. I just don't know how to be loved.'

'Clemmie's barely cold, Rupert. Do you think she'd be dead if you'd left her in the club you found her in that first night?'

'I wanted you to come so I could apologise about what I did in Greece.'

'I hate you, despise you, loathe you, but for my own sanity I'd like to pretend it never happened, at least for a little while longer before I have to . . .'

'Good, we're agreed it never happened then. It wasn't that bad. Barely anything. Just a one-night stand.'

The kitchen door creaked slightly when it swung open, as the waiter came out with heritage tomato bruschetta with aubergine caviar, and plates of ricotta and Parma ham with grilled peaches in a balsamic reduction. The wine waiter then appeared and filled a glass with a Sancerre before retreating to the kitchen.

'Ask me the question, I can see you're thinking it,' Rupert said, picking up his wine glass.

'Did you kill Clemmie?'

'No, I didn't.'

'But it works for you.'

'It works for us.'

'I've got to give a statement on Monday.'

'Do you know what about?'

'I'm assuming it's about your dead girlfriend.'

'Do you believe me?'

'I don't know what to believe.'

'Clemmie was pregnant, and it wasn't mine. I would've been rid of her finally.'

'That handsome detective came to my work.'

'What did you talk about?' Rupert didn't like the word 'handsome' being applied to that dolt.

'Jane Austen, mostly.'

'Really? You can turn any conversation to one about spinsters.'

'These peaches are delicious,' Nell said, taking a bite. It infuriated her that the food was edible. She was starving.

'I know about Alex.'

'Of course you know.'

'I hope he won't be sticking around.'

'I doubt he will once he realises how fucked up this all really is. Alex is a nice guy, he can do better. The sex is fun though. He's improved since university, he's had practice. You did know that, didn't you? That we'd slept together?'

'How's work?' Rupert ignored that last part.

'I've handed my notice in.'

'I thought you liked it? With the jolly man who talks about *Cats* all the time.'

'I used to. Got a bit bored. It's repetitive. Reading shit poetry every day makes you abysmally miserable.'

'What are you going to do instead?'

'I'm not sure. Maybe try and get a job in a busier publisher, keep on writing, do an MA in Journalism, or should I get down to that PhD finally? Something will happen.'

'You can start your own publishing house. I could set you up. You could specialise in novels by sexless spinsters? Start a cult magazine? Write angry feminist articles about blow jobs and racism?'

'How would you help me set up a publishing house?'

'I have my own money. I also know some people. It doesn't matter who, but they like to think of themselves as patrons of the arts. I could get you the funding.'

'Did they help you set up this restaurant?'

'No, I came into money from my mother's estate when I turned twenty-one. I use that for all my passion projects. We could open a little bookshop. Get you a fat tabby cat who sits on the till. You'd like that.'

'Whatever happened to that novel you were going to write, Rupert? The one that was going to define our generation.'

'I got distracted.'

'Eight years and I still haven't seen a full draft.'

The door creaked, and their empty plates were removed. Red wine was served. Malbec to go with the Chateaubriand that followed it out from the kitchen.

'Why are you not drinking?'

'I've taken up running,' Nell said, pouring herself a glass of water. 'Drink mine.'

'You're not a runner. You're not built for it.'

'I am now. I signed up for a 10k for Cancer Research in the autumn. I'm nearly thirty – I can't keep eating chips and hope my waist stays slim through God's will alone.'

'It's bad for the knees. You should try to gain muscle instead. That's what affects the metabolism.'

'I really should just stop going out for dinner. That would cut the calories.'

'Nell, you're above all that macro/micro-nutrient nonsense.'

'I'm really not. I'm just good at pretending that I'm cool. That I'm down for anything. How can you complain about Clemmie being a fraud, a fake femme fatale, when really you're complaining about having the privilege to see behind it all? You like to eat your steaks free from thoughts of the abattoir.'

'I wasn't allowed to break up with her. It got complicated by Clemmie's involvement in a, um . . . well. I can't explain the mess I'm in right now.'

'What do you mean, you weren't allowed?'

'Helena, will you marry me?'

'What mess? Rupert, are you in with a bad crowd?'

'Nothing. Forget I said anything, please.'

'What's for pudding?'

'Tiramisu.'

'I hate you. You know it's my favourite.'

'It's a nice ring.'

'She's not cold, Rupert. They haven't even buried her.'

'Think on it. It doesn't have to be a big wedding. We can just go to the registry office on the King's Road and put an announcement in *The Times* afterwards.'

'What about all the other girls?'

'What about them? There are no other girls. I promise you. It's only ever been you.'

★ ★ ★

The driver was used to this sort of thing working for Mr Beauchamp, but he had to turn the radio up to unprecedented levels. The young lady had seemed so quiet, so serious, on the way over, but she was really laying into him. She looked too polite to know so many expletives.

SUNDAY

45

Caius's flat

It was 5 a.m. and Caius had forgone his lie-in. A flexible American woman was talking him through the downward dog in his living room. YouTube yoga was a radical, revolutionary concept to him. Sod having to go to an expensive, judgemental studio; he just turned the heating up, put a woolly jumper on and streamed it through the television. He'd brought the judgemental gnome inside to motivate him.

Tread those feet. Don't think about the smell.

Feel the flex in your abductors. Don't think about the brown puddle that soaked through the living room rug and into the flat below.

Some of you might feel a tugging in your calves. Don't think about his floppy neck, his head pointing in the wrong direction.

Walk your hands backwards slowly until your legs are in a standing position and your neck and arms are hanging loose. Don't think about the foot poking out under the scrub.

Relax those arms. Don't think about Clemmie's unborn child.

Don't forget to breathe. Don't think about her mother and her father.

Breathe into your lower back. Don't think about how the blood around her neck looked like a delicate, lace choker.

Feel those shoulders release. Roll back up vertebra by vertebra. Don't think about Nell reading *Persuasion*. Don't think about the hideous joke you made about Rupert being a rapey swan. Don't think about the video. Don't think about the noise. Don't think about the moment when she stopped struggling and froze. Don't think about the lack of noise. Don't think of Clemmie standing at the door watching. Just watching. Don't think about the size of her eyes, wild with hate. Don't think about the video.

★ ★ ★

A prison guard escorted Ned Osbald into the room. He sat at the table opposite Caius. He didn't want to be there. He looked terrible.

'The food here isn't great, is it,' Caius said. Ned wouldn't look at him. 'I would've opened with a remark about the weather but that doesn't feel right with you locked up.'

Ned did not respond.

'I don't think you killed Clemmie. I think you've decided to take the fall for someone else. Probably because you felt guilty. You thought that your affair was likely the reason she was killed. Did Rupert tell you that your wife was the killer? You confessed to the crime to spare Fay. I mean, she wouldn't have killed Clemmie if you hadn't been having an affair with her. How very gallant of you. How very foolish.' Caius saw his jawline tense. 'He's a rapist. We can prove it. I dread to think what Clemmie suffered all those years. I bet she confided in you. Told you about the times when he was too rough. Told you about when she'd said no but he hadn't heard it. Did Clemmie ever come into work with bruises? I bet she cried at her desk quite a lot. He probably cheated on her constantly. Put other women on a pedestal. Made her feel worthless. Ridiculed her.'

Ned stared at a spot on the wall just above Caius's left shoulder. Caius could see his face turn more and more puce.

'Do you think this is the best way to honour Clemmie's

memory? To let her killer walk free. To let Rupert off the hook.'

'Don't you dare talk about Clemmie.'

'You loved her.'

'Of course I bloody loved her. I didn't know about the baby. I didn't know. I swear I didn't know.'

'I believe you.' Caius took a sip of water from a plastic cup. 'How did Rupert do it?'

Ned went back to staring at the spot.

'We know about Rupert's drug empire. We know he smuggles art.'

Ned laughed. 'That coked-up little shit can just about organise a fuck in a whorehouse. He's nothing more than a poxy middle-man. A petulant little boy who they all indulge.' Ned stood up from the table. 'I want my lawyer. I want my lawyer.'

46

The Police Station

Two slices of toast (white bread) with butter. That was it. Matt wasn't risking anything more interesting for breakfast today. A mug of tea with two sugars. Maybe a banana if he was feeling up to it. Perhaps a Lucozade if his stomach felt dodgy thinking about the smell. Definitely no omelettes. He wasn't ready to watch the video that Amy had found yesterday. There wasn't enough Lucozade in Britain to settle a stomach after that.

IT had got into Hereward's iPad and Matt was looking through his emails. There was nothing suggesting any illegal activity thus far. Hereward had donated books to the Oxfam in Islington using gift aid and had had a confirmation email. Matt had a delightful call with Doreen, one of their volunteers, who had put them aside for him to collect later that day. They were all still boxed up at the back, apparently. Hereward had made enquiries at three different storage units asking for quotes in the last month, but there was no email confirmation of him having taken out a unit. The one closest to Hereward's flat was the most expensive and the one furthest away was the cheapest. Convenience or price? Or would he split the difference and go for the third option? This was like one of those maths problems that his mum shared on Facebook. One of Hereward's neighbours had reported that they'd seen him having furniture and things loaded into a white van the previous Saturday morning. He was going to have to go to all three of them after the archaeologist arrived.

'You look less like an archaeologist than I thought you would,' Matt said to Dr Roberts, the specialist from the British Museum. She had a lot of tattoos and a huge silver ring through her nose like a bull.

'What do archaeologists look like?' Dr Roberts asked.

'I don't know, a cross between Indiana Jones and Charlie Dimmock.'

'Charlie Dimmock is a gardener, not an archaeologist.'

'I know, but she wears shorts and sturdy boots to scramble around in dirt.'

'I don't scramble around the dirt much any more.'

'Sorry, just trying to make conversation.'

'Chatter away. I tend to mostly do lab stuff now. It's nice to speak to a person.'

'Would you like a cup of tea?'

'Yes, please.'

'I'll get someone to bring the head in,' Matt said, leaving her in the room. He went to the kitchen and boiled the kettle. He had spent all of last night thinking about that lavender shortbread at the auction house. Tea made, he went back to give it to Indiana Dimmock, who had since received the head from evidence and was crying.

'Are you all right?' Matt asked, putting the tea down.

'Yes.'

'Why are you crying?'

'Where did you find it?'

'In a mop bucket.'

'I didn't think I'd ever get to see anything like this in my lifetime.'

'But it's creepy. Like your nana's garden gnome went a bit wrong. Did you ever have those paint a plaster-cast animal craft sets when you were a kid? I had a giraffe. It's like one of them.'

★ ★ ★

Caius came into the office to find Matt arranging rich tea biscuits in a fan formation on the one nice plate in the kitchen. There were eight cups of tea brewing on the side.

'Matt, *mon petit chou*. Are your aunties visiting?'

'You're here, *meine Kartoffel*!'

'Did the archaeologist come?'

'She's still here.'

'Why?'

'She saw the head and cried. Then she called another archaeologist, who called another, and they then multiplied by a factor of six. It's worth murdering over. Carry the biscuits through?' Matt asked.

★ ★ ★

'I think we should chuck the archaeologists out,' Caius said, closing the door swiftly behind him as if it contained a rabid Rottweiler.

'You're paid more than me,' Matt said.

★ ★ ★

Caius and Matt were standing in the grand pooh-bahh's office looking sheepish.

'Sir, we can't get rid of the archaeologists. I think you might have to threaten them,' Caius said.

'They're academics, Caius. Respected members of society with standing and position. I'm not threatening them, they're not used to that sort of thing. They're used to libraries and lecture halls.'

'They're feral, and they are refusing to leave. That mop bucket head is likely to be why Hereward Trollope-Bagshott was killed and they've gone gaga over it.'

'That's something.' The grand pooh-bahh leaned in close to Caius. Their conversation earlier that week had niggled him. He hadn't been a bad detective in his youth. 'I've been thinking about what you said about Osbald, and I thought I'd check with my daughter whether she took any sneaky pictures of the party. She's on holiday trekking in Nepal. She's probably halfway up a mountain by now, but I'll let you know if I hear anything. Right, I'll ask the archaeologists to leave. I'm sure they will respect my rank.'

★   ★   ★

Caius and Matt stood in the corridor waiting for the Chief Superintendent to reappear. The door finally creaked open, and he backed out slowly before gently shutting the door.

'Caius, get the riot gear.'

47

U-Lock-Up

Matt pulled up outside the last of the three storage units. Hereward went for convenience, it seemed. He'd taken one of Caius's Pink Ladies along for the journey and was carrying a sticky apple core in one hand – hoping there would be a bin for it inside – and a pair of bolt cutters in the other. Apples were a safe food. He walked into the office unit, where a young man was standing at the desk leaving a voicemail for someone who had asked for a quote online. The room smelled like stale coffee and Lynx Africa and contained a twenty-year-old with a blatant hangover.

'Hi there, can I help you?'

'Are you the manager?' Matt had had a blathering sales assistant at the last lock-up.

'Yes, I am.'

'Great. Have you got a bin?' Matt asked, waving his apple core around.

'Yes,' he said, picking up a waste bin for Matt and holding it over the counter. 'Are you interested in renting a unit?'

'No. DS Matthew Cheung. Did you let out a space to Hereward Trollope-Bagshott last Saturday?' Matt flashed his badge.

'Let me check,' he said, looking on the computer. 'Yes, he rented one on the second floor.'

'Can you take me there?'

'Don't you need a warrant or something? I don't want to get in trouble with Steve, the regional manager.'

'There are too many Steves in the world, aren't there? Here's the warrant to search the unit and to access your CCTV. You ring Steve while I wait for forensics. Deal?'

'Man, you're a lifesaver. He'd go ballistic if he wasn't here when it all kicked off.'

★　★　★

'Barry, does this look like a crime scene to you? It looks like a jumble sale to me,' Matt said, looking at the clunky hardwood furniture and boxes of crockery.

'Nothing obvious. We'll take it all out item by item and dust for prints. Anything interesting we'll send to the lab for further analysis. I sent over the post-mortem report this morning, have you seen it?' Barry's minions were going to be very busy.

'Not yet. We had a horde of hysterical archaeologists loose in the station this morning.'

'Cause of death was as expected. Other than the fingernail being torn out, there was a small fracture on the cheekbone suggesting he'd been punched.'

'Sounds amateur again. Hitting someone in the face will make it difficult for them to talk. I'm wondering if the removal men were the ones who killed him. They might have had rope to hoist furniture. Their fingerprints would be all over this stuff: it would be hard to pin down which prints were legitimate and which were the result of the crime. They'd have had access to the flat to search for the head.'

'What was the head in the end?'

'I am so glad you asked. Now I can share the burden with you too. According to the archaeologists, we have a sanitised idea of sculpture in the Ancient Mediterranean and a racially and culturally whitewashed view of the Hellenic world in general.

I got told to read a book called *Black Athena*. Anyway, statues of the gods and emperors were painted in bright colours. It's incredibly rare to find one with a visible trace of paint on it, let alone a full children's art project like the bucket head. I got another lecture about trace elements and pigment residue. It's a major find. They were working out which goddess it was through the hairstyle. Artemis is unlikely – something about a diadem thing – and the facial features don't suggest it's Athena. The hair is blonde, so they think it's Aphrodite.'

'That sounds exciting.'

'Does it? I don't know, I'm Chinese. We'd probably invented gunpowder or something way cooler by that point. Fireworks? Extensive civil engineering projects? Paper money? The printing press? Are you OK to work through the furniture, I need to collect a load of books from Oxfam.'

★ ★ ★

Matt had a playlist of piano covers of pop songs that he liked to play when reviewing CCTV footage. He was listening to Britney Spears as if Cole Porter were playing. The footage showed Hereward arriving in a white van with two young men. The young men then moved the furniture out of the van and into the facility. They did their job, Hereward paid them in cash, they shook hands and drove off. Hereward walked away towards the hustle of Islington's main shopping street. Probably to buy reduced ham from Waitrose. He'd set up an interview with the movers, but that looked like a normal interaction.

Matt moved on to Hereward's books. He felt bad for Oxfam; he'd robbed them of a considerable income. There were boxes of science fiction, bodice rippers and old-fashioned spy thrillers.

Biographies of Westminster grandees. Treatises on economics. Gender Theory. History, so much history. The books had been boxed and labelled according to genre. Hereward was such a considerate man. 'Egypt: from Rameses I to the Suez Crisis'; 'Sub-Saharan Africa: from Mansa Musa to the Biafran War'. He opened the substantial box labelled 'Art' and started looking at the titles; Renaissance this and Renaissance that. One book jumped out at him: *Motherhood*. Matt picked the book up; it was the accompanying text to the exhibition Fay had curated in Athens. Inside the front cover was a receipt for the purchase and a cut-out of an article from a Greek newspaper about the exhibit. Matt couldn't read the text, but the accompanying picture was an action shot of the press night with Hereward and Fay looking at a statue together in the gallery.

48

The Police Station

Caius, Matt and the Chief Superintendent were standing on the other side of the two-way mirror watching Fay Bruce-Osbald. She was nursing a mug of green tea and ignoring the plate of biscuits that Matt had put out for her. It was becoming a thing for him, plates of biscuits. Caius wasn't sure that their meagre budget would sustain this new habit that he'd acquired at the auctioneer's.

'What's your hypothesis?' asked the Chief Superintendent, leaning against the table. Much to Caius's dismay, he could see that the Chief Superintendent was wearing Christmas socks six months too early/late.

'She lied by omission about Rupert being her godson. I doubt it would get a conviction, but it might be enough to spook her,' Caius said, thinking about his socks. Were they too jazzy for work? They had a red and orange geometric pattern.

'Did she lie to protect him or herself?'

'Anyone who's capable of rape is capable of anything. We think Rupert may be involved in a drugs ring that Clemency was a runner for. He wanted to break up with her, but she knew too much.'

'We can also prove that Rupert interned with Hereward Trollope-Bagshott ten years ago. Fay Bruce-Osbald knew Hereward professionally, and we have evidence that they knew each other socially too,' Matt pitched in.

'If you want her to flip on the godson, tread lightly. People like her take that duty seriously. I take it there's an art connection to all this?'

'Yes, the mop bucket head is exceedingly rare. It should be Venus de Milo level famous, which suggests it was acquired illegally.'

'Where does this leave Ned Osbald's arrest?'

'I don't know,' Caius said.

'I don't appreciate being so out of the loop on this drugs angle.'

'Sorry, we were told to keep it quiet.'

'Told by who?'

'A connection at the NCA.'

'Do you work for the NCA?'

'No, I don't. Sorry, it won't happen again,' Caius said, staring at his shoes. They needed shining.

'I hope it won't. What did your connection say?'

'MI6 took over a separate investigation into a drug front masquerading as a charity called Help for Hippos from the NCA recently.'

'It's massive if they're involved. Has anyone from either MI6 or the NCA been in touch yet?'

'Not yet. I've been expecting it though.'

'Keep pursuing it until you get an official order. Your mate telling you something they've heard from someone else, who heard it from someone else down the pub, isn't good enough. Now go in there and make yourself look pathetic in front of Fay Bruce. She'll either take pity on you and be helpful or get cocky and mess up. Full Hugh Grant: tits, arse, bollocks. I'm late for another sodding wedding.'

* * *

'Thank you so much, Dr Bruce, for coming in. I hate to think that I ruined your Sunday,' Caius said, slumping in his chair. He did a little sigh that turned into a half-smile.

'That's all right. You look tired,' she said sympathetically.

'I am.' Caius took his glasses off and rubbed his eyes. He felt like he might be overdoing it. 'I, um, I got dumped a few weeks ago, and I'm not sleeping very well. I'm quite heartbroken.'

'Why am I here?'

'Yes, that, of course. Sorry. I understand that you freelance at Farleigh's Auctioneers?'

'I do, yes.'

'I'm very sorry, really I am, to tell you that Hereward Trollope-Bagshott has died.'

'Oh no, that's such a shame. I am very fond of him.'

'Did you know Mr Trollope-Bagshott quite well?'

'Yes, we were colleagues for quite some time.'

'Did you ever socialise outside work?'

'Yes, occasionally. They're an amusing bunch at Farleigh's. They like a drink on a Friday after work.'

'Did you know him well enough to go on holiday with him, for example?'

'No.'

'Did he talk about his private life with you?'

'Why are you asking?'

'Between you and me, they weren't that helpful at Farleigh's, and when we realised that you two might have known each other, even slightly . . . You're a direct woman' – Caius leaned in conspiratorially – 'and the thing is, the Mediterranean Antiquities Department just said things like "he read a lot and ate biscuits". Don't get me started on HR. If I'm honest, we haven't got a clue what happened to the old boy. I thought that maybe on the off chance he might have mentioned to you how fond he was of going to Chepstow or something like that?'

'No, nothing springs to mind.'

'Did he have any lovers?'

'I don't know. I really don't.'

'Any feuds with neighbours?'

'Again, I don't know.'

'Did your godchild know him well?'

'Which godchild?'

'Thingy, who you got the internship there.'

'Which one?' she repeated with a raised eyebrow.

'Rupert. You said he was your godson last time you were here. That you were very close as his mother died young. That's how Clemency got the job at the gallery. Remember?'

'Of course. Rupert did work experience there ages ago. I doubt he can remember Hereward. They had the poor thing filing paperwork. That's not really his skill set.'

'What is his skill set?'

'Oh, I don't know, he's like his mother. Lofty, has artistic ambitions. He's sweet but quite useless. He's probably fairly deft at writing in iambic pentameter, but that's about it.'

'How are you holding up? Have the support team been helpful?'

'Yes, very helpful.'

'Good, good. Well, thank you so much for your time. We might send you an email questionnaire about your experience.'

★ ★ ★

'Jeffrey, hello, this is DS Matt Cheung, from yesterday. I've completed that complaint form that you asked for. I was wondering whether you'd be able to check something for me? A few more records? If you could please ring me urgently once you've got this? It's really important.'

49

Thurstone

Nell was wearing last night's dress and drinking a cup of atomically strong coffee. Rupert bought the expensive stuff, and God, it was worth it. She hadn't slept. He had made her a cup before he got in the shower. She couldn't face eating anything but had had to sit with him in the kitchen while he poached eggs and proceeded to lecture her on how to do so correctly before he left her. She then stepped outside through the French doors into the neat back garden – such a luxury in London – and was sitting regally on an ancient-feeling stone seat underneath an old apple tree that was beginning to fruit. It was going to be a hot day; not one of her fellow clouds blighted the sky. She finished her coffee and walked back into the house. She had insisted that she slept on the sofa and her neck ached (not that the adrenaline had allowed her to sleep). Despite attempting to offer her the spare room, Rupert was surprisingly all right with that – he probably imagined that he was displaying self-control. There was a his-and-hers calendar hanging in the kitchen that had managed to escape the purge, a relic of Rupert and Clemmie's year. January – Clemmie did a lot of juice cleansing that month. February – they went to Venice for Valentine's Day, how clichéd. March – nothing too interesting, they had the carpets professionally cleaned. Nell flicked through it with disdain – their domesticity appalled her. There were a few charity galas here, a few dinner parties there. Gallery openings. Restaurant bookings. Theatre trips. Nell put the cup in the sink, found her shoes and left the house.

Walking through the garden gate towards South Kensington tube, Nell felt peculiar, like she could float. Perhaps she was a cloud after all. She thought she heard someone say her name from behind. The pavement felt remarkably reassuring as it rose to meet her.

'Nell!'

The sky was endlessly blue.

'Nell!'

She wanted it to swallow her whole, to envelop her and carry her away from this mess she found herself in. To pick her up and coddle her. To coo and stroke her hair. To be her sky mother.

'Nell, are you all right? Did you hit your head?'

She could feel someone softly touching her head and saying her name, but she couldn't concentrate on the other sounds she heard.

'I should take you to A&E,' Rupert said, wearing a pair of light grey jogging bottoms and nothing else.

'It's nothing,' she said as he helped her sit up.

'You just collapsed in the street. That's not nothing. Do you have any grazes?'

'I'm fine. I just tripped.'

'No, you didn't, you fainted.' Rupert stood up straight and puffed his chest out. 'You'd better come back inside at least. I'll make you some toast and we can watch *Troy* together on the sofa.'

'I'd rather watch *Rome* instead.' Nell got up as Rupert held her arm.

'We can watch both.'

'Why aren't you wearing a shirt? Or shoes? How improper.'

'You're the one who upped and left without saying goodbye. You only got three paces outside the front gate though,' Rupert said, pushing the gate open and leading her back into the house by the hand. 'You have terrible manners, Waddingham. You're lucky I am so easily offended that I would speed after you. Lord knows what would've happened to you splayed out on the street like this. Now, come inside. Have a shower and something to eat. The neighbours will talk.'

★　★　★

Nell was sitting naked on the edge of Rupert's bed. The bed that Clemmie had slept in only a week before and that she had been expected to sleep in the night before. Living and breathing Clemmie. Clemmie the philistine. Clemmie who scowled whenever Nell and Rupert talked about books. Clemmie who scowled whenever Nell and Rupert talked at all. Clemmie who would say things like, 'I love your dress. You're so brave. I couldn't pull that off and I don't eat gluten.' Poor Clemmie. Poor Clemmie, cold in a drawer in the morgue. He must have changed the sheets, right? Clemmie's toiletries had gone from the bathroom. The expensive cleansers, lotions and potions probably all thrown into the bin. There was an empty wardrobe so her clothes must have been disposed of. Clemmie was as transitory as Rupert always claimed she was. The house was emptier than Nell remembered it. Rupert's bookshelves looked bereft. Nell put her dress back on, sprayed on some of Rupert's deodorant and went downstairs to the kitchen.

'I scrambled you some eggs,' Rupert said, putting the dirty pan in the sink. 'Oh, and some bacon and toast. You look pale. Paler than usual. Are you sure you don't want to go to the hospital?'

'I'm just anaemic. Oh buggeration, I'm supposed to be playing tennis with my cousin Marina this afternoon.' She wasn't. She picked up her fork and began to eat.

'I don't think you should play.'

'I should probably go home though.'

'Stay. We can have a pyjama day.'

'I don't have pyjamas with me, I'm afraid. Where have all your books gone?'

'I've packed them up. I'm letting this place out and moving into my family's house in the Chilterns next week.'

'Of course. You own it now.'

'I've owned it for years. This whole square too – my father transferred all of the family's property into a limited company yonks ago so I wouldn't have to pay inheritance tax. I get a handsome dividend every year. The old boy was being funny about the house though. Wouldn't let me live there. I'm exceedingly rich. We'd have a good life.'

'You're everything that's wrong with this country.'

'I'm fine with that. I have a fancy house. Do you want to come and visit next weekend? You liked it before, right? The roses will be blooming, and I never did take you to see the folly that I told you about. You did just quit your job, so you won't have anything better to do soon. You could move out there with me? You can choose the wallpaper. It needs freshening up. Get you out of Casper's poxy flat.'

'Remember your twenty-fifth birthday?'

'I don't have the best birthday parties, do I?'

'Next year just stay in and get a Chinese,' Nell said, eating some eggs. She felt sick, but she forced them down. 'Poor Minty, I didn't see it happen, but it sounded awful. I like her, she's sweet.'

'Don't feel too sorry for Minty. She's a wolf in gardening gloves.'

'Can you call a taxi for me, please?'

'I'll ask the car to drive you, but I would prefer that you stay,' Rupert said, pulling out the ring box from his pocket again, putting it on the table and opening it up so Nell could see the obscenely large sapphire in the centre of it. 'Think on it. Please? We'd live a lovely life. Think on it. Take it home with you. Give it a spin.'

Nell started to cry.

'What's wrong?'

'Nothing,' she said, as Rupert handed her a piece of kitchen towel from the side. She dabbed the tears away, but they wouldn't stop coming.

'Waddingham, what is it?'

'I don't know.'

Rupert put his arms around her shoulders as she cried and cried and cried. He kissed her on the forehead. She crumpled into his chest. He texted his driver over her shoulder telling him not to come and pick her up after all as he felt his chest become a floodplain for her overflowing tears. He gently led her to the living room, found his boxset of *Rome* and put it on. He sat next to her on the sofa, and she put her head on his lap. She'd stopped crying.

'It'll be all right, Nell. Whatever it is. It'll be all right, I'll look after you,' Rupert said, stroking her hair. It had sounded like the correct thing to say in his head, but this made her cry again. He didn't know what to do, so he stroked her hair to the opening credits.

'Rupert, I'm . . .'

'Uh-huh?'

'Never mind.'

MONDAY

50

The Police Station

Caius was waiting to sign the Official Secrets Act in Conference Room 1. He'd been greeted by the Chief Superintendent as soon as he'd walked into the building, and Matt and Amy would be dragged in to sign it as soon as they arrived. The door opened and an officious-looking woman walked in and sat across from him.

'My apologies for keeping you waiting,' she said as she handed him a form to sign.

'That's all right,' he said as he took a pen out from his pocket.

'This is your debrief from the Clemency O'Hara case. The case will now be pursued by another government agency.'

'And what does a debrief entail?'

'You tell me everything you know, sign that piece of paper, and then you walk out of this room and never give another thought to this case again. You will, of course, be supplied with the official version of events.'

* * *

'Why did they ask us to tell them what we knew?' Caius asked Matt, as the two of them sat on a bench near to the station. They'd gone out for a cigarette. Neither of them smoked. 'They're MI6; they know more about Help for Hippos and the art smuggling than we do. Like Errol said, they've been investigating it for weeks.'

'It's a cover-up, isn't it,' Matt said, glancing over his shoulder. He'd pilfered two fags from the duty sergeant and asked a passer-by for a light. The lit cigarette slowly smouldered out between his fingers.

'I find it suspicious that they suddenly appear after we question Fay about her connection to Rupert. The evil bastard.' Caius stared at his lit cigarette, dropped it and stubbed it out underfoot. 'He must have some very powerful friends indeed to quash an investigation this public.'

'What are you going to do about Helena Waddingham?'

'The rape is a different case; I don't see why we can't progress with it. Oh shit, what time is it? I'm late.' Caius took out his phone and rang Amy. He asked her to stall with Nell until he got there. 'Come on, duckie, the station is going to pot without us,' Caius said, hauling himself off the bench and trudging back to the station.

51

The Police Station

'I like your dress,' Amy said to Nell, who was wearing a bright tangerine smock. It was short and it billowed outwards. She looked like a cross between a wild poppy and a piece of crumpled birthday wrapping paper. The effect was glorious. 'Where is it from?'

'Oh, I made it myself,' Nell said, looking around her. 'This is the first time I've ever been inside a police station. I didn't expect lavender biscuits.'

'The biscuits are a new phenomenon.'

Amy flustered her way through twenty minutes of small talk before Caius arrived.

'Thank you for waiting, Ms Waddingham. I got stuck on a call,' Caius said.

'That's all right, we've had a lovely chat comparing Waugh to Fitzgerald.' Nell smiled at him.

'This is yours.' Caius gave her back her copy of *Persuasion*.

'Did you like it?'

'I did, very much.'

'Not enough men read Austen. Not enough men read. This has all been very lovely, especially the biscuits, but why am I really here?'

Caius turned on the tape, said the date and all their names. 'During our investigation into the murder of Clemency O'Hara, we found a video recording that she had made of an attack against yourself by Sir Rupert Achilles de Courcy Beauchamp. The video shows clear evidence of rape and my suggestion, if you agree to press charges, is that we pass it on to the Hellenic Police for prosecution. If they decide to pursue it, which we have cause to believe they will, Sir Rupert will be extradited under a European Arrest Warrant. Do you want to press charges?'

'Can I see it?' Nell asked.

'Do you really want to?' Caius asked in turn.

'I need to see it before I make a decision.'

★ ★ ★

Caius had just shown Nell out of the station. She had met with the specialist support officer after watching the video, and Caius had waited outside in case he was needed. He wasn't. Caius had offered to get Nell a taxi to take her back home, but she had insisted that she was fine. He wasn't sure that was true, but he didn't know what to do. He couldn't bundle her into a car against her will. Caius had offered to call her father, or her cousin who she said lived nearby, but she repeated that she was fine. Nell thought she might press charges, but she wasn't sure. Caius could see her waver.

★ ★ ★

The Chief Superintendent pulled Caius, Matt and Amy into his office. 'Just to say that MI6 want us to hand over all physical evidence and proof of the investigation after lunch today.' Caius thought he looked puffed up – he was enjoying being involved with a case of importance to national security. 'If you could neatly and swiftly round everything up. They have tech people coming to wipe your computers.'

'What about our outstanding lines of inquiry? I'm expecting video footage from outside the bank at the bottom of Osbald's road,' Amy said.

'Hand it all over. Caius, you can't touch Rupert Beauchamp. They know you've been sniffing around him. He, like the rest of the people involved in this case, is off limits now.'

★　★　★

Caius was finishing a set of squats next to his desk – he'd been lax of late. Amy was scrolling through her Facebook feed as Matt gabbled at her about the auction house.

'I suppose I should try one of these infamous biscuits?' Caius asked. His suit trousers were a little too tight for any more squats anyway.

'Go on then,' Matt said, handing him the box. 'Why did MI6 let us do the legwork if they knew they were going to swoop in at the last minute? The Met has a specialist art crime department, you know. Why are they not involved?'

'Whoever ordered the cover-up didn't want real experts involved, just us bumbling plods, but we've got a bit too close for their liking,' Caius said, before taking a bite. 'These are delightful. Who knew you could eat lavender?'

'My life has changed,' Matt said, eating another.

Caius picked up Clemmie's panda-covered notebook and the museum guide that they'd collected from evidence and went to shove them into boxes as ordered. Instead, he started reading through the notebook. It was mostly shopping lists:

- YSL lipstick in '104'
- Dior chromatic bronzer in 'Sunrise'

- Prada sunglasses (a cut-out from a magazine had been paper-clipped to the page)

The lipstick was the same as the one they had found in her bag. He continued flicking through the book. More lists of luxury goods: a watch, perfume, shoes, even the handbag that had been found at the crime scene. He reached a second set of entries that were upside down. He flipped the book around and started reading. They were budgets done in pastel colours like a bullet journal, but the figures had to be wrong. In May's entry, under 'Gym' it said £24,550. The gym was pricey but not that expensive. Besides, Rupert paid for her membership. The figures for 'grooming' and 'socialising' were huge too.

'It's Clemmie's account of the drugs she was dropping off. Fay must have been paying her in luxury goods,' Caius said. It was frustrating making a major breakthrough on a case that was about to be taken from you, probably never to be heard by a judge. He picked up the museum guide and the cover protector flapped about. He went to tuck it back in when he saw that a series of numbers had been gently pencilled on the inside of the cover. It was a bank sort code and account number. Even more frustrating.

'Was Hereward selling the head on the side? Did he steal other stuff? That has to be why he was killed. Was there anything in the storage facility in the end other than clunky furniture? I rang Barry but they've been ordered to stop too. Is there someone else on the inside at the auction house now that he's retired? Who is the contract killer? I have so many questions and I'm never going to know now,' Matt sighed.

'Tell me about it. Why did Ned hand over Clemmie's things like that? He was either naive, unaware of what Clemmie and his wife were up to or he wanted us to work it out. And what exactly did he mean by "middleman"?' Caius said, sulking.

'Jesus Christ on a bicycle,' Amy said, standing up.

'What is it?' Caius asked, helping himself to another biscuit.

'Have you seen the *Mail Online*?' she asked.

'Nope. What does it say?' Caius stretched his calves out – his squats in too-tight trousers had given him a mild cramp.

'*Swooning Beauty: sexy Sir Rupert sweeps up damsel as more sordid details of Clemency O'Hara's affair with married sugar daddy are revealed.*'

'Wowser,' Matt said, leaning over her shoulder, 'are there any pictures?'

'Yes, there are. Poor girl! They'll never believe her if she tries to prosecute him now. He could say they were having an affair and it was all a game, a roleplay, and the jury would believe him.'

'Let's have a look,' Caius said, scrolling through the pictures – Nell leaving his house in a very glamorous dress, stilettos and the night before's make-up; Nell mid-faint; Rupert rushing out shirtless and barefoot to pick her up off the pavement. 'What's he got going for him? Besides a title, a fortune and a six-pack?'

'He's a bit evil. Sexually deviant, dashing and complacently confident. He's an archetypal Byronic anti-hero,' Matt said, picking up his tea. 'I hate men like him. They were told they could have anything they want, so they take everything. If only a fever would take him in Missolonghi.'

'I wonder what weights he does . . .' Caius was still looking at the picture of shirtless Rupert.

'Why was she there at all? Any half-decent defence lawyer would use this to prove that the rape wasn't half as bad as the video made it seem. Who would go to their rapist's house after

that? Why go to their birthday party for that matter? Denial?'
Amy asked.

'Denial is very powerful,' Matt said.

'Do you know what the worst thing is?' Amy said, staring at
Caius – he knew the answer but wouldn't admit to it out loud.
'Nell loved Rupert. In the video he kisses her, she kisses him
back, but then she changes her mind and tells him to ask her out
properly when they're back in London. If he'd done as she said
and stopped there that night, and then dumped Clemmie, they'd
be together now. She loved him, I think she still loves him a
touch, and I think she thinks the attack is her fault: if she hadn't
frozen, she could have stopped him from raping her and then
they'd be together. I could see it today when you were speaking
to her. If she does press charges, she is punishing herself not
him. He strung her along for years and yet . . . How do you love
someone like that?'

'With suicidal abandon.' Matt reached for another biscuit.
'Someone take these away from me. Save me from myself.'

Caius's desk phone rang. 'DI Caius Beauchamp.'

'You're my only call for the day,' Ned said.

'I'm honoured.'

'I thought Fay did it because she was jealous. I panicked. I
don't know. I was trying to be gallant I suppose. I didn't do it.'

'I know you didn't.'

'Whatever happens next, whatever they say about her, I just
wanted to tell you that Clemmie wasn't a bad person. He just
made her act a certain way. He made her a certain sort of cruel
sometimes. She was quite lovely.'

Osbald hung up.

52

Antigone Publishing

Nell hung up after leaving Alex another rambling voicemail asking for him to call her. She'd texted him too. He'd left her on read. What that meant for them she didn't know. She didn't know much: she could conjugate a verb, but she didn't know what she was going to do now. Nell walked through the doors of her office to the sight of Ali being accosted by a queue three deep of bicycle couriers all carrying various packages. They looked like three wise men with helmets instead of crowns.

'She's here. She can sign for them now,' Ali said.

'Hullo, what's this?' Nell asked.

'Are you Miss Helena Waddingham?' the first delivery guy asked.

'I am, yes.'

All three of them sighed in relief.

'We have all been told not to hand these over to anyone but you,' the second said.

'Apparently my signature isn't good enough,' Ali huffed.

'Sorry you had to wait for me,' Nell said, signing for the three packages in turn.

'Jonathan has been asking for you all morning,' Ali said, once they were alone. 'Are you all right? You look a bit off. Feels like you've had a crazy time recently.'

'You wouldn't believe me if I told you. Would you mind helping me carry these back to my desk?' Nell asked.

★   ★   ★

Rupert had gone on a spending spree and Nell was opening the resultant boxes at her desk. Champagne truffles from Charbonnel et Walker, three bottles of Bollinger, a pair of emerald earrings. Shoes that probably weren't to be worn for anything but fucking. Three dresses from Alexander McQueen, the cost of which she was going to google later. A ticket to the theatre for tomorrow night, one for the ballet on Friday and a train ticket to Bath at 9 a.m. on Saturday morning – for what she could only presume was either some sort of perverted weekend or an innocent day trip around the Roman Baths. Rupert had appeared to set up a Two Together Railcard for them. Such presumption. She looked around at the couple of thousand pounds he'd spent on her. Had she just seen Pemberley? Or should she leave the country? The video had brought it all back. She shouldn't have watched it. She knew she shouldn't have. She could have pretended, perhaps. Wiped it clean, sanitised it, remembered it as a bad one-night stand. Just a bad one-night stand. Just another bad one-night stand.

'Knock, knock,' Jonathan said through the door.

'Come in.' Nell leaned back in her chair.

'I just wanted to check in on you. I saw your email.'

'Wanted to check what exactly, Jonathan?'

'Well, I thought I should, I wanted, just to say . . .' he bumbled. He was going to get in trouble for this, he knew it. The chairman of the board would be furious if what had happened got out.

'Never mind, Jonny darling, never mind. It's just time for me to move on.'

'Yes, quite. Well, um. Yes,' he said, backing out of the door, shutting it quietly behind him. Nell heard him scuttle up the stairs.

Nell turned on her computer and opened her emails. Normally on a Monday morning her favourite thing was reading the responses to the rejections she'd sent on Friday. Not the polite ones. The angry ones. The sweary ones. The ones who the world hadn't been cruel enough to, yet – they'd never needed to become witty, never felt the need to become something more interesting because they hadn't ever squirmed in their skin, wanting to scratch it off their bones. Had they never been in love? Had they never been thrown aside for a girl with longer legs? Or blonde hair? A prettier nose? Been betrayed? Been kissed? Been despised? Despised themselves? How could they not despise themselves for sending in such drivel? Drivel, drivel, drivel. Drivel is an amusing word if you say it loud enough. If you lie on the floor of your pretentious office of your tedious job and yell it at the cornicing.

Nell went downstairs and curled up under Ali's desk as she answered the phones.

'Sweetie, are you going to come out of there? You're next to my runners and they don't smell great.'

Nell crawled out. 'They really don't smell great, do they.'

'Nope. What's up with you?'

'Did you read *Sleeping Beauty* when you were little?'

'Yeah, I suppose I must have.'

'They weren't meant to be children's bedtime stories. The Brothers Grimm were serious folklorists trying to collect the remnants of Mitteleuropa's Dark Age tales before industrialisation finished them off. The prince rapes her as she sleeps, and she only wakes up when she gives birth to twins.'

'That's not very Disney.'

'Can I run a hypothetical situation by you?'

'Sure.'

'Close your eyes. I mean that. Close them. Imagine you're a hard-working but lowly scullery maid, who is in love with a man. A prince. Blond. Shiny armour. He has a really impressive white horse and a fabulous jewel-encrusted castle.'

'The horse means something else, right? What sort of castle?'

'Fancy, proper fancy. Old tapestries. Ghosts in the rafters who crack jokes and help you cheat at cards. It's got a maze with a unicorn at the centre and a lake filled with singing mermaids.'

'Right, I'm on board with this.'

'He loves you back, but he can't marry you because you're merely a scullery maid and an evil witch queen has cast a spell on him to make him love her too.'

'That's shit.'

'Yeah, but because some part of him underneath it all knows that he really loves you he still calls you, and takes you out for coffee every couple of weeks just to see how you are, and sends you books in the post that he thinks you might like, and remembers your birthday every year. And then one day you're walking through a clearing in the woods together talking of nothing because now you're just old friends even though you're in love with him, and you can do that, you can pretend that you don't adore him, looking at the wildflowers, and then, and then he rapes you, because he can't bear being just friends with you any longer either.'

'Right. Well, he might be a prince but he's not a gentleman. Honey, are you trying to tell me something really important through a horribly laboured metaphor?' Ali asked. Nell ignored her, continuing her fable.

'The witch has transformed him into an evil dragon that breathes fire and hoards gold in his lair. He's committed many crimes under her influence – but then the wicked witch is struck dead by lightning. Her grip on him ceases but the damage has been done, and he spends half his day as the prince and the other half as a scaly beast – trying to claw his way back into the maid's affections. The dragon prince keeps turning up outside the kitchen window begging for forgiveness, but the scullery maid realises that the witch queen wasn't evil, she was actually under his spell too. A white knight appears who was in love with the maid all along, who says he can help her flee from the dragon prince.'

'Does the white knight slay the dragon?'

'Yes, he has to, it's a fairy-tale kingdom and that is how it works there. The knight doesn't know all of it, not really. He doesn't understand what happened to the maid.'

'Does the maid like the white knight?'

'She does . . . But . . .'

'But what? Sweets, come here.' Ali tried to place her arms around Nell.

Nell backed away from Ali. Her eyes were distant. 'Is it my fault? Did I do this to myself? I knew that in his heart he was a dragon from the very beginning. I just didn't think I would burn. He proposed to me, you know, on Saturday. Rupert, that is, Rupert the dragon prince proposed to me. He thinks he can make it right,' Nell said, fetching her phone out of her pocket and checking for a non-existent message from Alex. She had Rupert's ring on her finger. She twisted it. She'd carried the box around with her and put it on on the way back from the police station. She wanted to know what it felt like. What it felt like to be bound by a wedding band.

'You look like you need to sit down. We can go upstairs to your office and have a proper chat? Do you want me to call your family? What about your cousin who pops in?'

'No, no, no. I fancy an ice cream,' Nell said with a manufactured cheeriness. 'I'm going to the Co-op round the corner. Want anything?'

'I'm all right. Can I ring anyone for you? Please? What about the white knight? Do you want to talk to him? Shall I come with you?'

'If I'm not back in twenty minutes then I've been carried off by the dragon to be locked in a tower for eternity,' Nell said, leaving the building in a state of semi-conscious delusion.

53

The Police Station

Pizza: is it just pretentious cheese on toast? This was an opinion Amy hadn't expected to be so violently rejected by both Caius and Matt. They were trying to decide on what to get for lunch. Caius's healthy-eating regime had finally been defeated by the haunting feeling of having failed Clemency O'Hara that was stalking him like a spectre wherever he went about the station. He was afflicted with a sense of right and wrong that reality was not daunted by. Everything about these two cases felt inalienably wrong.

'Pizza isn't everything it's hyped up to be.' Amy couldn't backtrack now. She had stumbled across the hill that she was going to die on and was surprisingly fine with it.

'I think we should vote on it,' Matt said.

'But you're both going to choose pizza,' Amy said.

'Exactly,' Matt said.

'Amy, check your email,' Caius said, scanning his on his phone. 'We've got the footage from the bank at the bottom of the Osbalds' road. Look through it after 3 p.m.'

'My contact at the auction house has finally come through,' Matt said, turning to his screen. 'Oh shit. Look at this, Caius.'

'As has the Chief's daughter,' Caius said, opening an email attachment. 'Fucking hell, look at this picture of the party. The person who made the flowers for inside McDonald's made the flower crown too. How did I miss that?' Caius gave Matt his phone as he looked at the personnel file from Farleigh's on Matt's monitor.

Amy was speeding through the footage looking for a glimpse

of Clemmie. She found her and the itching feeling that had been bothering them all. 'Ned Osbald definitely didn't do it.'

Matt and Caius crowded round her computer as they watched Clemmie being lured into the van of a familiar redhead – and to her death.

Caius's desk phone rang. Matt looked up at him from Amy's computer and saw the colour drain from his cheeks as an Antipodean voice panicked at the other end. His phone rang again just as he put the receiver down, this time to say that Rupert was downstairs and demanding an audience with him.

★　★　★

'I would like to know why you hauled my fiancée in for questioning this morning,' Rupert said, leaning back in his chair nonchalantly. 'She isn't taking my calls. The only reasonable explanation for that is something slanderous that you said.'

'Your fiancée?' Caius was incredulous, until Rupert went to wipe his nose a few times in a row, with increasing twitchiness.

'Nell, Helena. We're engaged to be married.'

'What?'

'It won't be a big wedding. A quick ceremony at the Chelsea Register Office and then a marquee in the garden. I digress. What did you say to her?'

'Nell left her office an hour ago to get ice cream from a corner shop. Flowers from you were delivered to her office five minutes after she left by what Nell's colleague described as a "suspiciously fidgety" redhead. Nell's colleague went to look for her after thirty minutes. All she found was a solitary shoe and a box of white chocolate Magnums five metres from their offices.'

'Oh, bugger.'

'Uniform are on their way to Minty's house, her business premises and your godmother's house. I doubt they'll find Nell there. We've put a call out on the van. If you were a psychopath that was in love with you, which you sort of are, where would you take Nell?'

'Frithsden Old Hall – my house in the Chilterns,' Rupert confidently said, getting up and rolling towards the door.

'Where do you think you're going?'

'If you're going to rescue Nell, then I should be there too.' Rupert strolled out of the room.

'You don't seriously think you're allowed to come?' Caius asked, trailing after him.

'That house is a Tudor rabbit warren. There are priest holes and secret corridors.' Rupert allowed Caius to walk ahead down the corridor that led to the reception, where they were stopped by the sergeant on duty.

'Detective Inspector, I've been trying to ring you. We've got an Alex Adonis here who says he has info on the O'Hara case,' said the young officer, gesturing to Alex who was sitting on a squeaky chair in the waiting area. Alex rushed up and grabbed Rupert by the front of his shirt.

'Mate,' Rupert said aghast, as he tried to swat Alex away like a fly. Caius stepped in and stopped Alex from taking a swing at Rupert. 'I didn't realise that you thought so low of me.'

'I know what you did in Greece. Nell left me a voicemail. You're a monster; a giant lizard smashing your way through the city leaving nothing but rubble in your wake. How could you? How could you do that to her? How could you do that to Nell?' Rupert did not react but for the slightest flicker of shame that disappeared as quickly as it came. Alex turned to Caius, who was still firmly wedged between the pair. 'He did it, he had to. He killed Clemmie, not the man you have in custody.'

'Alex, you need to calm down,' Caius said, getting him to back away from the startled baronet who was now busy readjusting his hair. 'I'll get an officer to take a statement from you, if you'd just sit back down.' Caius looked up at the desk sergeant, who'd seen the whole thing and had started calling for an officer to take Alex to an interview room.

This calmed Alex, until he realised that he was being fobbed off by the smug look on Rupert's face as he followed Caius out of the station and to the car park, where Matt and Amy were already waiting in Caius's car.

'Where the fuck are you going?' Alex asked, as he charged after the unlikely Beauchamp alliance.

Rupert climbed into the back of the car. Caius had already clambered into the driving seat and had turned on the engine.

'You're showing them where you've buried all the bodies, huh?'

'Oh, fuck off, Alex. You're not needed,' Rupert said, as he slammed the car door.

Alex stood behind the car so Caius couldn't reverse out of his parking space.

Caius wound down his window and yelled, 'Alex, please move. It's an emergency.'

'What emergency?'

Rupert opened his door again. 'Minty has kidnapped Nell and we're going to rescue her.'

'What the fuck?' Alex stood still, unable to comprehend what Rupert had said.

'Oh, for fuck's sake, just get in too,' Caius yelled. It wasn't protocol to take civilians along in circumstances like these, but technically it wasn't even a police case any more so to hell with protocol. He couldn't have these two rutting stags slowing him down.

Rupert refused to move into the middle seat, so Matt had to squidge up between the pair of warring suitors.

'Can you turn on the sirens?' Rupert asked an incredulous Caius from the back seat. 'I'm deadly serious. I demand that you turn them on.'

54

M1 Northbound

Alex was staring out of the car window in silence. Caius was staring hard at the road in front. Matt was staring at the back of Caius's headrest. Rupert was staring intently at nothing as he rocked slightly. Amy was in the front passenger seat of Caius's car with her arms crossed.

'Did we have to bring him?' she whispered to Caius, as Rupert rhythmically tapped the back of her headrest. 'His pupils are huge.'

'Unfortunately, yes. Feel bad for Matt, their knees are touching,' Caius said quietly.

A voice came over the radio. 'Alpha Charlie One, vehicle spotted matching the registration plates heading north of Hemel Hempstead. Unmarked car following.'

Caius picked up the radio and said, 'Romeo Juliet Four, has there been a sight on Helena Waddingham? About five foot seven, wavyish, curly brown hair.'

'Alpha Charlie One, negative,' came the response.

'If she's dead . . .' Alex started but trailed off.

'Can I ask you a question?' Amy said, leaning over her seat and looking at Rupert.

'Why not,' Rupert said, peering at her.

'Do you feel guilty?' Amy continued.

'For what?'

'This whole situation?'

'Why? I didn't do a damn thing.'

'Do you miss Clemmie?'

'No comment.'

Matt shook his head at Amy to discourage her from continuing her line of questioning, as fascinating as it was, in such close quarters.

Caius tried to push the contempt he felt for Rupert back down to the pit of his stomach. He didn't feel like he'd ever got to really lay into him. 'If this was the 1970s, I would've punched you by now.'

'If this was the 1770s, Rupert would have owned you,' Alex said. Matt peered over his shoulder and saw that he was reading the 'Fainting Beauty' article.

Caius almost laughed, he felt that angry. He looked at Rupert in his rear-view mirror. 'I thought Fay Bruce lied about being your godmother to protect you, but she was trying to protect another godchild of hers instead. Araminta Gaunt. Minty. She's a family friend, right? You have a godmother in common.' Matt had been sent a scan of Minty's work experience record at Farleigh's that Fay had arranged during the same summer as Rupert's. 'Old family friends, the Gaunts? Take you on sailing holidays with them in the summer after your mother died? Have you over for the weekend when you boarded?'

'And why is my florist your concern?'

'Because you're shagging her. I got the angle wrong. I thought Clemmie was killed for who *she* was sleeping with, not who *you* were sleeping with. Who has their mistress deliver flowers to other women for them? Minty has already killed once because she can't let anyone else have you. She was at your house purging all traces of your life with Clemmie, ready to replace her. I don't think she'll have taken kindly to the photographs of Nell swooning into your naked arms all over her Facebook feed this morning. The flower crown has been bugging me all week, but when I saw the pictures of the party, it clicked. It was so beautifully made and from the same flowers as the ones at your party. Minty made both of them. I thought there was something wrong with your alibi even though I couldn't prove it. I was adamant that your friends were lying to protect you, but actually you were covering for Minty whether you knew it or not. I'm assuming that you were balls deep in someone that afternoon and it was convenient for you to go through with the lie.'

'I wasn't actually,' Rupert said. He opened his mouth to say something else but even through his coke-addled brain fog he knew to shut up. 'Oh, fuck off, Poirot.'

'I thought Nell was the only girl that you had strung along over the years, but actually there were two of them. Minty wormed her way in with Clemmie over the last year. We can see that on Clemmie's Instagram. She starts appearing more and more frequently. Maybe she felt like this was her last chance to get you to pick her instead before she was "past her prime"? Whatever that means. Everyone knew that before Clemmie stood by and watched you rape Nell, she was putting pressure on you to marry her. Minty probably didn't know that Clemmie was about to leave you after she saw what you were capable of . . .'

'I didn't rape Nell.'

Alex took a sharp breath. Matt felt his whole being coil into knots.

Caius continued, ignoring Rupert's interjection as the satnav on his phone told him to turn left up a winding country lane towards Frithsden Old Hall. 'We know that Minty followed Clemmie on your birthday. She waited outside her gym, followed her to Belsize Park, and then offered to drive her back to yours after she "happened to stumble across her". She probably took a "quick" detour to her workshop in Highgate so she could drug her with foxglove disguised as tea. We've got CCTV footage of Minty picking up Clemmie. She had access to your home. The last time you were fucking Minty in the stables, she stole the clothes, the bag and the shoes that Clemmie was wearing when we found her.'

'The London house doesn't have stables.'

Caius ignored that remark too. 'Foxglove makes people dizzy and confused, gives them diarrhoea and makes them vomit. A botanist like Minty would've known that – she was going to make Clemmie embarrass you at your party, so you'd have no choice but to break up with her.'

'We've decided that next year for my birthday we're going to stay in and have a Chinese instead,' Rupert said nonchalantly before looking at Matt. 'Is that offensive to you?'

'We?' Alex asked.

'Nell and I.'

'You're utterly delusional,' Alex said.

Caius pushed on, all that testosterone making the car feel hot with hate. 'She had a drugged Clemmie in the back of her van rolling around with bits of leaves from all the flowers she was transporting, so that when we found the body it looked like she'd been writhing around the undergrowth. En route to the party, Clemmie threw up and choked to death. Minty panicked, left the body in the van while you partied, and then her fairy godmother met her in the small hours. You and whatever the man who dressed like Toad of Toad Hall is called were passed out on Minty's sofas. We heard how drunk you were from the bar staff on your pub crawl to Minty's. You couldn't have been in a state to help with the disposal of Clemmie's body. You didn't notice Minty leave. Either Minty or Fay slit Clemmie's throat for good measure and put the flower crown on. You probably commissioned the crown for Clemmie to wear at the party anyway which means you've known all along who the murderer actually was, you just weren't going to say anything. It made the murder look more bizarre, bought themselves some time to plant the evidence on Bruce's philandering husband. Cheaper than getting a divorce.'

'Iphigenia,' Rupert muttered.

'What?' Caius asked.

'Agamemnon slit the throat of his daughter in a ritualised blood-letting so that the Greeks would be granted a favourable wind when they set out for Troy,' Alex explained.

'Fay's a classicist too. She probably thought she'd need a favourable wind to get away with it,' Matt said.

'I haven't got time for posh-boy nonsense,' Caius said.

'Beauchamp, we need to plan how to sweep the building,' Matt said.

'I'd start with the stables and the other outbuildings,' Rupert said. He rolled his eyes at the mispronunciation of his name.

'I meant the Beauchamp with a warrant card and a conscience. But yes, securing the outbuildings before moving towards the main house is probably a good idea.'

'Although Minty does have keys for the main house. She was helping me move my things in this week. She's probably gone there.'

Matt's stomach grumbled loudly.

'Amy, have a look in the glove compartment. There are some rhubarb and custards,' Caius said, as Amy searched for the boiled sweets. She chucked one at Matt and Alex.

'Can I have one, please?' Rupert asked.

'No,' yelled everyone else in the car simultaneously.

'Fine. I get that you all hate me, but do you know how hard this is for me?'

'I can only imagine,' Alex said, as he watched the suburbs disappear into the countryside.

'Can you explain the whole you-and-Minty thing to me?' Matt asked against his better judgement, as the boiled sweet rolled about his mouth. 'I haven't got my head around how your love life works . . .'

'It's quite simple. Minty and I just had a physical thing on and off. I don't have any feelings for her.'

'Was she fine with you being with Clemmie?'

'No, not at all.'

'Hence the Great Pond Incident,' Alex muttered.

'And what about you and Nell?' Matt asked.

'What about it?'

'I want to make sure I've got this right. You were living with Clemmie although you didn't like her that much, and you couldn't get rid of her because she was involved in your and your godmother's criminal empire.'

'I protest my innocence and deny all knowledge of any criminal activity carried out by a third party.'

'But the whole time you were knocking Minty off on the side and Clemmie knew about it? What about Nell?'

'I'm meant to be with Nell, but I wasn't there yet, you know. She's the only woman I could ever marry. Thought I'd sow a few wild oats first.'

'Don't forget about all the girls you pull in Mahiki every week.' Alex turned to Matt. 'Rupert is a direct descendant of Lord Byron.'

'Through my mother. But what does that have to do with anything?' Rupert asked.

'That makes a lot of sense.' Matt's phone rang. 'Hello, yep. OK, bring them in and log them as evidence.' Matt hung up.

313

'Uniform found Clemmie's gym clothes at Minty's workshop but no Nell. They'll go into the black hole with the rest of the evidence.'

'Was my twenty-fifth birthday really as shit as everyone keeps telling me it was? I had a dreadful time, but I thought everyone else enjoyed it,' Rupert asked Alex.

'I don't remember it, not even the Great Pond Incident. I woke up the next morning with a bottle of champagne in the middle of the maze. It took me two hours to get out.'

Caius's car wound up through steep, meandering country roads. Boughs of hawthorn shaded them on their ascent up through the Chiltern Hills and a lone walker was trudging along the opposite verge, clinging to a pair of funny skiing poles.

'Alpha Charlie One, suspect has turned through the main drive of the manor house. An armed unit has entered the grounds through a back entrance. Over.'

'Alpha Charlie Three, I'm in woodland to the east of the house. I have sight of the suspect and a young woman matching the description of Helena Waddingham. The young woman is not moving. The suspect is dragging her out of the back of the van and is loading her into a wheelbarrow to take her into the house. I can't tell if the suspect is armed. Over.'

'If your police officers break anything, I will sue you for damages,' Rupert said.

Matt looked at him with disdain.

'There are a couple of Turner's less thrilling paintings hung next to the coat stand. They're an asset. I can't worry about Nell now. I'm stuck in this tin can with you dolts. Nell's either dead or alive. If she's alive, bloody brilliant. If she's dead . . . then I ruined everything, again. As I am wont to fucking do.' Rupert recognised a landmark. 'If you turn left here then this

314

road takes you up to the tradesmen's entrance. You can park the car behind the old dairy buildings. We won't be visible from the house.'

Caius turned left and nodded at Amy to use the radio. 'Romeo Juliet Four, we are approaching the back of the house and parking behind the old dairy. Three plainclothes officers and two civilians. Over.'

The car pulled up to a squat stone building.

Rupert clambered out, flicked his hair like a prince from a Disney movie and rolled up his sleeves.

'Alpha Charlie One, armed officers entering through the main entrance now. Over.'

55

Rupert's twenty-fifth birthday party – five years earlier
Frithsden Old Hall, Hertfordshire

The flagstones in the entrance hall had paths worn onto them by generations of Beauchamps as if they were themselves like their descendant Rupert – aimless wanderers. Nell ran her hand over the wooden panelling as she walked down the hall looking at the paintings. She got a splinter in her little finger. She sucked it out as she stared at the painting in front of her. It must be a Turner, she thought to herself. The clouds. The light. It had to be. She dreaded to think how much it was worth. Art: commodities masquerading as higher thought. These paintings were merely an asset class to the Beauchamps that happened to brighten their walls. Nell could hear the party in the gardens begin: the faint tinkle of conversation and the gentle explosions of champagne corks popping. Nell opened a heavy oak door and continued down the walking gallery. She stopped at each portrait, searching each face: a nose here, an eyebrow there – these were most definitely Rupert's ancestors. Fat and comfortable. On horses. Strolling through the parkland as heifers grazed. Wearing their red coats – military and hunting. Stern-looking statesmen. Delicate ladies with willow-thin wisps of waists, cherubic children in tiny sailor suits on their knees. It occurred to Nell that it was probably rude to wander around someone else's house like this, but it was Rupert, so Nell felt no guilt. Passing by a distinguished-looking admiral, Nell went through the final door and into the library. She rolled past the shelves, looking at the titles.

Rupert was standing in the middle of the marquee he had hired. A battalion of waiters were handing out canapés – tiny swirls of smoked salmon and caviar, Stilton and heritage pear on rye toast, miniature beef Wellingtons with dabs of English mustard, and flutes of champagne – to a select group of a hundred or so members of his closest acquaintance. The air was full of early summer heat, grass pollen and jovial mirth. Clemmie was busy trying to be witty near the bar, flirting with Teddie from the college boat club. As if Teddie's attention could make him jealous. Rupert felt a broad hand grasp him on the shoulder.

'Bella is intense,' Alex said, downing the dregs of his glass.

'Bella? She's got cracking tits and goes like a rush-hour Pendolino.' Rupert's eye darted across the bar, scanning it for Nell. He'd hoped that Bella would've been better at diverting Alex's attention away from Nell for the evening.

'She recited the entirety of "Ode to a Nightingale" at me. I am all for girls who read poetry, but it was oddly erotic and there were tears in her eyes. Keats isn't a sexy poet. He's a bit feeble, pale and pallid, has a cough.'

'Al, you are a fussy man.' Rupert laughed and put his left hand in his pocket as he continued to survey the room. It had balled itself into a fist.

'Do you know where Nell is?'

'No, I don't.' Rupert finally turned to look at Alex. 'Why do you ask?'

'I don't know. She is an old friend and all that.' Alex stared at the bottom of his empty glass. 'She's single right now, isn't she? I thought I saw that on Facebook.'

'Is she?' Rupert feigned ignorance. 'How's work?'

'I'm thinking of making a change. Moving back to London.'

'Ask Nell out properly?' Rupert downed the champagne in his glass.

'Perhaps. I'm getting on, I'm twenty-five in a few months.'

'I don't think you're her type.' Rupert silently added 'but I am' and took Alex's empty glass from his hand. 'Would you like another? Can't have you sober at a party of mine, mate,' he said, before disappearing out the back of the marquee. He was keeping a case of Premier Cru out there for his own personal consumption – Clem didn't know about it, nor did she ever need to know about the good stuff. He took a little pill out of a packet from his top pocket and put it in Alex's glass. He watched it start to dissolve in the dregs. He popped a cork and poured for them both. Rupert slithered back into the tent and back to Alex, who was standing still, bewildered by the intense eye contact Bella kept trying to make with him from across the tent. 'Here you go, pal. I'd sip that if I were you, it's the good shit. Don't tell anyone it's out there.'

'Thanks, I'm honoured. How are you?'

'Not too shabby. Thinking of opening a second restaurant. Don't tell the old boy though, he thinks it's vulgar. Restaurants are businesses for immigrants, apparently.'

'Is your grandfather here?'

'Oh yes, he's holed up in the house and complaining rabidly about the party to anyone who'll listen. The poor housekeeper has had an earful over the last week. The gardener threatened to quit.'

'Why did he let you host it here then?'

'Some people take pleasure in having something to complain about. *Guardian* columnists, for example. The gays. My grandfather.'

Alex looked over and saw Clemmie playing with Teddie's lapels. 'How are things with Clemmie?'

'Shit. Fucking shit. I hate the bitch. She's trying to move in with me. She's living in a shared house in Clapham with that girl with the face like porridge' – Rupert pointed to a dumpy creature in an unflattering dress the colour of bile – 'but apparently she's ready for the "next step".'

'Might be better to break it off now rather than let it drag on. The longer these things go on the messier it gets.' Alex raised his eyebrows as he tried to control his face and not laugh at him. Rupert could never admit to an emotion. The hyperbole – the professed hate – was all nonsense. If Rupert wanted rid of Clemmie then he would just dump her. He couldn't admit to loving her. He couldn't admit to loving Nell either. Alex thought he loved them separately and differently, but his dishonesty with himself meant that he was never truly going to be with either of them in any meaningful sense – he'd always be caught halfway between the two until either of the girls made the decision for him. Alex had tried to explain this to him once, but Alex was drunk and Rupert was drunker. Somehow it had ended with Rupert taking a swing at Alex, and as such he vowed never to mention it to him again, only to steal Nell away if he could.

'Indeed.' Rupert couldn't find Nell anywhere in the crowd. He had caught a glimpse of her earlier from afar getting out of a car with Tabs, so she had to be here somewhere. 'I'm going to check on the old boy.'

★　★　★

Clemmie watched Rupert leave the marquee. 'Excuse me, Teddie,' she said as she started to follow him.

Teddie gently grabbed her hand. 'Where are you going?'

'After Rupert, in case he needs my help.'

'He doesn't.' Teddie stared at her. Her heart-shaped face. Her doe-like eyes. 'Look, you're a pretty girl – more than that, you're beautiful. You can do what you want, move on from Rupert. He won't be good for you in the end.'

'Move on, and then climb on top of you?'

'Something like that. Let's go for a coffee next week?'

'You know I love Rupert.'

'I don't think you do love him, and Rupert definitely doesn't love you.'

'Yes, he does.'

'Are you sure? He's been boffing Araminta for years. Half the girls in here have given him a blow job behind the quad in college. You were tucked up the other side of town on your own campus and he thought you'd never find out. Plus, we all know he's madly in love with Nell, but is utterly terrified of committing to her. The speeches he would give about her beauty when he was drunk after a regatta. Like a discount Dante describing Beatrice.'

'Fuck you, Teddie.'

'Clem, I'm not saying this to hurt you. You need to see the truth. Look, I may not be a baronet, but I am going to be a barrister. Surely that's good enough? I have my own flat in Islington, I go on lovely holidays to my parents' villa in Tuscany, I can cook a mean seafood risotto. Sometimes I say things that are funny. My dick's pretty big. Clemmie, I adore you. I'd put you on a pedestal, pander to your every whim. Just leave him.'

'Excuse me, Edward,' Clemmie said, as she left him standing on the edge of the dance floor trying to regain his composure.

'It's Edmund.'

A waiter waved some salmon under his nose, which he refused, and he went back to the bar with the aim of drinking bloody Rupert dry. Clemmie walked up the white gravel path towards the house. It was lined with fragrant English tea roses. She saw Rupert reaching the kitchen door and yelled after him. If he heard her, he didn't turn around.

★ ★ ★

Rupert saw that the door of the library was ajar; the old git was probably reading *The Spectator* and lamenting his useless grandson. He pushed the door open and was pleasantly surprised: Nell was perched on the arm of a chair reading. 'Nell, there you bloody are,' he said, sauntering over to her, leaving the door ever so slightly open, enough for Clemmie to hear everything. 'Everyone's been asking for you.'

'I doubt that; I'm terrible at parties. I can't do small talk. I can only talk about big things: elephants, black holes, apocalypses . . .'

'Trust you to find the library.'

'It's glorious.'

'What are you reading?'

'It's a first edition of *Pride and Prejudice*. Should I be wearing gloves? Shit, sorry, I couldn't help myself.'

'Take it home with you.'

'No. No. I can't. I really can't.' Nell put the book down on the side table.

'All right.' Rupert picked the book up, leaned over her and put it back on the shelf. His grandfather would be apoplectic if any books were left lying about.

'Happy birthday, Beauchamp,' she said, kissing him on the cheek. Her lips grazed the corner of his mouth.

'Thank you,' Rupert said, taking her hand in his and leading her to a corner of the library. 'I'm glad you're in here. There's something I've always wanted to show you. Push this panel here at the bottom.'

Nell pushed the heavy oak plank which swung backwards, revealing a draughty, black passage. She thought she could make out some steps going into the darkness, into Tartarus. 'Where does it go?'

'It comes out in the Temple of Venus in the grounds. One of my ancestors was a romantic. The story is that he was desperately in love with one of the milkmaids who worked in the dairy.'

'Because they didn't get smallpox?'

'Exactly. Beautiful skin, like yours. Anyway, he was married to an heiress who despite a glorious dowry was of rather weak constitution – that was often the way with heiresses, they're the survivors of a sickly litter. My ancestor still wanted to meet with the lovely milkmaid, and this was how he used to sneak out of an evening. He'd say that he was working in the library and was not to be disturbed. The servants would come in in the morning and find him conked out in his armchair. He'd leave a ledger open for good measure. Once the heiress finally perished from her weak constitution, he married the milkmaid and took up breeding Old English Sheepdogs. Everyone was a little pre-occupied with Emma Hamilton for it to be much of a scandal at the time. The Georgians were a racy bunch.'

'You're descended from a milkmaid?'

'I do have an affinity for cows.'

'Is that's why you're dating Phlegm?' Nell reached into her bag and pulled out a present wrapped in brown paper. 'I know you said not to on the invitation, but I bought you a present. It's just a little token. I thought you'd find it amusing.'

Rupert started carefully opening the present systematically, unfolding the creases that Nell had delicately folded. '*The Letters of Nancy Mitford and Evelyn Waugh.*'

'I saw it in Daunts and thought it was your sort of thing. You haven't read it already, have you?'

'No, I haven't.' Rupert put the book down on a side table and touched Nell's cheek. She closed her eyes and leaned in. He thought to kiss her but then something stopped him. 'Thank you. I'll enjoy reading it.'

'You're welcome. I should go back to the party. I've not seen Alex in six months,' Nell said, fidgeting with her hair. 'Sorry, I shouldn't have done that.'

'No, wait.' Rupert's arm snaked round her waist. 'What would you say if I told you that I was going to dump Clemmie tomorrow morning?'

'I'd say that Casper and I broke up on Thursday.'

'Shall I leave her?'

Nell stared at the oriental rug on the floor. Her cheeks flushed. Why couldn't they be together? Why was he asking her permission? Hadn't she been clear when she tried to kiss him? 'Rupert. Why did you have to say that? This could've been one of those fleeting moments that I sigh over when I'm in my nursing home forgotten by my ungrateful children.'

'Be serious, Nell.'

'What would I say if you said you were finally dumping Phlegm? I'd say that was nonsense. I'd say that you've been reciting that line to me for the last five years, and you never have followed through. I'd say that if I had any sense at all, this is the last time I ever see you, and that I'd forget you. I'd ring Casper, take up his offer and move in with him. I'd forget that I love you. Loving you makes me hate myself. It makes me miserable.' She stopped, breathed and looked into his burning blue eyes. 'I wouldn't say that. I wouldn't say any of it, even if I know I should. I'd have you in a heartbeat.' Nell broke free from his gaze.

'We could run away?'

'Run away? Run away from what? We don't need to run away, Rupert. I hate this. I hate that you're scared.' Nell swept away from him and through the door back to the gallery. She ran down the corridor, ignoring the haughty stares of Rupert's forebears. Not one of them was a milkmaid.

'Do you really hate me?' Rupert followed her out of the library, his voice getting louder the quicker Nell ran through the gallery.

'How could I not?' Nell yelled back to Rupert, as she continued to dash through the house. She stopped in the entrance hall, her voice carrying in the hollow eaves. 'I always knew exactly who you were, who you would become, and still I flew to you like some unfortunate moth to a suburban patio light. No Zephyr picked me up and abducted me, took me to your palace. I adore you and it's a horror. I'm sorry if I'm not acceptable to you, and you feel like we'd need to run away. I yell. I do colourful things. I'm an angry bluestocking. I talk about spinsters whenever I get the chance. I'm untidy. I have a collection of postcards from exhibits under my bed to send to friends, even though I only have two real friends. When I get drunk, I talk in circles about Stalingrad, and I recite poetry in the bath, and I won't eat blue food because that colour doesn't exist in nature – apart from blueberries, but they're really purple. You can't expect anything else of me.' Nell pushed open the kitchen door. She felt at sea. The kitchen was capsizing. The boat was flooded. 'You don't get to make me feel like this any more. You have no right to. I won't allow it. I'll just go. I'll fade away, I'll disappear in the mist,' she said to the flagstone tiles on the kitchen floor. 'What am I doing?'

'You're showing a remarkable lack of decorum.' Nell froze as she realised that Rupert's grandfather was at the kitchen table eating beans on toast. 'But I am as convinced as you are of my grandson's failings.'

'Sir Edgar! My apologies, I did not know you were there.'

'Not at all. I like hearing the boy whipped.'

Rupert leaned against the door frame. 'Of course you're here for this. Dinner and a show.'

'We have met before, haven't we, Miss?' Sir Edgar put his copy of *Private Eye* down on the table.

'Waddingham, Helena Waddingham.'

'Yes, you were at college together, weren't you. I don't know any Waddinghams,' he said to Nell, before rounding on Rupert. 'This is the sort of girl you should marry, not that bubble-headed clot who was just here. I have been watching her prancing about out there as though she's in the dressage category. I think Miss Waddingham may be too bright to have you though. Shame, she's got sturdy legs. Good breeder, I bet. Have you got many siblings? Always good to have a couple of children in reserve in case the eldest son is a lost cause. That's where your parents went wrong.'

'Grandfather,' Rupert started, but was cut off.

'Miss Waddingham, you don't want to miss the party, do you? You look charming tonight. Might be a nice civil servant who enjoys cryptic crosswords and owns his own motorcar out there for you. Perhaps a nice solicitor. Do not have a dalliance with my grandson. No greater bounder have I ever met, and I played cards with Lucky Lucan when I was young.'

'Good evening, Sir Edgar. It was nice to see you again.'

'I'm sure it was,' he said, signalling to Nell to flee the kitchen.

'Grandfather, I love her.'

'And? What do you expect me to do about it?'

'What?'

'I'm not going to take the poor thing out to dinner, am I? Thirty years ago I would have, but I am too old for all that now.'

'Well . . .'

'Well what, Rupert? If you like the girl then do it properly. If you want to go into politics like we discussed, a normal wife would be a virtue. Makes you look relatable. The papers don't like fillies with too many teeth like that sad little Gaunt girl any more. Makes you look out of touch.'

'I have a problem.'

'What sort of problem?'

'A Clemmie-shaped one. She's, well, you know, in a certain condition.'

'Is it yours? That's a problem that can be solved quite easily these days. Have you spoken to your godmother? She's very good with such advice. Send her to a clinic to have it dealt with. You need to break it off cleanly. Can't have the tabloids dragging you through it all over again in ten years. At least we know that you're capable of that. We don't want the line to end with you. Now, it's your birthday. I suggest you go and celebrate with those people you call friends, and I can finish my beans in peace.'

★   ★   ★

Nell walked down the gravel path back to the marquee through the sweet-smelling roses. She stopped at one particularly heady, scented tea rose and picked it. She pricked her finger again as she beheaded it. She dug the thorn out with her thumb, placed

326

the rose behind her ear and carried on to the marquee, sucking the blood. Music thumped, and the sound of braying echoed around her. Soft-footed dusk was encroaching on them. Nell walked inside and straight to the bar, got herself a whisky and then hid in a corner. The marquee opened up on the one side so that it overlooked the large pond. Nell wasn't sure what the difference was between a large pond and a small lake. It could well have been a lake for all she knew. She wandered outside to find Clemmie standing there alone. Nell turned around to go back inside.

'I hate you,' Clemmie said to Nell's back.

'Why don't you leave him?' Nell turned around and looked at Clemmie.

'I can't,' Clemmie said, touching her belly.

'I can.' Nell went back into the marquee as the DJ announced that the fireworks were about to begin. She snaked past the moving throng and went to the bar. Rupert entered the tent. She ignored him. He ignored her. She finished her whisky, left the glass on the bar and started up the path back to the house. The fireworks began, but instead of oohs and ahhs Nell heard a large splash and gasps from the crowd. Chattering chaos ensued. Nell didn't care. She walked back to the main house and upstairs to the room that she was supposed to be sleeping in. She gathered her things and called for a minicab to take her to Tring station. Nell looked out of the window towards the party and saw the spellbinding spinning of Catherine wheels. She picked up her bags and left the house, setting out down the driveway to the main road where her taxi was waiting.

★ ★ ★

Alex didn't feel great, he felt bloody fantastic. What champagne! The bubbles had gone straight to his head and he himself felt like he was going to float out of the tent and pop. He heard a muffled announcement about fireworks and headed for the pond with everyone else. Alex found himself standing next to Clemmie. He threw his arm around her shoulder.

'Clemmie, how are you? You dumped Rupert yet? You should do. He's a cunt and you're better than him.'

'Hello, Alex,' she said, removing his arm from her person. 'You wouldn't lie to me if I asked you a question, would you?'

'Depends on the question.'

'Is Rupert fucking Minty?'

Alex took a moment to think. 'I am not certain, but if you have a suspicion like that about Rupert it will be true. He is not a subtle man.'

'Thank you.'

'Can I ask you a question?'

'Sure, Alex.'

'Have you seen Nell?'

'She went to find the pagoda in the middle of the maze.'

'Cheers, Clem. Clem, dump him,' Alex said, retreating back to the bar, the marquee now empty. He didn't hear the splash. He leaned over, picked up a bottle of unopened champagne and set out for the maze to find Nell, moving more and more unsteadily as he went.

★　★　★

Rupert appeared outside just in time for the beginning of the fireworks. He sidled up next to Clemmie and held her hand as if she hadn't heard him say any of those things to Nell in the library minutes before. As if she hadn't known it all before anyway.

'Hello, beautiful,' he said, squeezing her fingers. 'I love you.' It sounded like he meant it.

Clemmie wriggled free and turned to the plain girl standing next to her. Surprising her, she seized her by the hair, undid the bow holding the poor girl's dress up, exposing her pale naked body to everyone gathered, and threw her into the pond hair first. Minty gaped like a carp as she splashed through the muddy waters. Initial gasps of shock were followed by a rousing chorus of 'get your tits out for the lads'.

'Minty!' yelled Rupert, who gallantly dived in after the floundering topless girl as the fireworks began. Some of those flashes were cameras, not rockets.

Clemmie withdrew with a fistful of red hair and walked back to the house, her point made and her dignity mangled.

56

Caius barrelled into the entrance hall. An officer from the armed response unit was staring at the door that led to the walking gallery. The wheelbarrow was overturned, and the bloody shards of a blue-and-white china vase were scattered over the floor next to it. His radio crackled:

'Library clear.'

'Ballroom clear.'

'Wine cellar clear.'

'Drawing room – I think that's what this is – clear.'

'Sorry, had to drive from London,' Caius said, flashing his badge and catching his breath. 'I've sent two plainclothes officers round the back. Do we have sight of either of the women yet?'

'Not yet. I'd say that the girl in the wheelbarrow was playing possum, sprung up, grabbed the first thing she could and then smashed the other one over the head with the vase,' he said, looking at a dust-free circle on a large oak cabinet next to the wheelbarrow. 'That door to the library was open. I thought one of them would be in there, but it's clear.'

Alex and Rupert fought each other to get through the door first. Rupert kicked Alex in the shins.

'For God's sake, Rupert,' Alex said, clutching his leg.

'It's my house and my fiancée that is in peril.'

'She's not your fiancée, creep; she's my girlfriend.'

'You're very fast, detective,' Rupert said, a hint of envy edging into his voice as he caught up with Caius. The hero had to be the quickest man. Rupert noticed the shards of the vase on the floor. 'Did you break that?' Rupert sneered at the armed officer, squaring up to him. 'I'd make you buy a new one, but I doubt you could afford it.'

'Out of courtesy, I'm pointing out that he has a gun, and you have an obnoxious attitude. I wouldn't care if he shot you, but I want to save myself the paperwork.' Caius took a moment to breathe before asking Rupert, 'The door leading to the library was open. Is there another way out of that room?'

'There's a passageway behind a panel in the wall that takes you to the Temple of Venus in the grounds. It's past the lake. I showed the library entrance to Nell once.'

Caius pulled out his radio. 'Amy, Matt, you there? Over.'

'Yes, over,' came Amy's voice.

'There's a fake Greek temple in the grounds. There's a tunnel from the house. Nell might be trying to get out that way. Over.'

'Venus was Roman, actually . . .' Rupert said.

'I can see the temple. Shit, Matt, look over there.'

'Amy, what's going on?' Caius asked. He was interrupted by one of the armed officers radioing in.

'Blood in the kitchen. It's on the door leading to the gardens. There's a fair bit – is there an ambulance on standby? Requesting back-up in the grounds.'

Caius, Alex and the first armed officer followed Rupert's lead to the kitchen, where there was indeed blood all over the sage-green door to the rose garden. It was smeared on the counters and the drawer handles. The knife drawer was wide open. The armed officer charged out of the door after their colleague; Caius sped after him, leaving Rupert and Alex panting behind him. Caius jogged through the rose garden, noticing that some of them had been beheaded. There were tiny spatters of blood on the leaves and a trail of petals leading down the path. He continued along the gravel until the lake came into view. He could see Matt running down a grassy slope towards Minty. Minty was standing staring at the lake from a steep embankment. Blood poured down her face from a gash in her forehead. Two armed officers were hanging back as Caius approached them. As he got closer to Minty, he could hear an out-of-breath Matt trying to talk to her.

'Minty, remember me?' Matt wheezed. 'I'm DS Cheung, the detective you spoke to last week.'

'Yes.'

'I want to help you, Minty. I can help you get out of this. Where's Nell?'

'I don't know. She hit me and then she ran. I didn't see where she went. I like her. I like Nell.' Minty went to touch her head but was too fearful.

'Minty, put the knife down, we can talk more freely then.'

'No,' Minty said, raising the knife to her chest. She was holding a bunch of white roses in her free hand; the thorns had torn her hands and Caius could see blood dripping down her little finger.

'It's all right, Minty. We know what happened. We know that you didn't mean to kill Clemmie. You just wanted to embarrass her. It was an accident.'

'I didn't mean to hurt her. She choked. I didn't want to kill her,' Minty said, staring at the lake. 'She pushed me in, and he came in and rescued me. She ruined my dress. I was covered in mud, but Rupert didn't care. He dived in and saved me.'

'Don't pin your hopes on Rupert this time, Minty. You can get yourself out of this one. Just put the knife down.'

'No.' Minty looked away from Matt and towards the magnificent head of blond hair that she had longed to see, to come and save her, as it came into view. He didn't have a white charger, but he was wearing a pair of white jeans which was good enough for her.

'Minty, you've got a head wound. We need to stop the bleeding. Put the knife down and I can help you,' Matt said.

'I hated Clemmie. He hated her too. He kept saying if only she were dead, then he could get married to the girl he always wanted to, but he didn't mean me. I thought he meant me. He meant Nell. She's got a ring,' Minty said, as Rupert and Alex puffed up behind Caius. 'But perhaps I was wrong.'

'Minty, what the fuck are you doing?' Rupert said sternly, as if he were telling a naughty puppy off for pissing in his slippers.

'Rupert!'

'You're not going to get in trouble for this. It'll get swept away. They'll send you to rehab for a month or two and then business as usual, darling. Now don't be daft. Drop the knife and come over here.'

Minty lowered the knife and took a step back from the edge of the lake.

'Good girl.' Rupert turned and smiled at Caius; a grin that said, 'See, I told you I was the hero of this epic.' Rupert caught sight of Alex furtively backing away from the scene and turn towards the Temple of Venus. 'Where the fuck are you going?'

'To get my girlfriend.'

'Leave my fiancée the fuck alone.' Rupert leaped at Alex, unaware that everyone else's eyes had widened in horror at the effect that callous noun had really had. Rupert launched himself onto Alex, taking a swing at him and wrestling him to the ground as Minty plunged the kitchen knife into her stomach with all the violent force needed to fight the desperate itching urge to live. Her hands fell away as she tumbled into the water.

Matt dived in after Minty. Pulled her to the side and tried to stem the bleeding while the first armed officer started CPR.

Caius managed to pull Rupert off a bloody-nosed Alex and tried to restrain him as one of the armed officers took out a pair of handcuffs. Rupert elbowed Caius in the teeth as he broke free and started running to the temple. The other armed officer tasered him.

Rupert pissed himself.

★ ★ ★

Amy had finally reached the temple after climbing up a steep hill overlooking the horrors of the lake. She had seen Matt rush through a meadow of poppies and hoped he had made it in time. She rattled the wrought-iron gate with its intricate swirls and swung it open. She entered the temple and looked around. There appeared to be an altar on which there were some dead roses, what looked like incense, a few rotten apple cores, and weirder still what looked like a burnt old dog's bone. Caius said there was a tunnel connecting the temple to the house, but Amy couldn't see any obvious entrances. She wandered behind the altar and noticed a brass handle embedded in one of the stone tiles. Amy heard a faint noise from under the slab – it sounded a bit like 'shit'. She hooked her finger over the crest of the wave and pulled hard, revealing a dust-covered Nell.

'Hello, officer. I bet you don't like my dress now,' Nell said from within the tunnel. She was holding the bloody neck of a broken vase in her hand. Amy gave Nell her hand and hauled her up. Nell leaned against the altar and touched one of the wilted flowers. 'Trust Rupert to make offerings to a love goddess in a joke temple. That's where he went wrong,' Nell said to Amy, as she staggered outside the temple and threw up.

57

Hemel Hempstead Hospital

Following his heroics, Matt had been cocooned in one of the shiny blankets given to people after natural disasters. He'd been taken to A&E to get checked out for waterborne diseases – maybe get a hepatitis vaccine. He'd looked a bit pale after all that. Caius had spoken to his girlfriend, Freja, who was on her way. Rupert was also in A&E, but he was handcuffed to a constable. They were getting him checked out before charging him with assaulting a police officer. A patient Amy was there with him, waiting for a nurse to find him some scrubs to change into now that he was starting to smell of stale piss. Caius was outside Nell's hospital room, waiting to be given the all clear to see her. Alex, whose bloody nose had been deemed a minor injury, was with him too. The nurse left Nell's room and signalled to Caius that he could enter.

'Minty, did she . . . I saw them doing CPR,' Nell asked. She was propped up on a bed with a drip in her arm.

'I'm sorry, Nell. Minty is dead.'

'The poor girl. I hit her so hard with that vase. I didn't know what else to do. I tried to reason with her in the van but . . . She killed Clemmie, but it's Rupert's fault. He killed them both really.' Nell stared at the tiled ceiling. 'I want to press charges.'

'About that—'

'It's getting swept under the carpet, isn't it. Some pal of Rupert's . . .'

'I wouldn't be surprised if that's what happens. Between us, the case has been officially taken away from my team. Out of curiosity you don't happen to know about Rupert's involvement in something called Help for Hippos, its drug dealing, or whether he ever spoke about obtaining and selling classical sculptures?'

'No. As far as I know, he inherited his money from his mother and was just playing at being a restauranteur.'

Caius felt guilty. If only he had put her in a taxi and sent her home, then there would be one less woman in a hospital bed and one less in a body bag. Caius wondered who the 'they' was that Rupert had referred to when trying to talk Minty down. Fay, perhaps? Someone else? 'If it helps, we're arresting him for taking a swing at me. I doubt it will stick, but we can keep him in a cell for a bit.'

'I see,' Nell said, noticing that she'd chipped a nail, hiding her disappointment and her left hand from him. 'Did someone ring my dad?'

'Yes, he's driving down from Warwick now.'

'You'd like my dad. He's direct, upright, sees the world in the plainest terms: good and bad; right and wrong.'

'There's much more nuance to the world than such a binary view allows.'

'Not if you were raised by strict Baptist, Jamaican parents. Whereabouts are your family from?'

'Kingston.'

'My dad's parents were from St Elizabeth. I have green eyes and wavy hair. I pass as white, as you do pretty much. Your surname was the giveaway. Too posh. Things are easier for us; we don't get hassled. People like to ask where in Italy or Greece or Spain I'm from. They don't assume I'm shoplifting, just bilingual.'

'A few years ago before Matt, I had this vile DS. HR got involved. He told me that there was an old "nig nog" waiting for me at the front desk. It was my grandfather; I'd lost the keys to my flat and he was dropping off the spares. He hadn't realised what I was, who I am. We came to blows. They sacked him, of course. Took a while though: he was popular, and the Chief Superintendent made me do a whole course of anger management. I've been thinking about quitting ever since.'

'To be mixed race is to carry the burden of your History as a proper noun, an ancestral wound, while being complimented on your tan in January and the thickness of your hair.'

'I grew up in London and never once got stopped and searched, unlike my friend at school who it happened to six times in one year – all because of a quirk in my melanin. You know what, never mind. I don't need to tell you; you've got the same story. Can I ask you a question?'

'On the record?'

'Off the record. I'm asking as a concerned individual, not a police officer. You're not going to go back to Rupert, are you?'

'Why do you ask?'

'The fainting, and the throwing up.' She'd splashed some sick on Amy's shoes.

'It's Rupert's, before you ask.'

'Don't marry him. I know the house is something else, and that ring is spectacular (I'd pawn it if I were you), but he's a Wickham not a Darcy, and you're definitely an Elizabeth Bennet.'

'You have been reading your Austen, detective,' Nell said, hiding her hand under the covers.

'I have.'

'I did something bad when I stayed at Rupert's house.'

'What?'

'I took something. Rupert's been writing this novel for a decade. I was curious. He always rattles on about it being "era defining". I found one of his notebooks stuffed in a drawer. It had the ending in it. He wrote it by hand – so there isn't another copy. He won't miss it for a while, not while his things are all boxed up between the two houses.'

'Right?'

'I threw it into a skip in Hackney. I threw part of him away. I took a decade of his life and wasted it.'

'Was it any good?'

'Unfortunately, it was brilliant.'

'That's a secret I'll take to the grave.'

'He can never know it was me.'

'I won't tell a soul. Nell, whatever you decide to do about the baby, you're better off on your own than with Rupert. Two dead bodies – don't be the third.'

She took the ring off her finger and gave it to Caius. Caius looked through the glass window in the door and saw Alex pacing the corridor.

★ ★ ★

Amy was escorting Rupert to the marked car that was going to take him back to the station to be charged when Caius appeared.

'I found enough coke to knock out a small horse in his wallet,' Amy said.

'A small pony in his case. Charge him with possession if it's not enough to charge him for dealing,' Caius said, pulling out the ring that Nell had given him to return. 'Detective Constable Noakes, I am placing in your care this engagement ring to be returned to Sir Rupert Beauchamp once he has been bailed. If he's bailed.'

Amy took receipt of the ring.

'Where did you get that?' Rupert asked, as Amy got him into the back of the car. A bruise on his cheekbone that he'd received in the kerfuffle with Caius had started to bloom.

'Ms Waddingham gave it to me and asked that I made sure it found its way back to you.'

'Is she OK? Did she say anything? Did she mention me?'

'Only that if you ever tried to speak to her again then she'd get a restraining order.'

'Was she joking?'

'No, she wasn't.'

'Shit. Are you sure she wasn't laughing behind her eyes when she said it? She can be quite dry.'

Caius leaned in towards him – he was close enough to get a whiff of the lingering stink of ammonia. 'The coroner owes me a favour; I wonder if I can get her to put the cause of death as "Rupert Beauchamp's callousness"?'

'You filthy oik . . .'

'Language like that, from a gentleman? Particularly from one who stinks of stale piss.' Caius leaned on the car door, looked Rupert square in the eye and held him there. 'You destroyed Minty today. The poor thing died of a broken heart. You as good as murdered Clemmie too. You'd already raped Nell, but why not get her abducted and nearly killed as well?'

'I'm not responsible for Minty's actions.'

'Yes, you are. You did that to Minty. You pushed an unstable young woman into committing manslaughter and two counts of kidnap because you like easy sex with vulnerable women. All this carnage, this circus of death, is all your bloody fault. Rupert, you did this.'

'Fuck off, did I.'

'Who's the "they" you told Minty would make her go to rehab and then this would all be forgotten? The ones you've been acting as a middleman for?'

'The same people who'll make these stupid charges disappear.'

'Give me a name.'

'No.'

'If you think this is the end of this, the end of me pursuing you, then you're nothing but naive. I'll get you one day. Even if it's in ten years' time. It may be for not paying your parking tickets, for urinating in public – as petty and low as I have to go, I will. I swear to God, I will get you.' Rupert snorted in disbelief. 'How can I explain this in a way your boarding school-warped mind will understand? I am a Fury snapping at your heels no matter how fast and far you run. I will dog you, plague you. I swear on Styx that I will ruin you. I am fucking inescapable.'

Caius slammed the car door, nodding at Amy as he did so.

WEDNESDAY

58

Brompton Oratory

The church was heaving. Clemmie's was the most popular funeral in town. Caius wasn't convinced that all of the mourners were genuine – bound to be a journo for a red top in here some-where. Both Rupert and Nell were missing – Nell had gone home from the hospital with her father early that morning, and only God knew where Rupert could be. Rupert's charges had already disappeared into the ether, but Caius doubted that the bruise on his face from when he'd fallen to the ground being tasered had. Matt was convinced that Rupert would appear and do a big woe-is-me set piece, but perhaps they had underestimated the effect of that article on his reputation. The world knew his business. Rupert could wash his hands of poor Clemmie now that it was widely known she was carrying on with her boss – who was still under arrest. Caius was expecting Osbald's charges to be dropped any day now and to release him back to Fay, who was living her halcyon days of freedom. She was probably in Harvey Nichols right now spending her drug money. Caius knew in his gut that they had barely scraped the surface of Help for Hippos. He had so many questions. Who was really in charge? Getting so close to a coked-up Rupert had made him doubt their assumption that he was the ringleader. Caius wondered what MI6 would do with the information they had gathered. He'd just have to wait and see what happened next.

Matt whispered to Caius that the pallbearers were all old rowing buddies of Rupert's, including Alex. A priest gave a sermon – life cut short, lived to the fullest, etc. No one cried.

Caius found funerals without sobbing and wailing odd, but that's the English for you. The ancient pianist played 'Abide With Me'. A girl read out a speech from a set of tiny yellow cards about how Clemmie was her best friend, how much fun they had at Oxford Brookes and living together in Clapham – the brunches they ate, the margaritas, the taxis they fell out of. It wasn't the most elegant speech Caius had heard, but she meant it. He was glad that poor Clemmie was going to be missed. The church was beautiful: vaulted ceilings and stained-glass miracles. 'Amazing Grace' began. The pianist had picked an odd key, but that was it, Caius was off. It was the only sure-fire way to make him cry. His Jamaican grandmother used to hum it on Sundays after she'd been to church. He looked at all the pale faces near him and did not see true comprehension of the words they were singing.

Clemmie's father got up and made a speech about his little girl. 'Jerusalem' played:

> *And did those feet in ancient time,*
> *Walk upon England's mountains green:*
> *And was the holy Lamb of God,*
> *On England's pleasant pastures seen!*

Did England have any mountains? Real mountains like the Himalayas, not gentle inclines. Caius wasn't so sure it did. He was, however, very sure that Jesus definitely never came to this wind-battered, gloomy backwater of the Roman Empire.

> *And did the Countenance Divine,*
> *Shine forth upon our clouded hills?*

Caius liked the Old Testament God more than New Testament God. Old Testament God was violent and angry. Liked to be paid in blood. Needed constant affection from his children. Old Testament God understood persecution, understood the slave – that's probably why every Jamaican family has a great uncle Isaac. Old Testament God is more like Zeus. Perhaps New Testament God is Zeus too. Impregnating virgins with rays of light. Very Zeus-like, that. Maybe that was what happened. Zeus got bored of Olympus, its petty toings and froings, and wanted to go it alone. Caius was a bad Catholic, which in turn made him a good one.

And was Jerusalem builded here,
Among these dark Satanic Mills?

Caius shook his head at the thought of those dark Satanic Mills processing American cotton and manned by beleaguered peasants new to the city after the commons were enclosed – all to make the mill owner rich and for the workers to die with fluff in their lungs.

Bring me my Bow of burning gold:
Bring me my Arrows of desire:
Bring me my Spear: O clouds unfold:
Bring me my Chariot of fire!

That was a good movie. Caius wondered if it was on Netflix.

I will not cease from Mental Fight,
Nor shall my Sword sleep in my hand:
Till we have built Jerusalem,
In England's green and pleasant Land.

345

The funeral service over, Caius, Matt and Amy speedily filed out of the church before the throng of mourners slowed them down. They paid their respects to Clemmie's parents, making sounds but not promises that they'd solve the case, and headed back to the car. Caius put the radio on. Chaka Demus & Pliers was playing. The three of them bobbed their heads along to 'Tease Me' but that felt a bit odd after 'Jerusalem'. Caius changed the station to Radio Four, something more subdued in mood. They listened instead to a discussion on farm subsidies for a good thirty minutes as they headed back.

'They released Minty's body this morning. I got in touch with her family about the funeral, but they want it to be close relatives only,' Matt said, staring out of the window.

'Poor woman,' Amy said, fiddling with a split end. 'I know she killed someone, but she can't have been in her right mind. I can't help but feel sorry for her.'

'How do you love someone that much? Burn for them,' Caius asked, trying to unclench his jaw. Matt saw how firmly he was gripping the steering wheel. 'Or, more specifically, how could anyone love Rupert Beauchamp that much?'

'I don't get it either, but then I don't really like men,' Amy replied.

'I think we all need a treat. McDonald's?' Caius said, forcing himself to smile as they crawled through Camden. The fake smile seemed to work, and he put a more cheerful radio station on.

★ ★ ★

Amy slurped her cola under the flickering fluorescent lights and Matt chomped on chicken nuggets as Caius dipped fries into his chocolate milkshake. Amy looked at him with disgust, but Caius

346

just laughed. He'd been doing it since he was seven. He saw a blonde woman go to the till and order. For a moment he thought she was Clemmie.

'Why do we do this job?' Caius's mood had shifted. 'There's this whole criminal conspiracy that we've barely uncovered but now can't touch. It's powerful enough that they can just make those charges against Rupert disappear. Rupert told Minty that Clemmie's death would just get swept away, that there would be no repercussions. How did he know that?'

'Because it's happened before?' Matt wondered.

'That's exactly what I'm worried about. How bloody big is this? How many more bodies are there? How are we supposed to come into work and do our jobs when we know that justice is fucking subjective? How are we supposed to sleep at night?' Caius got up and left the table. 'I need to pee.'

Once they were on their own, Matt turned to Amy and said, 'You might have heard this around the station already, but Caius's older sister was murdered a decade or so ago. It was never solved. It's why he does this job, and why he's also always on the verge of quitting. He's got the highest conviction rate in the station, but he doesn't cope well if he can't solve it – he managed better at the funeral than I thought he would. I think he's learned to detach more, although he did then bring us straight to the very same McDonald's that Rupert had his party in.'

'Poor Caius. I didn't know that about him.'

'He won't talk about it, so don't ever mention it.'

Caius came back to their table.

'I am looking forward to having tomorrow off,' Amy said, stretching her legs out of the side of the cramped banquette. 'Caius, what happened to Paris? Are you going?'

'No, I'm going to have a staycation. Potter around my flat. Might buy a house plant or six, learn to bake bread, read a book or two. That sort of thing.'

'But what about your big romantic gesture to get Héloise back?' Matt asked, before grimacing. 'Sorry, I probably wasn't supposed to say that out loud.'

'Amy's a good detective. She probably worked that out a while ago.'

'You're not exactly an emotionally subtle person, are you,' Amy said, taking a bite from her burger.

'Nope, I am an open book for all to read,' Caius said, grinning to himself – a hint of sorrow creeping into his eyes. 'I'm not going to Paris. I don't want to go any more. I think Héloise cheating on me may work out for the best, eventually. I really don't know what I want. Do you believe in fate? Love at first sight? True love?'

'Star-crossed lovers?' Amy asked.

'And all the messy bits in between.'

Amy paused for a moment before saying, 'It's comforting to think so, but I've seen too many crime scenes for that sort of whimsical thinking. I've taken too many statements.'

★ ★ ★

Caius returned home following an afternoon of paperwork and drudgery to find a surprise waiting on his doorstep.

'*Merde*,' Caius said to *la belle femme* waiting patiently on his doorstep with a half-drunk bottle of Badoit, a dog-eared novel and a small overnight bag.

'Hello, Caius,' Héloise said, standing up and brushing imaginary dirt from her skirt. '*Comment ça va?*'

'*Très bien.* I didn't think I'd ever see you again.'
'Me neither.'
'Do you want to come in, Héloise? I think we need to talk.'
'*Oui, mon coeur.*'

Acknowledgements

First and foremost, my long-suffering husband deserves more than acknowledgement. He puts up with an awful lot. Thanks, Ben. You poor git. Thanks also to my wonderful sister-in-law Katie and my mother-in-law Tina for keeping us going. Thank you to my late nan, Juliet. We spent hours together watching adaptations of Agatha Christie when I was child. We both loved a good murder. I can't even catch a glimpse of David Suchet without missing you. I wouldn't be who I am if it weren't for my wonderful aunties: my Auntie Dee, a fellow book-hoarder, kept a small girl up to her ears in imaginary worlds; my Auntie Rose, always there with a kind word and a chicken sandwich – the best cooker; and my Auntie Michele whose constant encouragement and support has kept me going on this journey. Thank you to my dad, all small children should watch that many documentaries on WW2. Thank you also to Wendy, Di and Lesley for their early feedback. Thank you also to my dear friends Sasha Kundal, Hettie Bray and Sarah King for letting me waffle on at them about the book. You're all too kind to me.

I have been extremely fortunate to work on this book with one outstanding person after another. My agent Jon Wood is a marvel – thanks for taking a chance on me. Thank you Safae El-Ouahabi for all your hard work. The team at Faber are brilliant. Thank you so much Libby Marshall, I'm very lucky to have you as my editor. Thank you to Louisa Joyner, Sara Helen Binney, Hannah Turner, Phoebe Williams, Rachael Williamson and Claire Gatzen. I could not wish to work with better people.